SUPERNATURAL™

ONE YEAR GONE

SUPERNATURAL™

ONE YEAR GONE

REBECCA DESSERTINE

WITH FOREWORD BY ERIC KRIPKE

Based on the hit CW series SUPERNATURAL created by Eric Kripke

TITAN BOOKS

Supernatural: One Year Gone
ISBN: 9780857680990

Published by
Titan Books
A division of
Titan Publishing Group Ltd
144 Southwark St
London
SE1 0UP

First edition May 2011
10 9 8 7 6 5 4 3 2 1

Visit our website: www.titanbooks.com

Did you enjoy this book? We love to hear from our readers. Please email us at readerfeedback@titanemail.com or write to us at Reader Feedback at the above address.

To receive advance information, news, competitions, and exclusive Titan offers online, please register as a member by clicking the "sign up" button on our website: www.titanbooks.com

A CIP catalogue record for this title is available from the British Library.

Printed and bound in the United States.

FOREWORD

So here's the thing. The book that you currently hold in your hot little hands (or are reading virtually on your hot little tablet doo-hickey) was written by the *Supernatural* staff member who knows the inside of my sticky skull better than just about anybody. Better than Sera Gamble or Bob Singer, that's for sure. You see, Rebecca has the unenviable job of my assistant. Which means she has to tolerate my bellowing rants, my hurling hot coffee in her face. Just kidding—I'm not really that kind of boss— more the compulsively neurotic type—a less photogenic Albert Brooks, if you will. But I digress. In truth, I interact with Rebecca more than anybody on the show— all my notes and drafts go across her desk, she performs crucial research, she contributes brilliant show ideas—and most of all, she sees how our grubby little series is made, from a catbird seat like no other. On top of it all—she's smart. Damn smart. Damn good writer, too. And all of this adds up to the book (or hologram) you are currently grasping in your meathooks. I think you'll enjoy the corner she's staked out within our weird little universe. Because she lives inside that universe as much as any of us. Hell, maybe more. Anyway, have fun. And send a silent prayer to Rebecca—she needs it—after all, she's got to put up with me.

Eric Kripke
Creator & Executive Producer, *Supernatural*

PROLOGUE

Winter 1692

A pale sliver of crescent moon pinches at the sky. A lone pair of footsteps crunches over a snow-encased field. Through spindly black brush, a young girl emerges and makes her way over the frozen earth. Her full black skirts scrape hieroglyphic shapes into the powdery snow. She stops and studies the ground before her; a covered mound pushes upwards from the earth. Scraping off the moss with her mitten-covered hands she reveals a grave. Despite the cold she proceeds to kneel down before it.

From beneath her coat she takes out a folded piece of purple fabric. Unwrapping the triangles of cloth, she lays it ceremonially on the frozen earth. Out of her pockets, she produces various objects and sets them precisely on the shroud. Faint moonlight glints off a silver outline of the pentagram extending to the corners. The girl pulls forth several black candles, fighting the wind as she lights them.

Into a small brass bowl she drops various feather pieces, stone, crystal, and herbs. Then she pulls a small dagger from her coat and presses the blade against her palm. Wincing slightly she slices the soft skin from her index finger to the base. Blood drips into the bowl covering the objects.

From her pocket she produces a worn book, two fists thick. Nervously, she lays it on her lap, brushing the pages apart with her gloved hands. Her voice wavers as she starts to chant, softly at first, tracing the words with her finger as she reads.

The wind whips up, steadily increasing to a screaming gale. The girl shades her eyes from the blowing snow but continues to chant over the howl of the cold air. The flakes before her begin to gather, as if attracted to one another by an unseen force, becoming denser and denser. The whirlwind slowly takes on a shape.

With each howl of the wind more snow coagulates until the figure of a woman solidifies before the girl. The girl peers up at the tall figure. A faint gasp escapes her blue lips. Her eyes move over the vestige of rotting flesh before her She bows.

"Madam. I've missed you so. I serve only you."

The specter's glassy, dead eyes seem not to register the plea.

The girl continues. "I've done exactly as instructed. I've tried so very hard." She wipes away a small dribble of mucus from her nose. "Council me. I know not how to make more provisions for him."

The corners of the specter's mouth turn upwards into a curdled smile.

"Why child, know what ye must. Raise us all."

The color drains from the girl's face.

"I… What if I cannot?" Her tear-streaked face turns upwards. "I'm not as strong as you."

The specter's lips prune into a rotten scowl. Raising her arm, she gives a quick flick of her wrist. The girl catches her breath as if someone startled her from behind. Her hands fly to her throat as a phantom grip tightens down onto her doe-sized neck. Blood rims her corneas, she fails to draw a breath.

The woman leans down, eye to eye with the girl.

"Well then, if you cannot do it, I will find someone else."

She slowly turns her hand. The girl's eyes dilate to saucers as the vertebra in her neck go POP, POP, POP, snapping like chicken bones.

At that moment, from behind, a dark figure emerges from the tree line. She approaches the girl silently, produces a knife and with one hand grabs the girl's neck as the blade slices across her throat. Her small body falls limp into the snow, lifeless dark eyes staring out across the white expanse.

The pages of the old tome flap like the wings of a downed bird.

The figure holds the knife downward as blood drips from its blade. She picks up the book and continues the incantation as the blood petals over the white snow; spreading and soaking the purple cloth.

"Deviser of Darkness, *imus adque deportamus…*"

As the woman continues the chant, the specter darkens and materializes. With each word the figure becomes more corporeal: Her limbs take shape. The rancid skin on her face smoothes and tightens. Her rotting, torn clothes repair themselves.

The woman stops chanting, and looks at the creature before her.

"Dear mother, I've missed you so."

The old woman nods, and the two walk off across the field together.

Snow wafts over the young girl's dead body. Gradually, the snow covers the slight figure, blending it into the white landscape.

PROLOGUE

2010

Dean and Sam swig from a bottle as they barrel-ass down a dark country road. Dean cranks the tunes. Sam smiles and lays back into the Impala's passenger seat. All is right with the world.

"How long till we get there?" Sam asks.

Dean casts a sidewards glance at Sam. "Dude, you're my personal Garmin, figure it out."

Dean smiles, he loves making Sam feel like the little brother. But Sam doesn't respond.

"You're my co-pilot. Just without the uniform."

No answer.

"Sam? You in there? When are we going to get there?" Dean asks, a flicker of concern on his face.

Sam turns toward Dean.

"We'll never get there, Dean. It's over. All over. I'm gone."

* * *

Dean woke with a start. His flailing arm hit the quarter-full glass of Scotch on the bedside table. A brown spot on the cream-colored sisal rug widened to a stain. *Crap.*

Hefting himself up off the bed Dean reached for the towel that was draped over the chair by the window. But as his feet hit the ground, the sheets wrapped around his ankles, impeding his progress. Tied and tripped up, he landed on his face.

"Perfect, another kick-ass way to start the day, Dean," he muttered to himself.

The bedroom door creaked open. Dean studied the pair of feet sporting nicely painted toenails that moved into his eyeline. He looked up. Lisa Braeden stood over him with a pitying smile on her face. Dean had grown quite accustomed to the expression that he induced almost every time they spoke. It was the same face Dean was met with when six weeks ago he showed up on her doorstep, after God knows now many years. They hadn't been serious, it was just a couple of dates, years ago. But Dean and Sam had come to her rescue when her housing development had been taken over by a serious case of deadly child-nappers.

"Nice to see you made it this far out of bed today. That's farther than any day this week."

Bleary-eyed, Dean nodded. This is his life.

ONE

"I'll make you some eggs," Lisa said as she picked up a pair of jeans from the floor. "We're going to Morse Reservoir today, if you want to come."

Dean heaved himself back onto the bed.

"No thanks. I'll just stay here."

Lisa's eyes flicked over Dean's unshaven face.

"Why don't you come? It might be fun. Remember fun?"

Dean smiled tightly, the levity of the conversation almost making him nauseous.

"Besides, you haven't talked to Ben in a week." Lisa sat on the bed next to Dean, taking his hand in hers. "I don't mind you staying in our spare room, but it's like living with a ghost. I told you I wasn't going to push you—"

"You're right, you did." Dean cut in, immediately regretting his tone. "I'm sorry. I'm trying."

"I know you are. So am I. That's why I'm asking you if you want to go to the park."

She brushed the light hairs on the back of Dean's hand. The pure emotion made his stomach twist.

Dean withdrew his hand from Lisa's.

"Give me a couple minutes."

Lisa pursed her lips, as though she wanted to say more. Instead, she kissed Dean on the cheek and stood up. At the door she turned and held up Dean's discarded jeans.

"Just in case you care to join us, I'm going to throw these in the wash."

Dean nodded.

Lisa closed the door to Dean's room, slowly clicking the lock. She stood there for a moment wondering whether she had made a mistake when Dean came to her front door and she let him into her and her son's life. Ben was twelve, impressionable and sensitive. She knew deep down how kind and generous Dean was, but she also knew that the years of hunting had calloused his ability to commit himself emotionally. She thought that perhaps she could get through to him. Two months on, she wondered if she had done the right thing. Emotionally, Dean was an out-of-control rollercoaster with faulty brakes. It was only a matter of time before he ran off the rails.

Dean sat on the edge of the bed, then lay back and closed his eyes. In his head he played over again the vision of Sam jumping into the pit of Hell: the fiery opening swirling and writhing in the middle of the cemetery. He had been there for his brother, but there hadn't been anything he could do to stop him. Talk about being impotent. Sam *had* to jump, but an acidy feeling of regret constantly swirled in Dean's stomach. He should have stopped him. But there wasn't any other way. Every so often, like every two minutes, Dean's heart would palpitate and leap into his throat. The reality was constantly there, Dean's brain wouldn't let it go: Sam was gone forever.

The smoky Scotch he drank in large gulps helped his cause. But frequently, mid-morning, after Ben had gone to school and Lisa had left to teach an early morning yoga class in Carmel, Dean's mind would clear enough so that once again he remembered, moment by moment, Sam jumping into the pit.

There had been no other way to save the world. Sam had said "yes," and Lucifer had taken over Sam's body. The plan rested on the tenuous idea that Sam could somehow gain enough consciousness that he could hurl himself, with Lucifer within him, into the hole. The brothers had collected all four horsemen's rings—Death gave Dean his ring outright—and together the rings opened up the portal to Hell.

But it didn't go down like that. They weren't able to get Lucifer into the portal. As was their fate, Lucifer and Michael met on the battlefield, ready to duke it out. The collateral damage would only be a few hundred million lives, and no one would need Pay-Per-View for this fight, it was going to be right outside everyone's front door.

But on that field, in the middle of the fight, somehow Sam had gained enough control of his own body, while possessed by Lucifer, to hurl himself into the cage. And there he would stay for eternity.

With that act, a hole had opened up in Dean's soul and there was no way to fill it. The Scotch only anesthetized him for a few hours. After that, the thoughts would come flooding back. The panicky guilt would set in and Dean would race down the stairs to the kitchen looking for everything and anything to drink in order to knock himself out again.

Once, Lisa had found him on the kitchen floor in just his boxers: a bottle of cough syrup spilled onto the linoleum beside him, a glass smashed on the floor and several shards embedded in his feet. Lisa had patiently brought him upstairs and put him into the shower then waited until he had sobered up enough to get into bed.

The next morning when Dean woke, Lisa was perched on the side of his bed watching him.

"Not your finest moment yesterday," she said.

"Yeah, sorry about that. Maybe it wasn't the best idea coming here."

"Maybe, but I want you to get better, Dean."

Dean drew his fingers across his brow and pinched them together.

"I don't think you can get better from something like this. That's why I should probably leave." Dean made a move to get out of bed.

"You're not leaving. You can stay here as long as you want. But you have to make the decision if you want to move past this."

"You can't just move on from something like this, Lis. I let him do it."

"There was no other way. Remember you said that? I can't forgive you, Dean. You have to do that on your own." Lisa got up and turned at the door. "You couldn't have done anything else."

Dean shook his head. "I'm not so sure about that."

"No one could have." Lisa's hand hovered over the doorknob. "I'll bring you up some coffee." She shut the door, leaving Dean with his heart beating in his ears.

Day by day, Dean had started to rejoin the ranks of the living: he got up a little earlier rather than sleeping until noon, at night he would join Lisa and Ben while they were watching TV, still with a bottle close to hand, but drinking a little less every day.

Dean's relationship with Lisa thrived through Dean's self-imposed confinement.

"I know how to do laundry, Lisa." Dean leaned against the washing machine as Lisa separated out the whites and coloreds.

"No. You don't. Everything you wear is that same olive grey because you don't separate your whites and coloreds."

Dean looked down at his olive-gray T-shirt. She had a point. "I like this color," he said. "I look good in it."

"It's fatigue green. Let's go get you something in blue or even red."

"I'm not wearing red. It's a shade of pink."

"It's not," Lisa said, smiling as she leaned over to grab the laundry detergent, her face a few inches from Dean's.

Dean looked into her dark eyes and grabbed her arm. A pull inside of him wanted to do more, to hold her. But he just couldn't.

"I don't want to mess up your life," he said.

"You're not. And I won't let you. Now let me go. I have to put in the fabric softener ball."

"What the hell is that?"

Lisa grabbed the powder-blue ball, snapped off the cover and poured fabric softener into the hole.

"What does that do?" Dean asked, genuinely perplexed.

"Fabric softener, to make your clothes softer." Lisa smirked.

"I didn't know that was really a thing. Making clothes softer."

"Oh young Jedi, I have so much to teach you." Lisa slammed the washer shut, spun the dial and gave Dean a kiss on the cheek.

It was the first moment of levity that Dean had felt for weeks. But even as Dean's life normalized, thoughts about Sam haunted him.

"Never thought I would see you reading a self-help book."

Dean opened his eyes. He had fallen asleep on the couch in the living room. On his chest a copy of *Chicken Soup for the Soul* was flipped open. That night Lisa had said, "Why don't you read this?" She pulled it from a shelf and handed it to Dean. "It helped me when my grandmother died." Dean accepted the book reluctantly, but after reading a couple of pages he sort of got into it.

Sam leaned over and pulled the book from Dean's chest.

"'101 stories to open the heart and rekindle the spirit'? Really Dean? That's lame, even for you."

Dean peered at his brother through sleepy eyes. Sam stood before him in bloody clothes, with his face looking like a wild animal had ravaged it. Sam's lip had been torn— more like bitten off—his teeth peeked through beneath. His left ear had shriveled and darkened and on his left arm a swath of skin peeled from shoulder to wrist. His body had been scorched from top to bottom, layers of raw skin stuck to his clothes in slick black patches.

On some level, Dean knew he was imagining his brother standing before him. His dreams had been tormenting him like hounds. This evening was no exception.

"Sam."

"Long time no see, bro. Of course, as you can see, I'm having some trouble. They burned my eyes with pokers. I can only really get a good look at you if I go like this." Sam turned his head slightly to the side. His eyes were scarred into cataracts. Dean winced. Sam swung around, checking out the room. "Nice place. Comfy. Lot nicer than where I am. 'Course it's a little different for me down there being pulled apart fiber by fiber by a thousand rabid demons. No worries, though. I'm glad *you're* comfortable up here."

"It's not like that, Sam. I tried. What else am I supposed to do? Cass is gone. How am I going to get to you?"

"No. I get it, Dean. Don't worry about me. I'll be okay.

I'm fine being barebacked by Lucifer every second for the next couple of hundred millennia."

"I would do anything to get you out."

"You sure about that? It looks to me like you are just doing what you always wanted." Sam growled, but the force of the movement proved too much. He shook his head and spit a molar out into his hand. "Never did get my wisdom teeth out. They're taking care of that right now."

Dean was now up off the couch, face to face with the specter of his brother.

"Sam, you told me to come here to Lisa's. Remember? Barbecues, football games."

Sam winced.

"What's wrong?" Dean asked.

"Oh nothing, just a pesky demon who keeps playing the Operation game with my liver. I lost my funny bone first, wouldn't you know. Maybe that would have helped me get through this with a sense of humor."

"Sam, tell me what I can do. There has to be someone down there that knows how to break you out."

"Don't worry about me. Have a good life, Dean."

With that, Sam vanished.

Dean woke up in a cold sweat. His hands had clenched the book so tightly, the paperback was waded into a ball. The room was empty.

Dean swung his heels to the floor and hung his head. He felt as if someone had reached inside and pulled out his intestines through his eyes. The excruciating pain, the guilt, was beyond anything he had ever experienced.

He heard footsteps and looked up to see Lisa appear at the bottom of the stairs.

"You okay? I heard you scream," she said anxiously.

"I'm fine. Go back to sleep." Sweat dripped down his forehead.

Lisa walked across the room and sat down next to Dean on the couch.

"It's not your fault," she insisted gently.

"Lisa, please. I'm fine."

"We talked about you seeing someone before."

"I'm not seeing a psychiatrist. I'm fine. Really."

Lisa nodded and then left him alone.

Lisa had been trying to get him to see a therapist since he showed up. It was part of the normal mourning process, she told Dean. Not that the Winchester family had ever had a *normal* mourning process. It seemed to Dean as if they had died and come back so many times. Dean wondered how long it would be until he finally *did* crack. Until his soul finally fractured under all the pain he had seen, caused, and felt.

TWO

"It's normal to feel guilty when a family member passes, especially under extraordinary circumstances. Your brother died how, exactly?" Dr. Hodes took off her glasses and peered at Dean, slouched on the patterned couch opposite her.

"Um. Mining accident. We were both miners and he fell into a pit."

"Terribly sorry. That's an awful way to pass."

"Yeah. It is. Listen Doc—"

"You can call me Linda."

"Linda. I just need to know when this is going to go away. I'm putting my girl—well, my friend through hell. I'm staying at her place and I just need to be set straight again."

"Dean, I'm sorry, things don't work that way. We live in the real world where no magic power is going to restore your brother or take away your pain. What we need to focus on is why you have this guilt."

"How about angels?"

"Excuse me?"

"Nothing. I'm sorry. I think this was a waste of time." Dean rose from the couch and dug into his pockets.

"Dean, why don't you sit down? Let's talk about how therapy might help you so it doesn't feel like the weight of the world is on you and you alone."

"It's not anymore, Linda. It was on my brother and he took care of that. Thanks for your time." Dean pulled a wad of cash from his pocket, counted out some bills and placed them on the coffee table. He then grabbed his jacket and left the office.

When Lisa returned home that night Dean was on the couch surrounded by a pile of books.

"I see you found the library," she said putting down her purse and peering into the kitchen. "Where's Ben?"

"He's in bed," Dean said flipping a page. "We ate macaroni and cheese, watched *30 Rock*, then he conked out."

"So what's all this?" Lisa already could tell she was going to regret asking the question.

"Um. Nothing really."

"So you're just doing some light reading?" Lisa picked up a Carl Sagan book, then put it down. "Why, Dean?"

Dean looked at her.

"Because I want to know that I've exhausted every possible way of getting him out of there."

"By what? Turning back time? I mean this is…" Lisa looked around wide-eyed. "This is even a little too much for me."

Dean set down the book he was reading.

"I tried it your way; Dr. Melfi didn't work. Let me exhaust this as one last option. Please?"

Lisa shrugged, what else could she do. These past weeks Dean had seemed more connected to her and Ben. If he needed to do a little reading, perhaps it wasn't the worst thing in the world.

"Okay. I'm going to bed. Night," she said.

"Night," Dean said, already engrossed in another book.

"You know I'm not coming back," Sam said. The light from oncoming cars flickered over his face.

"Yeah. I'm aware." Dean clenched his jaw.

"So you've got to promise me something."

"Okay. Yeah. Anything."

"You got to promise not to try to bring me back."

Dean couldn't believe what he was hearing. What awaited Sam in Hell made Dean's time down there look like the ball pit in a McDonald's playground; fun but a little smelly. It wasn't going to be the same for Sam. Sam was going to get the royal treatment. He would be toast. Dean couldn't just let his brother rot in Hell.

"So, what am I supposed to do?" Dean asked.

"You go find Lisa. You pray she's dumb enough to take you in. You go have barbeques. And you go to football games. You go live some normal apple pie life, Dean. Promise me," Sam said, looking at his brother.

Far away lights blinked in and out over the cornfields of Michigan as the Impala raced past. They were rocketing toward their destiny. Sam knew it. Dean knew it.

Dean's throat was dry. He wasn't supposed to even *try* to get his brother back?

Dean lay in bed for twenty minutes staring at the ceiling, thinking about Sam. Downstairs he could hear Lisa and Ben getting ready to go to the reservoir. Dean knew life was precious, at any point they could go and most likely be gone forever. Then somehow whatever was holding Dean back, the bind finally dissolved. A weight lifted off him. Dean decided he should join Lisa and Ben. He would do this for Sam.

"Hey, buddy," Dean greeted Ben gruffly as he appeared in the kitchen doorway freshly showered and shaved.

Ben looked up from his breakfast. He beamed an accepting smile at Dean.

"Hey. Are you coming with us today?"

Lisa looked over from the stove, a wordless communication passed between them and Dean nodded. She understood him. Her limitless patience and acceptance was not the only thing Dean appreciated. As Lisa turned back toward the scrambled eggs Dean couldn't help but admire her tightly jean-clad backside. He quickly turned his attention to Ben.

"What's on the agenda at the park?"

"Fishing," Ben said, devouring the last bit of toast. "But I'm always the one that has to hook the worms for Mom."

"I'm squeamish with anything squishy," Lisa said, glancing over her shoulder.

"Well, we can't have that," Dean said, taking a place on

a stool next to Ben. "I mean, it's every man for themselves when it comes to fishing. Right Ben?"

"I've tried to teach her, but it's useless."

"I have a Winchester method that my father taught me." Dean lightly tapped Ben on the arm. "We'll get your mom up to speed. Next thing you know she'll be on *Bass Masters*."

Lisa set down some eggs, toast and a cup of coffee in front of Dean.

"I'm not going to be on *Bass Masters*."

Dean took a scoop of eggs.

"If I had known there was this type of service around here, I might have come downstairs more often," he said.

Lisa smiled. "The chef serves, the eaters wash up."

Dean made a face at Ben.

"I cleaned up last night," Ben said, taking his plate to the sink. "That means it's your turn."

Lisa leaned over the counter and sipped at her coffee. She chided, "Gotta pull your own weight around here."

Dean shoveled more eggs into his mouth. He might be able to do that.

"Ben, go get ready. Pull the tackle box and rods from the garage and set them out front. Okay?" Lisa said.

"Okay." Ben slid off the stool and disappeared through the laundry-room door leading to the garage.

A silence fell between Dean and Lisa. She put her hand on his knee.

"Thank you."

Dean set down his fork and peered into Lisa's dark eyes. He gently brushed a lock of hair from her forehead. Dean had been sleeping in Lisa's guest room for two months and never once had she asked why Dean had chosen her.

"Lisa, Sam told me to come here. To be with you."

"Are you telling me you're only here because Sam told you to come?"

"No. Initially, I didn't know where else to go. But also, yes, because he wanted me to be with you. Because even if I didn't want to admit it, he knew I wanted a life where I didn't have to worry if there's something around the corner ready to jump me. Sam knew me better than I knew myself. I'm sorry. I should have told you this weeks ago."

"I don't care if you're here because Sam said so. You wouldn't have stayed unless you wanted to. Right?"

Dean nodded.

"Then I guess it means you want to stay. Maybe you should start accepting that, rather than beating yourself up about it. Moving forward isn't a bad thing, Dean. And if you want to move forward with me and Ben, well... I'm willing to try that. You get what I'm saying?"

Dean understood. Even though the very fabric of his soul resisted the idea that he deserved good things, perhaps he couldn't suffer any longer. There wasn't anything he could do for Sam now except what he had asked: to be happy with Lisa.

THREE

"Moo shoo pork?" Dean called. He pulled the food container from the box on the kitchen table.

"That's mine," Ben yelled, racing from the living room to the kitchen, "and I want white rice."

"Brown rice. It's better for you." Lisa said, spooning rice onto a plate for Ben.

"Okay, whatever." Ben grabbed the plate and carried it back to his position in front of the television.

"Whoa, what's the rush?" Dean asked over his shoulder.

Ben turned up the sound.

"Not so loud," Lisa called, taking her place across the dinner table from Dean. She smiled as Dean cracked open a beer and dug into his chow mein.

"Not a bad place," Dean said, between bites.

"And you wanted to go to the Golden Palace again." Lisa smiled. "I don't know why you like it so much. You think that waitress is cute, don't you?"

"She doesn't have anything on you," Dean said, picking up Lisa's free hand and kissing her palm.

The last couple of weeks with Dean had been, if anything, simply idyllic: Dean had found a job refurbishing old buildings in nearby towns, and he was even cooking every once in a while. Life with Dean was great, even after everything they had been through in the beginning. Lisa never thought that Dean would walk back into her life, but here he was. It was strange. Years ago she had resigned herself to being a single mother. She had practically mastered being a single parent: she went to Ben's softball games, covered the parent/teacher conferences, stayed up late with Ben when he had the stomach flu. She handled a lot: the carpooling, lugging sports equipment, even the science projects which she never really understood. Lisa did it all. But it was the loneliness she felt at night that made her really want a partner. Then Dean showed up and all that changed.

Dean had never lived a normal life except those first years in Lawrence, Kansas before his mother was killed. Life with Lisa was exactly what he had imagined domesticity to be. There was no denying it; Dean was happy. He was like a regular guy: he had bought a truck and retired the Impala, and had even taken Ben to a couple of Indianapolis Indians baseball games.

Lisa had introduced Dean to the next-door neighbors. As summer approached cookouts became commonplace and Dean wholeheartedly took part in all suburbia had to offer.

On those summer nights Dean manned the grill while the neighborhood kids and Ben ran around menacing everyone with super soakers. And as the spring days dripped away into nights buzzing with the sound of cicadas, Dean's dreams about Sam stopped. For the first time in months Dean had slept through the night.

"You've got to help me, sis!" An inflated music score of a network show blared out from the television.

"Ben. Turn it down!" Lisa pulled her chair around and stared at the back of Ben's head. He was thoroughly engrossed and ignored the command. Lisa sprang to her feet.

"I'll get it." Dean stuffed an egg roll into his mouth and crossed to the living room. "Ben, your mom is talking to you."

Ben nodded but didn't make a move. Picking up the remote, Dean pointed it at the TV to turn down the volume.

"Carrissa, please." On the screen a blonde clad in black leather pants was being whipped around by an invisible force. "Use the *Necronomicon*!"

A brunette girl flipped through the elaborate pages of a large grimoire. "I'm trying. Here it is!" She began a Latin incantation. The wind subsided and the blonde dropped to the floor. The girls—sisters, Dean gathered—hugged each other. They had just escaped some sort of supernatural force and both of them wanted to go home. But how would they hide this from their mother? The two girls quipped a couple of lines of tween banter.

"What's this?" Dean asked.

"It's a new show. It's about two teenage witches." Ben blushed a bit. "But they're badass, not like stupid witches."

"What's it called?"

"*Spell Bound.*"

"*Spell Bound*, huh?" Dean sat down, and paused the show.

On screen, the book they called the *Necronomicon* hovered in digital stasis. During all of his obsessing over the past couple of months Dean hadn't thought about the *Necronomicon*.

The book had been thought to be a work of fiction by twentieth-century occultist and novelist H.P. Lovecraft. A Wikipedia search could bring up enough facts about it to make any Hollywood screenwriter seem sufficiently knowledgeable about the work; thus its appearance in the pop-song scored, tween show of which Ben was a fan.

But in truth, the book had existed over millennia, though it had been called a couple of different things: *The Red Dragon*, *The Great Grimoire*. These texts had all been combined, picked apart, then combined again. But the original text was thought to have come from one man, some seven hundred years before Christ's birth in Sumeria, what is now Iraq. It had been recopied, abridged and added to over centuries. The original was in an ancient form of Arabic, but it was later translated into Latin, Greek, German, and French by other scholars, monks, and priests.

The book contained ancient rights and spells with which to bind gods, which were in actuality demons. When the book was translated by Christians it was interpreted with less mysticism and more religion. The unorthodox nature of the text made many Christian scholars nervous, so they added locks and safety measures into the text, but it still stayed powerful.

Despite the changes made to the incantations, the text included spells for necromancy, raising the dead, the binding of demons, and mastery over the earthbound. If someone knew what they were doing the book was as potent as the day it was written. But there was one spell in particular—the only spell in the *Necronomicon* which Dean was interested in—a spell that could raise Lucifer.

The brothers had toiled to get Lucifer into the cage, but the *Necronomicon* was written to release Lucifer and bind him—a whole different story to raising Lucifer and starting the Apocalypse. It had never been done before because all sixty-six seals had to have been broken. But Sam had taken care of that and that meant that, in theory at least, Lucifer could now be raised and bound.

If Dean could get Lucifer out of Hell, he would be getting Sam out of the cage as well. Lucifer would no longer have to fight Michael, so he might have lost his spunk and perhaps could be lassoed silent for enough time for Dean to expel Lucifer from his brother's body. But the first step would be freeing Lucifer.

Dean thought about where he could find a complete enough version of the book. The brothers had run into a *Necronomicon* a couple of times, though usually only abridged, watered-down, fit-for-public-consumption pamphlets. An elementary version of the book had been used by the teens who had switched Sam into the body of a suburban geek a couple of years ago. It was witchcraft all right, but the pesky, pimpled kids had probably picked up their copy in a head shop.

The actual *Necronomicon* was locked up in a cloister somewhere in Europe. Chances were that H.P. Lovecraft had made most of his version up, since reading from the actual text is often fatal—it can only be used by someone very practiced and powerful. Dean was pretty sure that Amazon wasn't selling the originals. He had to find a real one.

And then who would help him cast the spell? He needed someone who knew how to handle powerful magic. Witches and those who practice witchcraft had used the *Necronomicon* and texts like it since ancient cultures developed an alphabet. The lineage of the sorcerers familiar with the book trickled down from ancient Sumeria to today. But where was Dean going to find a witch? He couldn't ask Bobby to point him in the right direction, and he and Sam had ganked every other witch that they had encountered. Finding a witch that was powerful enough and willing to help Dean might be difficult in Cicero, Indiana.

Dean sat down next to Ben, who again commandeered the remote.

"You want more?" Lisa called to Dean. "If not I'm saving it for leftovers."

Dean didn't answer, he was thinking about his brother.

FOUR

Sam peered at the house through the Impala's rain-splattered windshield. They had followed their mark home, but there hadn't been any movement since he went inside.

"What do you think he's doing in there?" Sam asked.

"What else would a guy who has killed everyone in his family be doing?" Dean said.

"You think he did it?" Sam asked.

"Totally. You're such a softy, Sam. You think he's in there making a fluffer-nutter and sitting down to watch *Frontline*? No, he's getting ready to go out and eat more human flesh. He's the last man standing. Of course he did it. He's gotta be a rugaru or a shapeshifter or something."

Sam wasn't so sure. Granted, Nick Warner *had* been found in the house where all three of his family members were found dead. But he claimed that he was sleeping and didn't hear anything. Plus, the police had cleared him. However, in all of Sam and Dean's travels they had come across stranger things. It could be a case of amnesia. Certainly in werewolf cases they had encountered the infected people didn't remember anything when they turned back. Maybe Nick Warner didn't remember killing his family.

"We have to just wait and see."

"Well, I've had enough, I'm going in," Dean said as he kicked open the car door and grabbed his sawed-off from the back seat.

"Dean, wait. What're you gonna do? Just walk into the guy's house? That's breaking and entering," Sam said, following closely behind his brother, shotgun in hand.

"Not the way I do it. The way I do it, it's just breaking."

Dean stomped up the steps and yelled, "Nick Warner, we know you're in there. Come out with your hands up or we're coming to get you!"

"What are you going to do when he comes out and sees you're not the police, Kojak?" Sam asked.

Dean ran his fingers through his hair. "Just let me handle that pa—"

A horrible scream came from inside the house. Followed by the sound of breaking furniture.

"Watch out!" Dean cried.

He stepped back, then hurled his shoulder into the door. The lock splintered away, revealing the dark interior beyond.

"Mr. Warner? Nick Warner?" Sam called.

The house had fallen silent. Dean motioned that he was going to check the back rooms, and he indicated that Sam should sweep the upper floors. As Sam crept up the stairway, a dark streak crossed quickly before him. A door slammed at the top of the landing. Sam stood before the door with his shotgun at the ready, then slowly turned the door handle and entered the room.

On the bed a nasty old crone crouched over a tied and bound man, who Sam assumed to be Nick Warner. She was up to her elbows in Nick, her hand jammed into his mouth. Nick was turning blue. She was trying to tear out his heart.

Sam pulled the trigger back and aimed at the crone's back. But she was quick. In moments, the old hag humped on top of him and overpowered his large frame. He struggled beneath her weight, her putrid breath wet his face with corpse-smelling saliva.

"Dean!" Sam yelled.

The crone was stronger than her bony body suggested. Both Sam's arms were pinned to the floor. She bent down and examined Sam's face. Sam half expected her to tell him how pretty he was. Instead she said, "I'm going to eat your heart."

"Talk about cliché," Dean said from the doorway.

The crone's dark pupils swept over Dean.

"You're next. But first I'm going to take his liver," she cackled.

She shot her arm down Sam's throat. His eyes bugged out, and he fought against her with his one free arm.

BLAM! The bullet blew apart the crone's head. Her body slumped over. Sam gagged and threw the body off him. He rubbed his tongue with his hand, trying to get the taste of the old woman's disgusting limb out of his mouth.

"Yum. Croney," Dean said.

He took one look at Nick Warner and his smile vanished.

"Let's get this poor guy to the hospital. He's lost a lot of blood."

"I almost lost a liver. I can still feel her fingers touching my stomach lining," Sam said with a grimace. "So, I guess Nick wasn't to blame."

"Nope, guess not," Dean said, untying the poor man from the bed. He then hoisted him onto his shoulder. "Come on, let's get going."

Later that night, as Dean and Sam drove out of the small North Dakota town, they both enjoyed a moment of quiet contemplation. The feeling that they were doing good in the world.

Dean woke from his reverie.

"You seem far away." Lisa leaned back in her lawn chair and regarded Dean.

It was a very warm day, summer was in full swing and Ben was out riding his bike with friends. Dean had been staring into space silently for a good twenty minutes without speaking. His mind *was* far away, in a different dimension entirely, he was thinking about breaking Sam out of the cage. The terrible dreams about Sam had stopped, but Dean's obsession with springing Sam had not.

"What's going on in there?" Lisa tapped Dean's head with her index finger.

Dean dusted away the cobwebs.

"I'm good. I'm good. Don't I look good?"

"Yes. I was just wondering what you were thinking," Lisa

said, then held up her hand in defense. "I know it's one of the cardinal sins of relationships to ask a guy what he's thinking. But I figure I have a kid, I'm way past stuff like that."

"I'm thinking…" Dean in fact knew he couldn't tell Lisa what he was thinking. *The* Necronomicon, he thought. *I'm thinking about how I'm going to find a powerful ancient book, steal it, and then use it to bounce my brother—who is probably already ripped to shreds—out of Hell. I know I said I would stop obsessing about Sam. But I just can't help but think this book could get me my brother back.*

Now of course finding a copy will prove difficult, there might not even be one in the United States. Even if I do get my hands on it, I'll have other problems, like figuring out how to get Lucifer out of my brother's body. I'm hoping the binding spell in the Necronomicon *will help me cast Lucifer back, just not in Sam's body.*

To top it all off, thinking I need to find a powerful person, most likely a witch, to help me with the whole thing. So basically I'm thinking about doing the impossible—getting Sam out of Hell.

Dean knew he couldn't say all that to Lisa. So he said the thing that every woman likes to hear.

"Let's go on vacation."

Lisa sat up to face him. "Really? Dean, that would be so wonderful. Ben would love that. The last vacation Ben and I had was when he was six. We went to a water park in Michigan and I got the flu and couldn't take him on any of the rides. A vacation would be perfect." She leaned over and kissed Dean on the mouth.

"Wow, if I'd known I'd get that reaction I would have mentioned it weeks ago."

"Where are we going to go?" Lisa asked.

Where would we go? Dean thought about it. He responded with an answer that was impossible to disagree with.

"It's a surprise, been planning it for a while. I'll let you know."

"Dean, that's great. Ben is going to flip."

Lisa was happy. Mentioning a vacation was a symbol that Dean was finally moving on from his past; putting away the crazy life that he had led for twenty-five years. Normal people take vacations. A vacation would mean Dean had finally joined the ranks of the normal and he'd retired from hunting monsters and killing things.

Of course, Lisa would never tell Dean how she felt about his old life, in fact she had always told him to do what he wanted. She didn't want to mold Dean. He was unmoldable. But if Dean made changes himself she was more than happy to accept them.

Dean smiled. A vacation would be nice. But even as he thought about where they should go—Disneyland, Yellowstone, New York—there was something that unnerved him. For the past few months Dean had been in self-imposed exile. Even though he had begun to play suburban Ken—he had begun working, his life with Lisa and Ben was happy and fulfilled, and the memory of Sam had become less like a gnawing and more like an slight stitch that panged his soul—Dean still felt guilty about truly enjoying himself. And the idea that the *Necronomicon* could possibly liberate Sam from Hell was tantalizing.

"Salem?" Lisa peered at Dean over breakfast.

"Sure, I mean, look. They have the beach, restaurants, and old clipper ships. It will be educational. Ben will love it. Really." Dean pushed the AAA brochure over to Lisa.

She stared at it skeptically.

"It's not a vacation destination though. Is it?"

"Of course it is, look at all the tourists in this picture!" Dean beamed.

Lisa looked at Dean's satisfied face. She couldn't really argue about it, any vacation would be nice.

"Okay. Salem it is."

"Ten AM. Everyone ready. " Dean took the last swig of his coffee.

"Really?" Lisa asked. "You want to leave now?"

"Sure, why not? What are we waiting for?" Dean wanted to be heading east as soon as possible. He could have driven the fifteen-hour car ride in one sitting, but he knew that Lisa would balk at that. They would probably stop halfway through New York State. After that it would be an easy five- or six-hour drive.

Thinking about it the night before, Dean had realized that to find a witch he was going to have to go somewhere legendary—Europe was out of the question, but the next best place was Salem. That town had to be teeming with witches. He could have a nice family vacation with Lisa and Ben and also find a witch that could help him raise Sam from the dead.

Lore said that a *Necronomicon* had been burned during the Salem witch trials in 1692. Chances were that someone in that town still had one. Dean reasoned if he could find the book, he'd find the witch. But he would have to be prepared.

"I'm going to go out and pick up a couple of things," Dean yelled, grabbing the keys to his truck. "I'll be back in a half-hour. Be ready."

Dean knew he had to have plenty of protection once he was in Salem; a *Necronomicon* wasn't something to fool around with, and the person who would be powerful enough to use it wouldn't be either. He decided to stop off at the local garden store; there was no better place to find mandrake, hemlock or monkshood. Not only were these things essential for making hex bags and protection spells, they all made excellent perennial ground cover.

After shopping, Dean sat in his truck outside the garden store. He snipped off the plants' tops and threw the pots of soil out his truck window, drawing stares from the store employees. Feeling guilty, he got out of the truck and took the pots back inside to be recycled. *Wow*, he thought, *I am a suburban douche-dweller.*

Back at home Dean took the cut plants and some of the weapons he kept in the trunk of the Impala, and packed them into his duffle.

Dean didn't touch the Impala anymore. He had shoved it into the garage and covered it with a tarp. It was best he not be reminded of all the time he and Sam had spent in it.

Instead he climbed into the driver's seat of Lisa's CRV. Ben hopped into the back seat. As long as Ben had his videogame player he was happy. Lisa took her seat beside Dean.

"Family vacation, huh?" Lisa said.

"Yeah, I'm so Chevy Chase right now. Holiddaayy Roooaad," Dean sung at the top of his lungs.

"Okay Sparky, let's go."

Dean gunned the engine. Pulling out of the driveway he admired Lisa's little house; he was hoping that the next time he saw it he would have his brother with him. Maybe they both could stop hunting once and for all, together.

FIVE

The Indiana clouds hung low like charcoal smudges wiped against a newsprint-colored sky, threatening rain.

Sam looked southward. He was twenty miles away from Dean. It would be a short drive—thirty minutes at the very most. Sam could make an excuse, slip away from Samuel and be there at Dean's front door. He'd embrace him. Sam would tell him he was back, he didn't know how it had happened, but he was back.

Sam looked in the direction of Cicero; Dean was there with Lisa. Of course, he knew he should make every effort to see Dean. But strangely he didn't really want to. Sam wondered what he was feeling: Was it comfort that Dean was safe and finally happy? Was it happiness that he was alive and brought back from the dead? Sam had said "yes" to Lucifer and on that field he fought with every fiber of his being to gain enough control of his own body in order to throw himself into the pit. It seemed that was the last time he felt... anything.

* * *

"You coming, Sam?"

Samuel Campbell leaned out of the door of his truck and stared hard at his grandson. Sam always seemed so far off. He couldn't quite put his finger on it. Or rather he didn't want to. He hadn't ever met the boy before. *Maybe that's how he always was.* Though Samuel couldn't quite convince himself of that. It was strange how he had found him in the first place, but despite the strange situation and the strange grandson, Sam was family.

Samuel sighed, the reality of this weird existence hitting him again. Most days he hated waking up. He didn't think it was a miracle that had brought him back from the dead; there was too paralyzing an ache inside him for this to be a true blessing.

What bothered Samuel was walking the Earth with the knowledge that his daughter, Mary, was dead. The regret and the loss stung him every day. All he wanted was to see his daughter, her radiant face ringed with blonde hair. She always looked like a cherub to him. He didn't have the chance to see her grow past the age of twenty-one.

It's said that it's awful for a child to die before a parent, but Samuel thought it was more terrible to come back to life and be told of your child's death. And to know that she was killed by the same demon that had killed him was even worse. What he would give to go back to 1974 and murder Yellow Eyes! Samuel knew that he should be overjoyed that he could spend time with his grandson. In any regular person's life dying ten years before your grandchildren are born ordinarily precludes being able to spend time with them—but not if you're a Campbell.

"I'm coming!" Sam swung around and got into his grandfather's truck.

"Why you dilly-dallying?" Samuel cast Sam a sidewards glance, trying once again to see what was behind that blank stare, but as usual it betrayed nothing. He just had to hope he was getting through to the kid. Much depended on Sam being at his side.

"You can't see him, you know that right? It would be dangerous."

Sam nodded. "I just wonder how he's doing."

"He's doing *fine*," Samuel said. They had been over this a half-dozen times since he had met up with his grandson. Dean was happy and the most important thing for Sam to do was to keep hunting. Sam would be putting Dean and his girl's kid in danger if he contacted them. True or not, that's what Samuel repeated to him and most of the time it seemed to work.

Samuel shook his head. Talking to his grandson he sometimes felt as though he was trying to get through to a block of wood. Sam was distant. But it was his inability to be *warm* that worried Samuel. He wondered what he had gotten himself into.

At other times, however, Samuel was outright floored by Sam's facility for hunting. He had never seen anything like it. In the past couple of months hunting with Sam had proved to be a marvel. Killing werewolves, vampires, and wendigos, even ghost hunting was almost easy with Sam. He intuited the prey's next move and was there in an instant; the capture or the kill was vicious but surgical. It was as if Sam's deftness at killing was drawn from some lifeblood deep within him. It almost bordered on the uncanny.

It was for this reason that Sam had become a leader of sorts to his cousins: Christian, Mark, and Gwen. They were second and third cousins to Sam and a tough trio, an extension of the more scrappy side of the Campbell family tree, and it was no small feat to impress them. But Sam had earned their respect.

Samuel was impressed with Sam; if pressed he might admit that he was also a little scared of him. But the sheer number of monsters Sam was able to take down required Samuel to look past that. He needed Sam.

Samuel and Sam headed back toward the compound and pulled into the gated driveway just before dusk. The compound was a collection of industrial and agricultural buildings, strongly fortified with cement and rebar. A good place to take a stand against monsters. It served as an unofficial hunting headquarters for the Campbell family. When Samuel came back from the dead, he took up heading the family and had been sleeping there ever since.

It turned out he had to stay close to base because things had changed from the days when he was a hunter. There were more monsters than ever before. The needle had been pinging up in the red zone for months. They were on monster overload. Perhaps it was just lucky happenstance, as this was all good news to him. Samuel wanted to hunt as much as possible; he had made a deal that depended on it.

SIX

"Jez, this place is a dump. Though, I *do* know a lovely designer who could do wonders with the sparseness of the space. Maybe an Eames lounger or two?"

Samuel spun around and found himself face to face with Crowley. Crowley was a dandified turd in Samuel's book, a despicable thing that blighted the earth. Even when Crowley was human, he had to have been an ass.

But Samuel needed him. He had been playing the demon's games since he got back and his patience was starting to wear as thin as a crick, but he had to keep going. There was a light at the end of this tunnel—a big light. If Samuel helped Crowley amass a fortune of monster souls, Crowley would bring back Mary.

"What the hell do you want?" Samuel sneered.

"I just dropped in for a jelly roll and some of that delicious coffee with powdered milk you have out there." Crowley motioned to the main space next to Samuel's office.

"No fussing about the nibblets though." The demon dusted off a chair with his handkerchief. "You and I have some business to attend to."

"I think you and I have said all we need to say to one another," Samuel grunted as he eyed a salt-filled shotgun that was within arm's reach. How he would love to stick it into Crowley's mouth and pull the trigger.

"Don't even think of blowing me away old man. Then where would you be?" Crowley cackled. Then, as though with the flick of a switch, he turned serious. "You need to have a talk with Dean. You remember him right? Your *other* grandson? The one with an actual... heartbeat? I know, I know. Dean's just a regular old human so you might not have any use for him. But I need you to talk to him."

"You know I can't do that. There is no way I can do that," Samuel said firmly.

"*How* you do it is not my problem. Just that you *do* it. Dean has a funny little idea in his head and you have to make sure he doesn't go through with it." Crowley crossed and uncrossed his legs as he spoke.

"How do you know?" Samuel asked.

"You don't need to know that. Only that I do. He thinks he's going to be able to raise Sam from the dead using a pisser of an old text."

Samuel realized immediately what Crowley was getting at.

"The *Necronomicon?*" he exclaimed. It hadn't occurred to Samuel before but now that he thought about it, that book *could* cause them some trouble. In the wrong hands, the wrong spell would raise Lucifer. *Those boys would do just about anything for one another,* thought Samuel. *I guess that does run in the family.*

Crowley's voice cut through his thoughts.

"Look here, mate, you and I are wearing the same jersey, yes? So just make sure that Deany-boy doesn't get his hands on that one tiny little spell. Because let me tell you, that would be a crapstorm of epic proportions. There is a chance that spell, with enough battery power behind it, could actually raise Lucifer in whatever state he's in. If that old boy gets loose again… Well then, all bets are off between you and me. Understand?"

"How am I going to stop him? I can't control what he does."

"No, but you can control who he has access too. So make sure he doesn't get his hands on that book." Crowley stood. "I'm a little grumpy that I have to keep repeating meself," he added, moving so he standing nose to nose with Samuel. "Just do what I tell you to do. Okay?"

The demon's cold breath stung Samuel's face.

"Fine," Samuel said.

"Well, good. I'm just chuffed to bits." Crowley stepped back, all light and breezy again. "This went well. As always, I enjoy your company Samuel. It's nice to have another old fella about."

If Samuel had been up on the latest ways to tell Crowley where to stick it he would have, but since he wasn't, he stayed silent. Crowley smiled, and in an instant he was gone.

Samuel plopped down into a chair. He hated that guy, almost as much as he hated Yellow Eyes.

"Oops, one more thing!" Crowley suddenly reappeared, so close Samuel couldn't even stand up. The demon leaned over him while tapping on the crystal of his watch. "Dean is taking the fam' on a little vacay to Salem, Massachusetts. You understand the implications?" Crowley cocked his head questioningly.

"I have to follow him," Samuel said solemnly.

"Smart man. No wonder you're the patriarch of this cursed and screwed clan." Crowley patted Samuel on the cheek with his palm. "You're taking a road trip. Chafed ass, corn nuts, having to hold your pee for fifty miles. Such fun. Get your fanny-pack." And with that the demon disappeared again.

"Damn it." Samuel pinched his brow. Then he called out, "Sam! Sam!"

A few moments later, his grandson opened up the steel door of Samuel's office. His bulk almost filled the entire seven-foot doorframe.

"Yeah?" Sam asked.

"We have to go. Reconnaissance mission," Samuel said, hefting himself out of the chair and toward the wall that served as his mini-armory.

"For what?" Sam asked.

"We have to follow Dean," Samuel said.

"What? Why?"

"Because he's…" Samuel trailed off. He didn't know if he should tell Sam that Dean was trying to resurrect him. Would that cause Sam undue pain to see his brother manically searching for a way to bring him back from the dead? Samuel wasn't sure. Sam was so cold and calculating, it was hard to know how he would react. But reconnaissance wasn't a good enough carrot on a string for Sam, he had to pique the boy's hunting instincts.

"Witches," Samuel said firmly. "We have to find some witches."

"What does that have to do with Dean?" Sam asked.

"He's after them too, and we need to get there first."

"What are they doing? I mean, they're kind of small fry compared to the monsters we've been hunting."

"They're trying to create monsters. Just trust me. We could pull in the motherload with this one." Samuel was peeved he needed to give any explanation at all. "Go tell the others they're on their own for a few days—and you and I are going to need the van."

Sam shrugged and left the room. It was hunting—that was all that mattered to him.

Outside he stared out across the fields that surrounded the camp. He wondered why he felt disconnected from the thought of following his brother. Was it for the same reason that, though there was a breeze, he couldn't feel it on his face? Did it have to do with the fact that he hadn't slept since he got back? And though he had been eating, as sort of a facade so he wouldn't freak the others out, he hadn't been hungry. Not even once. Did it have to do with that?

And that other feeling Sam remembered having—when he and Dean would come out alive after a particularly nasty

SEVEN

The only thing Sam *did* feel was the intense need to hunt. It was almost as if an animal within him had woken up. He could literally *feel* the move a monster was about to make, and be there before it was. Sam was singular in his drive. Hunt. It was as if he no longer needed to intellectualize the right and wrong of it. All he cared about was getting the monster. For this reason Sam really was Samuel's perfect weapon. Except Sam's new nature wasn't without its dangers.

Three weeks ago he and Samuel had been hunting down a monster that had taken up residence in a halfway house full of recovering drug addicts and alcoholics. The local paper had covered a murder-suicide and another unexplained death at the house. Police thought the deaths were due to the unsavory characters of the residents, most of whom had been in and out of jail or had some type of police record, but Sam knew better. He talked his grandfather into going with him to investigate.

The next morning they arrived at the door of the facility posing as priests.

"May I help you?" A short-haired, round woman answered the door.

"Bless you, child. I'm Father Tipton," Sam introduced himself, "and this is Father Halford. We're with the Cumberland County Prayer Outreach Center. We were hoping to come and help your residents in their time of need. Two deaths in three weeks. Terrible."

The woman assented with a pudgy-cheeked smile. She introduced herself as Beverley and led them into a meeting room, where they talked her into letting them take a look around the house.

Seeing that each room was outfitted with a floor grate, their first thought was that the monster had been moving from room to room through the heating system. But the grates were wrought iron. Since ghosts can't pass through iron and demons don't like to either, they were confused. What was it? There was no way to be sure. Sam proposed they act as bait.

With a little persuasion, they were allowed to stay the night.

"I'll stay up. You go to bed," Sam said to his grandfather. He and Samuel had been given a room to share in the halfway house.

"Naw, I'm fine," Samuel said, though Sam could see he looked tired.

"Okay, just saying. I don't need much sleep."

"Right. Maybe I'll just shut my eyes," Samuel said,

relenting. He lay back on the bed and moments later his breathing slowed and he began to snore gently.

Sam held his salt-packed shotgun in his lap and stared into space, waiting.

Then he heard it. A deep moan from the bowels of the house, as if someone was trapped within the walls, trying to get out.

Without waking his grandfather, Sam crept out into the hallway. The residents' rooms were all located off the upstairs corridor.

A door slammed. Sam whipped around, but didn't move an inch further. He listened again, and heard the same moaning noise. Sam peered into the gloom at the end of the hallway. A grey mass appeared out of nowhere and gradually took shape in the dirty dark.

Sam trained his shotgun on the specter, but in a blink it was gone.

Sam ran down the corridor to the spot where the thing had been. There was no heating grate, no nothing—nowhere for it to go. Above him a single bulb flickered. He moved to touch it, but the bulb suddenly got brighter and brighter until it popped.

The thin shards of glass broke in Sam's face. He calmly picked them out of his skin with his fingernail.

Down the hallway underneath a door, Sam saw a light. He moved toward it and kicked open the door. A girl, about his age, stared at him, her mouth open in a silent scream.

Without hesitation, Sam spun around and aimed his gun at the ceiling above him.

BLAM!

The shot missed the creature as it dropped on top of Sam.

A shtriga, he realized. Sam struggled but the shtriga stuck its putrid face into his, and started to suck. It pulled, its beetle-black eyes rolling into its head. But there was something wrong, nothing was happening, no soul was being sucked out of Sam.

Sam smiled and with his right arm aimed the gun at the monster's head. The shtriga avoided the shot and skidded up the wall, still facing its unbeatable prey. Sam aimed again but it was gone.

The girl on the bed finally let out a nails-on-a-chalk-board scream.

"Shut up," Sam barked.

She did, cowering back away from Sam. Sam opened the bedroom door, but despite the screams and gunshots, the house was silent. He flicked the light switch.

"Don't do that. It might come back! What if it—" the girl squealed.

"What did I say?" Sam spat. She shut up again.

Sam closed his eyes. There were twenty people in the house. It was the perfect place for a shtriga to feed—beaten-down people who had given up on life. Easy prey. Like the shtrigas' taste for children.

Sam crept back into the room where Samuel still slept; somehow the noise further down the corridor had failed to wake him.

Sam quickly loaded a couple of iron bullets into his gun—the only thing guaranteed to work on a shtriga. Then he turned out the light and leaned over his grandfather.

Sam knew the monster would be attracted to a body that wouldn't put up too much of a fight. He took a pillow from underneath his grandfather's head. He held it over Samuel's face and lightly pushed down. He needed to slow Samuel's breathing enough so that the shtriga would be drawn to his body, on the brink of dying. Samuel's eyes popped open. He struggled against Sam, but his strength was no match for his grandson's and in moments Samuel was unconscious.

Sam released the pillow and checked Samuel's pulse—it was weakened, but still there. He was fine. Sam then got down on his hands and knees and shimmied underneath the bed.

A few seconds later, the lamp on the nightstand started to flicker and the air filled with a heavy weight. From his position, Sam could only see a foot of space between the floor and the underbelly of the bed.

Slowly, the dripping grey matter of the shtriga appeared, fluttering a couple of inches above the floor. It was singularly focused on the unconscious old man lying on the mattress above.

Sam heard the shtriga's large mouth open, followed by a hollow sucking. Samuel gurgled. The life was slowly being drained from him. Sam silently pushed his way to the opposite side of the bed, and pulled himself into a crouch. With his finger poised on the trigger, he sprang up from the floor and fired.

The shtriga emitted a high-pitched, inhuman scream as the iron bullet exploded through the top of its head. Dusty rag-like pieces stuck to the wall behind it. The body fell on top of Samuel.

"Ahhhhh!" Samuel coughed as he sat up. "What the hell did you do?"

"Used you as bait. Had to," Sam replied.

He stood up and threw the monster's body off Samuel's legs.

"You what?"

"I used you as bait. Had to slow down your heart rate to make you weaker, so it would be attracted to you." Sam put the shotgun away.

"Not only did you kill the damn thing, but you almost killed me in the process!" Samuel spluttered, glaring at his grandson.

"I just wanted to kill it. I knew it would go after you. You weren't in any danger."

"Fathers?" Beverly stood in curlers and a bathrobe at the doorway to the room.

Sam shoved past her.

"All set here. The souls of your residents are all saved."

"But what is that?" Beverly asked, pointing at the splattered body of the shtriga.

"Dead cat," Samuel said, flashing her a cursory smile. "Sorry about that. The church will cover the clean-up costs. Thanks for letting us stay."

Samuel moved past her and followed Sam out the door.

Sam thought about how many miles he had traveled with Dean. Thousands, millions. He didn't know. He didn't care.

All Sam wanted was to get to Salem and take out as many witches as Samuel told him to.

It made perfect sense to him that witches would be creating monsters. It seemed like there were a lot more of them around these days. Old Sam would have wanted to know why there were more monsters. New Sam just liked hunting them. Old Sam wouldn't have almost killed his grandfather to gank a monster. New Sam, it didn't faze him much. According to his grandfather, he had messed up. He moved on. He didn't feel guilty about it like old Sam would have.

Sam did remember having that feeling, guilt. A sick aching in his stomach, a flutter in his heart that would make him tremble and go weak. Guilt was an awful feeling, and being with Dean those past couple of years he had felt it *constantly*. Now, Sam didn't have that feeling any longer. He was free. Free to run after something, kill it and then move on. He was no longer tied to the push and pull of his mind and heart, weighing whether what he was doing was right or wrong. Instinct was the only feeling that was driving him.

THRUMP. THRUMP. THRUMP. Sam drove the van as his grandfather slept in the back. The road stretched out before him. Truth be told, he liked being without his brother. Hunting. Sam only wanted to hunt.

EIGHT

As Sam drove, he thought back to three months before.

He lay on the cold grassy ground looking up at the gray sky above him. A cold sensation was shooting from his back around his spine, and invading him through his blood. He was dizzy, as if someone was pushing him on one of those spinning carousels in a playground. His entire body hummed like a thousand tuning forks were being held to his bones. He tried to move his fingers, but wasn't sure if he was able.

Thirty minutes went by before he could roll off his back and sit up. All around him the grass was scorched black and flattened by the epic fight between the two powerful angels. Everything was super bright, his eyes burned.

A car drove past on the nearest road, the sound startling him. He realized his ears were still ringing. He had no clue how long he had been gone. Or how he'd got out.

He pulled his shirt off his shoulder—but there wasn't

a hand-mark on him like Dean had had when he was brought back by Castiel. He didn't have a bruise or a scratch on him. How had this happened? The last thing he remembered was jumping into the pit, and then a soul-searing pain. That was it.

He stumbled out of Stull Cemetery disoriented and alone. He headed north and hit Route 70. A big rig had picked him up and offered him a ride down the road to Topeka. Once in Topeka he had realized he wanted to check on one thing.

Sam caught the date on a flat-screen TV in a coffee shop and realized he hadn't been gone for very long at all.

Though not much time had passed, there was a profound difference in the way Sam felt. Namely—great. He felt like his legs had a strange sense of purpose, like they were more self-assured. He held his body differently, he felt stronger, broader, more vital. Yes, there was definitely a difference in Sam.

He quickly realized the potential of his situation; he could be anyone, do anything. No one was waiting for him any longer; there was no one to tell him he was messing everything up—again. No one to tell him that he couldn't do something or that he wasn't living up to what was expected of him.

Like Dean.

For the first time in a long time, Sam felt free. But he needed to check and make sure. For that reason, he went to Lisa Braeden's house and confirmed that Dean had shown up. He saw Dean, glass of Scotch in hand, sitting at the dinner table and Sam knew this was how it should be. Dean should be in there, and he should be outside. In the world. A new person.

It took him two days to get new credit cards and pick up a new Dodge Charger courtesy of some falsified loan documents. Sam didn't want to go to any of their old haunts so he found a different black market, a small brick warehouse on the south side of Chicago, where he purchased a couple of unregistered guns. Sam knew what he had been brought back for. He was here to hunt. There was an ache inside him and he knew exactly what food to feed it: pure, unadulterated hate.

Sam holed up in a crappy motel with a new computer, he guessed Dean had kept his old one, and started combing the local news.

He stayed up all night, meticulously looking at each picayune site. And then he found an interesting little tit-bit. A whole spate of cow mutilations in a small town in North Dakota. Every animal was found drained of blood, the throat ripped out, but there weren't any signs of tire tracks or animal prints. Could be a werewolf, or something cryptozoological. Whatever, it was a case.

Sam started his investigation by examining the dozens of comments on the news site. Just about all of them complained that the new sheriff, Sheriff Littlefoot, wasn't doing anything to help the local ranchers. They blamed his inaction on him being an out-of-towner who didn't understand the town's need for answers.

Sam roared into town in his Charger, sussed out which ranchers had been victimized and swiftly interviewed them.

Not that it told him much. The hard-working, hard-living ranchers were fed up with guys in offices not doing anything for them. They needed answers.

Posing as a park ranger, Sam rented a four-wheeler and went out to the site of the mutilations. The sky was big and the plains were wide. Even as he stood knee-deep in cow intestines, for the first time in a long time Sam felt he was *enjoying* his life.

That night Sam kept vigil on a barstool in the local saloon. He had been eyeing the cute waitress in the jean-skirt all night. She had given him a couple of glances, but nothing that told him she was interested. That was, until closing time rolled around.

Sam had downed what he thought was a good amount of beer, but he was as lucid and sober as he'd ever been. Her name was Jodi, and Sam chatted with her as she closed out her night and counted her cash tips. They shared another drink and then Sam invited her back to his motel room.

Sam was amazed. It was usually Dean who bagged the chicks. Sam had never had much of a taste for it. But something had changed. He enjoyed himself. In fact, it was the best sex of his life. And he didn't understand why. The girl was cute, but by no means would you stop the car to look at her. She had a good body, but it wasn't like she was a keeper. Sam couldn't understand what had changed, until he realized that emotionally—he felt nothing.

He didn't feel bad about leading her on and telling her that he had a new job in town and was looking to settle down with the "right girl." He didn't feel bad when he lied and said, yeah, he thought she was beautiful. He didn't feel anything but pure physical pleasure. No guilt. Usually, if he had sex with a girl, he would immediately think of Jessica and the moment would be ruined. But now: nothing. No guilt. It was the most free he had ever felt in his life.

But more pressing things demanded his attention. He was pretty sure there was a werewolf in town somewhere. The question was—where?

The next morning he decided to visit the infamous Sheriff Littlefoot, posing as a fed this time, so as to outrank him. Sam walked into the sheriff's dimly lit office. The metal blinds were cinched shut and made it difficult to see. The sheriff was a tall man of Native American descent. He was handsome but had grown paunchy around the middle.

"Mind if I open these up?" Sam said, moving toward the windows.

"Actually, I do. Sorry, stigmatism in my eye. Doctor says it's best to keep the light low."

"I've never heard that before," Sam said as he made himself comfortable and let the Sheriff sweat a bit.

The Sheriff ran through the usual nervous questions and answers a small-town law officer asks when a federal agent is in their jurisdiction. "What was this about?" "These things happen all the time in ranching areas, it's just wild animals." "I've seen this a million times before and it's usually over-active imaginations."

Sam listened, then asked to look at the files and if the Sheriff would mind if he stopped by at his house to drop them off later.

The sheriff resisted, saying, "Me, my wife, and the boy might be having dinner."

Sam assured him that he wouldn't interfere, he just wanted to get the files back in the sheriff's hands as soon as possible.

That afternoon, Sam sat outside the sheriff's house until the evening. It was a nice neighborhood; kids played in the streets, mothers pushed baby carriages. Sam registered this and continued to gaze intently at the sheriff's house. But the small clapboard house was silent all afternoon, the curtains drawn tight.

About seven in the evening, when the sun had gone down, and the prairies surrounding the town gave off a silver sheen, the lights inside the house clicked on, and the sheriff's little boy came out to play for the first time all day.

Shortly thereafter the sheriff came home. Sam slid low in his seat. The sheriff gathered up his son and went inside.

Sam took out one of his new guns and made sure it was loaded with a silver bullet and then approached the house. As he got closer a sickening baying came from inside. Sam tried to peek through the window but the curtains were still drawn. He needed to find another way in.

On other side of the house, Sam pushed open the small bathroom window. Through the open doorway and down a hallway he could make out the faint outline of a regular living room, complete with a small TV and worn couches.

Sam silently hoisted himself in through the window and crept across the room. Across the hallway there was another, smaller parlor and behind that the kitchen. The baying stopped. Sam thought he could hear the slick, wet sound of teeth pulling flesh apart.

Pressed against the wall, he edged down the corridor until he was on the other side of the kitchen door. Sam knew he was going to have to act quickly.

Just as he was about to kick the door open, the sound of breaking glass crackled from somewhere in the house.

A chair scraped—someone was getting up in the kitchen to investigate the sound. Sam needed a way out.

He ran up the stairs, and pushed open the first door he came to. He hid in what looked like the kid's bedroom. He waited a short while, then crept back down the stairs. Outside the kitchen door he drew in his breath, readied his gun then—

"This is my hunt, boy," a voice whispered.

NINE

Sam spun around and came face to face with a man who looked very much like his grandfather. Sam had only seen Samuel in pictures, but the resemblance was unmistakable—though in the earlier photos Samuel had a lot more hair.

Sam's face fell. He looked at the kitchen doorway on the other side of which he assumed there was a family of very hungry werewolves, then back at his long-dead grandfather.

Samuel leaned in and whispered in Sam's ear, "Hope that's not a silver bullet in there. The little one is a Native American god—you'll need something else to kill it."

Sam looked at his grandfather and then inclining his head to indicate the other man should follow him, he silently slipped out the front door.

Once outside, he checked to make sure his grandfather was behind and retreated a little way down the block.

Then Sam turned and took a good look at the other man. No question, it *had* to be Samuel Campbell. He was broad and in good shape, and most definitely alive. But it soon became clear that Samuel had no idea who Sam was.

"Why you edging onto my hunt?" Samuel demanded. "Who sent you? Did Mark and Gwen think I couldn't handle this myself? Jesus H. Christ, I've hunted for two lifetimes more than them, and they still coddle me like an invalid."

"Hold on. I didn't expect anyone else up here with me," Sam protested.

"Well, obviously neither did I," Samuel retorted.

"We can probably clear this up pretty quick," Sam continued. "I'm John."

"Well, John, nice to meet you. I'm Samuel Campbell." Sam's long-dead grandfather held out his hand.

Sam shook it, and smiled gainfully. He didn't know who was pulling what but he wasn't going to get caught in Hell again. In an instant, he raised the barrel of his sawed-off and cracked Samuel in the nose. Samuel dropped onto one knee holding his face, blood dripping onto the sidewalk. A couple out for an evening stroll quickly reversed their direction.

Sam pulled out a flask of holy water, grabbed Samuel's chin and forced it down his throat. Samuel choked a bit, but he certainly wasn't smoking from the inside out. The old man tried to get up but Sam kicked his legs out from underneath him. Samuel fell heavily onto the ground.

He was still trying to staunch his bloody nose when Sam grabbed him again and sliced his forearm with a silver knife. No sizzling.

"Jesus Christ! What the hell are you doing?" Samuel cried.

"You're supposed to be dead," Sam said, aiming his gun between Samuel's eyes. "So you're either an angel, a demon, or something in between. Which is it?"

"Jesus, boy. How do you know that?"

"Know what?" Sam said.

"How do you know I'm supposed to be dead?" Samuel said, pushing himself off the ground, while still trying to stop the bleeding from his nose and forearm.

Sam hesitated.

"Because you're my grandfather," he said eventually.

Samuel looked into Sam's eyes. "Sam?"

"Dean told you about me?"

"Dean told me *all* about you; Stanford, your girlfriend, what a great hunter you are."

"Dean said that?" Sam asked, truly skeptical that his brother would have complimented him.

"He said that you have a good head on your shoulders. You're fast, but mostly people trust you. Kind face, I guess. You're the brains, the yin to Dean's yang."

That's one way to put it, Sam thought. "Yeah, well, he never told me that."

"Where is he anyway?" Samuel asked. "I thought you guys were a team."

"Yeah, um, not anymore. Dean decided to pack it in and settle down with his girlfriend."

"Girlfriend? Really? Well, that's wonderful. I would love to see him," Samuel said. "But of course, things are a little different now. You know since... I've come back."

"Yeah, how did that happened?" Sam asked. He needed to know. Two people from the same family being resurrected, one from a cage in Hell—surely it couldn't be a coincidence.

"No idea. Woke up in a field somewhere. I called my niece—she was the only one I could think of that would be young enough to be alive—and she took me in. She was hunting. Met the group that she hunts with. Just sort of fell back into it."

Samuel pulled Sam in for a hug.

"It's great to meet you, son."

Sam pushed him away. Enough of this family reunion crap, it was time to get back to business.

"So the kid is a god?" he asked.

"Yeah. No need to kill the kid though, just chase the god out," Samuel explained. "He's the incarnation of Malsum. It's an Algonquin Cain and Abel story. The incarnation of Malsum comes every generation, takes the form of a wolf and mostly mutilates cattle as a kind of trick."

"So you weren't there to kill him?"

"Not at all. It's just killing cattle, not people. We have to chase the god out while it's in the wolf form, not as a child."

"Then why were you sneaking into the house?"

"I was going to hide under the bed until he changed, then use this on him." Samuel held up an elaborate bone and herb garland. "Wrap it around his neck, say a prayer three times and it's supposed to send Malsum back to the dark world."

"Let's just wait in the car then. If he moves, we'll get him," Sam proposed.

They sat in Sam's car for another hour or two. Sam wasn't in the mood for talking, but after thirty-odd years of being dead, it seemed his grandfather had plenty of questions. Sam responded as politely as he could, but he kept to himself the fact that he had been Lucifer's chosen vessel and had taken Lucifer on and jumped into the pit.

At around ten in the evening, the Sheriff's little boy appeared on the front doorstep. Sam and Samuel hunkered down in their seats as the Sheriff and his wife carefully peered up and down the street. They then ceremonially kissed the child on each cheek and handed him what looked like a small snack. The child turned his back on his parents and in an instant turned into a silver wolf.

"But the god is a bad god, right?" Sam whispered.

"I guess so. He's Cain," his grandfather replied.

"Good," Sam said. He got out of the car with his shotgun drawn. The Sheriff looked up, saw Sam, and yelled at the wolf to run. The wolf glanced at Sam and took off across the street and over the prairie beyond.

Sam was almost as quick. He ran swiftly after the creature, leaving his grandfather far behind.

The wolf leapt over a twelve-foot-wide irrigation ditch and kept going. Sam jumped, but hit the ground a little short, sliding down the embankment. But moments later, he found his footing and raced up the hill back onto the prairie. The wolf was far ahead now, so Sam leveled his gun and shot. The silver wolf went down.

Satisfied, Sam approached his victim. The creature was breathing heavily, blood draining from the back of its leg out onto the dry ground.

"What did you do?" Samuel yelled breathlessly as he reached Sam's side.

"Give me the wreath, you say the prayer," Sam directed.

Samuel did as his grandson said. Sam wrapped the herbs around the wolf's neck as Samuel said the prayer three times.

The wolf lifted its head one last time then laid it back down on the ground.

"You killed him, Sam. You killed a *child*," Samuel said. "What is wrong with you? *You don't kill people!*"

Sam looked down impassively at the wolf then unwrapped the herbs and bones from its neck. The body of the wolf disappeared and in its place was the young black-haired boy.

Silently, Sam scooped him up. The boy's breathing was faint. Sam strode rapidly back across the prairie to the Sheriff's house, put the child in his father's arms, then got into the car. His grandfather was waiting in the passenger seat. Still without speaking, Sam started the engine and sped onto the highway.

Eventually Samuel broke the silence.

"You shot a boy," he said.

"I killed a nasty god. The boy will be fine," Sam replied. He gripped the wheel.

"The fact that you could have killed him means nothing to you? Who taught you that?"

"No one did. I did what needed to be done," Sam said, staring at the road.

"What happened to you, boy?"

Sam shrugged. "I was sent to Hell."

TEN

The rhythmic thrumming of the tires over the cracks in the Eisenhower-era road lulled Dean into a reverie. This stretch of sun-baked cement was like the thousands of miles Dean had logged with Sam at his side. Dean's mind swerved again toward that afternoon at Stull Cemetery. He gripped the steering wheel tight and tried to forget. But like an unbalanced axle, he slowly got pulled to the side that his mind favored— Dean thought back to the days before Sam jumped.

"For the record, I agree with you. About… me. You think I'm too weak to take on Lucifer. Well, so do I. I know exactly how screwed-up I am. You, Bobby, Cass—I'm the least of any of you," Sam said earnestly. They'd had this conversation multiple times and each time Dean had said, "No." He wasn't going to let Sam say "Yes."

"Sam—" Dean began, but he didn't know how to carry on. His brother wasn't the least of them. He'd just taken one too many turns for the worse over the last two years: he had drunk demon blood, shacked up with Ruby, let Lucifer out of the cage. Dean couldn't deny that Sam had messed up. But who on Earth could take on Lucifer? Dean just couldn't bear to see his brother killed.

Sam continued. "It's true. I'm also all we got. If there was another way… But I don't think there is. There's just me. So I don't know what else to do. Except just try to do what's gotta be done."

And then Dean had lied to Death's face; told him he would let Sam jump.

When Dean spoke to Bobby later, he was surprised to find that Bobby agreed with Sam.

"Look, I'm not sayin' Sam ain't ass-full of character defects. But—"

"But what?" Dean asked curtly.

"Back at Niveus? I watched that kid pull out one civilian after another. Must have saved ten people. Never stopped, never slowed down. We're hard on him, Dean. And we've always been."

Dean knew that Bobby was right: At his core—his very core where his heart beat—Sam was a good person.

"So I gotta ask you, Dean. What are you afraid of exactly? Losing—or losing your brother?"

Lisa had become accustomed to that look in Dean's eyes. She had deliberately overlooked the history of Salem, the witch trials and all the supernatural activity they promised, when Dean mentioned it as his planned vacation spot for them.

A vacation in Salem is better than no vacation at all, she reasoned. *And a change of scenery is good. He will be okay. This will be okay.* She forced herself to ignore the feeling that perhaps Dean wasn't telling her the whole story.

"New York State! Just crossed into New York, Ben. Ben, you listening?" Dean said, checking the rearview.

"Whatever." Ben glanced up from his handheld PSP. "It looks exactly like the last state."

"Ben," Lisa said, giving him a motherly warning to not act out.

Ben heeded his mother's tone.

"It's cool. Very cool," he said, clearly trying to sound more enthusiastic.

"Good," Dean said with a smile. "Seven more hours and we're there."

"Seven more? Are you sure you're okay to keep driving? Shall I take over for a while?" Lisa asked.

"I'm fine. Better than fine," Dean said. And he was. The closer they got to Salem the closer he got to finding someone to help him raise Sam. Dean was focused on one thing and one thing only—getting his brother back.

"Dean," Lisa chided, "I know you can spend days straight in a car, but Ben and I can't. We need to stretch our legs and it's almost nine. Ben needs to go to bed."

"I can sleep back here," Ben offered.

"A proper bed. Please Dean, can we stop?"

Dean looked at Lisa. He didn't want to stop, he wasn't used to staggering journeys and waiting around. He just wanted to get to Salem. But he had other people to consider on this trip, it wasn't just him and Sam, driving through the night to another hunt. He was supposed to be on vacation.

"Sure, no problem. Next town or rest stop, we'll find a room. Okay?"

"Thanks," Lisa said, putting her hand on Dean's arm.

An hour later they pulled off the highway and into a little one-street town. Dean stopped the car in front of the only hotel he could see. It had a Western-style feel to it even though they were in western New York State, not Arizona.

"You check in, I'll drive park around back," Dean suggested.

Lisa and Ben hopped out and Dean pulled the car left, back into the street.

SCRREEECH!

Dean stomped on the breaks as a white van careened out of nowhere and past the car.

"Jesus H. Christ, Sam! You think you could maybe not hit your brother's car while you're still pretending to be dead," Samuel spat.

Sam had pulled off Route 86 a couple of minutes after Dean. He hadn't been following him the whole time, but had spotted the car halfway through Ohio. Samuel had said that they should follow Dean and keep an eye on him. If they got to Salem before him, they risked losing him or worse, being spotted.

"It's that damn Daddy Caddy. Dean never drove like that in the Impala," Sam said, scowling.

He held his course and pulled the van into the parking lot of a park a couple of blocks from Dean's motel.

"Let's get the MREs and hit the road right after them in the a.m.," Samuel said.

Sam ate his Ready-to-Eat meal sitting on a picnic table while his grandfather sorted through their equipment in the open back of the van.

Sam looked out over a buzzing little park pond, he liked doing everything himself these days and he didn't feel the need for company. As much as he trusted his grandfather, he trusted himself more.

Sam bit into a hard foil-wrapped brownie. It was tasteless to him, or maybe it was just tasteless. It didn't matter. The only hint of a feeling Sam could really understand was satisfaction. He liked getting a job done. He thought about Dean only a couple of blocks away. Whatever Dean was after, if they had to get there first and do it better, that was fine by Sam.

ELEVEN

The next day Dean, Lisa, and Ben were on the road early. They stopped at a fast food drive-through for breakfast and then were on their way. Four hours later Dean finally pulled off the interstate.

"Here we are. This looks good enough," Dean said as he angled the car into a Sunshine Inn parking lot. It was located off a bleak mall and gas station-stuffed suburban thruway.

"Oh Dean, I forgot to tell you," Lisa said, with a slight smirk. "I made reservations at this cute bed and breakfast in the heart of town. Here's the address." She handed him a piece of paper printed out from the Internet. "I think if you pull out of here, take a right, and then take your next right at Waters Street, that will take us right into town." Lisa gestured the route Dean was to take.

Dean stared hard at the piece of paper. Reservations? He'd never made reservations before. *For anything.*

"What's wrong with this place?" Dean said, even though

he knew full well the rooms inside were most likely witch-themed, dirty, and smelled of old cigarettes.

"Dean, please. It's our *vacation*. I wanted to stay somewhere nice." Lisa turned her mouth into a little pout. She hated resorting to female trickery—but she wasn't going to stay in a flea-bag hotel.

Dean shrugged. "How can I say no to that face?"

In the back seat Ben rolled his eyes and slumped further down.

"Gross," he mumbled.

Dean did as he was told and followed the directions into Salem proper. The town was a nice old colonial village with tree-lined streets and lots of federal-style brick houses with flat fronts, colonnade porches, and small windows. But commercialism and chains had grown like weeds and it was clear that the town didn't shy away from its dark past; in fact it did everything it could to capitalize on it.

They found the bed and breakfast easily enough, across the street from a big grassy expanse called Salem Common.

"Is that where they hanged the witches?" Ben asked, putting aside his video player and looking out of the window.

"No, actually they hanged the witches on a hill on the southwest side of town," Dean replied. "A place called Gallows Hill, though they're not sure of the exact location. Of course, none of the people they hanged actually were witches." Dean's voice betrayed a slight hint of having too much relish in the topic. Lisa shot him a look.

"That's cool. Can we go see it?" Ben asked.

"Of course. Do you know anything about the Salem

witch trials?" Dean asked as he parallel parked the CRV into a too-tight space.

"Not much, a little in school."

"Well then, I have lots to show you," Dean said.

They piled out of the car and Dean grabbed most of the bags. He wasn't used to actual luggage, he and Sam always traveled light, one duffle bag a piece at the very most. Now Dean really did feel and look like Chevy Chase.

The inside of the inn was tastefully decorated in a display-everything-your-grandma-likes kind of way. But Lisa didn't seem to mind.

"Hello, hello. You must be the Winchesters. I'm Ingrid," the tall middle-aged proprietor chimed from behind the inn's counter.

"Yes, we are. I made a reservation for two adjoining rooms," Lisa said.

"Aww, I can stay in a room by myself," Ben grumbled.

"Sure you can, buddy," Dean said, looking at Lisa. Dean and Sam had stayed in hotel rooms by themselves since they were seven. Ben was twelve, he could handle that.

"No, he can't," Lisa said.

Ben mumbled under his breath, then crossed the foyer to sit in a high-backed chair near the door.

"Two adjoining rooms will be fine," Lisa said, turning back to Ingrid with a smile.

"Great. Would you also like to schedule one of our ghost tours? We offer a full paranormal tour of our inn. We're the only inn on the East Coast with our own ghosts!"

"Your own ghosts?" Dean said, eyebrow raised.

Lisa paled. "Oh Dean, I didn't know!"

"We're the most popular inn on the square," Ingrid continued proudly. "People come from all over to take our spooky ghost tour and meet our otherworldly residents. There is Sally, the little girl who lost her bonnet. And Captain Chancy, who fell asleep and never woke up. He still thinks it's 1697 and he's sailing the high seas!"

"Great," Dean said flatly. It was so not great.

"We can go somewhere else," Lisa murmured quietly to Dean.

"No, it's fine," Dean said. The spooks sounded harmless enough—if they even existed at all.

"Real ghosts?" Ben jumped up in anticipation. "Dean, you can teach me how to kill 'em!"

Ingrid looked at Dean questioningly.

"He means I can... um... kill 'em with teaching him the rich history of your beautiful inn," Dean said through clenched teeth. He shot a look at Ben. "Adjoining rooms sound great, the spookier the better," he added with a forced grin.

"Lovely. Here are your keys." Ingrid handed Lisa a set of keys with a clipper ship key ring hanging off them. "Go up the stairs and to your right. Your rooms are the third and fourth doors on the left, overlooking the historic Salem Common."

"Thank you so much," Lisa said. They picked up their bags and trudged up the wide wooden staircase to the inn's second-floor rooms. Lisa opened the highly polished wooden door with brass numbers on it. She smiled gamely at Dean and walked into the room ahead of him.

"I think this is pretty. Don't you?" she asked, throwing open the blue-and-yellow-flowered curtains.

Dean surveyed the large garish floral bedspread and the ruffled pillow shams. This in fact wasn't his idea of comfortable, he felt like he was back in Ypsilanti, Michigan, in the Carrigan's house. They had been pagan gods of the Winter Solstice, and their design aesthetic was similar to the room: like someone just vomited up a quilting bee.

Dean smiled. If this was what made Lisa happy that he would cope. Besides, he wasn't here to relax, he wanted to get started searching for a witch as soon as possible. But Lisa had other plans.

"I'm starving, let's go get some fried clams and French fries," she said with a smile. "It's a gorgeous day. I don't want to spend a minute inside."

What was Dean going to say? As much as he wanted to start his mission, he knew that he had to spend at least a little time with Lisa and Ben.

"Okay then," he said.

Outside the sun was shining. As they made their way through the narrow streets, tourists crammed the brick sidewalks. Dean wondered at all the people enjoying their lives—oblivious to how much Sam and Dean had sacrificed so that they could continue on as normal. Would they even appreciate it if they knew? Dean doubted it. He didn't get a chance to walk among the masses very often and he was pretty sure he hadn't missed much as he watched tourists munching ice cream cones and shoving their bratty kids in front of buildings and statues to be photographed. For a moment he wondered why he even cared about saving all these schlubs' lives. It made him itch to get Sam back all the more.

"How about here?" Lisa asked.

"I'm starved," Ben added.

They tramped into a fish and chip shop called "Old Clappy's Clam Shacky." A wooden sign hung above the doorway: a drunken-looking cartoon sailor and a clam clung to one another in what looked like mid-song.

At the back of the restaurant a creaky covered porch hung out over the water. The bay was blue and still. They placed their order and then sat down at a brown-paper-covered picnic table. To their right, a couple of old clipper ships bobbed next to an ancient blackened pier.

"Are those pirate ships?" Ben asked, looking out over the water. "I totally want to go on a pirate ship."

Dean smiled smugly at Lisa as if to say, "I told you so."

"Sure are. You and your mom can take a tour of them this afternoon if you want," Dean said.

"What about you?" Lisa asked.

"I thought I'd… you know, look around town and find fun things to do. Plan the rest of our trip," Dean said casually.

Minutes later, toasty piles of fish, clams, and chips heaped in paper baskets were placed in front of them by a young girl who looked to be a little older than Ben.

"My name's Perry. Just let me know if you need anything else," she said with a smile directed at Ben. Ben blushed.

"Thanks," Lisa said with an edge.

Perry bobbed a little curtsey and returned to her place behind the ordering counter, Ben's eyes followed her.

"Don't even think about it," Lisa said gently as she squeezed ketchup onto a plate and dragged a fry though it. "She's five years older than you."

"She's not five years older. She's like fifteen," Ben said.

"How do you know?" Lisa asked.

"I'm twelve, Mom. I know," Ben retorted. "Besides, she was just being nice. You're always saying it takes a special person to make a lot of friends. Right?"

"Kid has a point. I've heard you say that," Dean said, grinning at Lisa as he teased her.

"Whose side are you on?" Lisa asked, poking Dean light-heartedly in the ribs.

Dean dug into more of the food and enjoyed the moment. He liked looking out across the water. He and Sam had never spent much time on the coast.

Ben polished off his food in minutes.

"I'm still hungry," he declared. "Can I have five bucks to get some more?"

"Oh, now you want more clams?" Dean smiled, reaching into his pocket and handing Ben a five. "I can see why. She's cute."

Ben blushed again.

"Naw, I just want some more fries. What's the big deal?"

"Just act casual. Like you haven't even noticed that she's good-looking," Dean confided.

"Really?" Ben asked.

"Absolutely. Pretty girls hate when people fawn over them. Just act natural. Like you couldn't care less about her."

Ben nodded earnestly and went up to the counter.

"Are you teaching my son to be a player?" Lisa asked half smiling, half serious.

"Kid has to know how to flirt. I'm just teaching him the basics. We haven't even begun the master class."

"Master class, huh?"

Ben came back with a large smile plastered across his face.

"We're going to the movies," he said proudly.

"I'm sorry, I didn't hear a question in there," Lisa said.

"Can I go to the movies?" Ben rephrased, rolling his eyes.

"Wow, that girl sure moves fast," Dean said, impressed.

Ben and Lisa went back and forth about whether it was a good idea for him to go to the movies in a strange town with a strange girl. Ben accused his mother of once again being overprotective.

Dean decided to sit this discussion out. Instead he watched the girl as she chatted affably with other customers. The teen kept stealing glances at him, like she was appraising something. She gave off a much more sophisticated air than a regular teenager. In that respect Lisa was right, Dean thought. But he figured Perry was a savvy, towny chick who regularly asked boys out in order to get a free movie and some popcorn. No harm in that.

They left Old Clappy's Clam Shacky and wandered around the square before following the throngs of people down one of the touristy little street, crammed with gift shops and cafés.

"Witch museum? We gotta go there." Ben pointed out a tall, large, stone-faced building towering above them, with a stream of people queuing out the door and around the corner.

"Looks popular. Yeah, you guys should definitely do that," Dean said.

"Dean, I thought we were here to spend time *together*?" Lisa said quietly, out of earshot of Ben. "We didn't come all this way so you could wander off alone."

Dean knew she was right, and he didn't want to upset her. But he had come to Salem to raise Sam, and he had to find a way to do that without Lisa finding out his real motive.

"Lis, I'm just saying," Dean said gently, "I might want to go off and do a little exploring myself. Like boring stuff. You know I'm a big history buff. They have some great historical reference libraries in town. I might want to hit those."

"You're a big history buff?" Lisa looked at him skeptically.

"Yeah, totally. Ask me anything about the Bible—I bet I know it," Dean countered.

"I'm not going to a library on my vacation," Ben chimed in.

"See, what did I tell you. Kid doesn't want to go to a library," Dean said. "Don't worry about it, we're totally Brady Bunch Does Honolulu this week, except of course minus like seven people."

"Six. Minus six people," Lisa corrected him with a grin.

"Who're you counting? Alice's boyfriend didn't go to Hawaii with them," Dean said.

They continued to argue the specifics of the Brady Bunch Hawaii trip as they passed a quaint shop with bay windows filled to the brim with witchy tchotchkes and a whole bunch of other stuff that all looked to Dean like worthless crap.

"Let's go in here," Ben said, veering in through the front door.

Lisa and Dean followed him into the store.

As far as Dean could see in the gloom, they were the only customers. Other tourists must have been put off by the slightly odiferous shop with its cloister-like atmosphere and creaky floorboards.

Across the back wall of the store, large apothecary jars full of herbs lined the shelves. Dean noted the handwritten tags identifying the contents—many of them could be used in black magic: calamus root, mustard seed, valerian root, black pepper, licorice root chips. But a lot of them were harmless potpourri fillers too: lavender, lemongrass, sandalwood. Dean wondered if this store catered for the local witches.

The store also had a lot of other junk found everywhere in New England, including the all-pervasive Yankee candles, cheap Chinese-made cut-glass candy dishes, and black soap shaped like cats and witches' hats.

"Hiya!"

A young girl of about twenty appeared through a door covered with a bead curtain. The strings of glass moved and clinked together as the Perky Polly jumped behind the counter.

"Welcome to 'Connie's Curios and Conversations,' what

can I do you for?" The girl was dressed in a long hippy-like skirt, with a couple of scarves wrapped around her waist. She wore a little charm on a black-leather bracelet around her wrist.

"Whoa Mom, can I get this?" Ben said, holding up an alligator foot.

"What on earth for?" Lisa responded.

"Hoodoo spell, brings luck, sometimes love. Wouldn't be the dumbest thing to carry on your date tomorrow," Dean said to Ben.

"You're not helping!" Lisa glared at Dean. "It's not a date, is it, Ben?"

Dean winked at Ben over Lisa's head. Ben shook his head.

"Nope, Ma. It's not a date. I promise," he said with a smirk.

"Let me know if you need anything!" the girl called again. "You know your witchcraft," she added, eyeing Dean.

"Yeah, you know. I just dabble," he said as he looked around the store. "You're well stocked. Got any puppy heads?"

"Dean!" Lisa swung round and looked at him.

The girl behind the counter suddenly lost her perk. Her face tightened.

"No we don't," she said brusquely.

"Oh okay, just wondering," Dean said. He fingered the gris-gris bag in his pocket. If this girl was a witch or tried to mess with him, he was protected. Puppy skulls, ground puppy skulls, were used in some of the darkest spells, specifically in hoodoo, to bind demons. And by making the material into a ball, covering it in sulfur, and burying it where a person would walk over it—some believed that it could kill.

The girl held up a jade necklace with charms hanging from it.

"You know what? This would look gorgeous on you," she said to Lisa.

Lisa appraised it. "It's pretty, I don't know if it's my style though," she said.

"You want to try it on?" the girl asked.

Dean stepped closer to the counter and leaned over toward the girl.

"It's not really her thing," he said. "Let's go guys."

Dean walked out of the store, Lisa and Ben following behind.

"What did you do that for?" Lisa asked, falling into step with Dean.

"That necklace had a black cat's bone on it," he said.

"Really?" Ben said. "Cool."

"It did? What would that do?" Lisa asked.

"It would have helped her trace where you were. Sort of like a witch GPS. I should go in there and bust that shop up," Dean growled.

"Dean, really, I think you're mistaken. I'm sure she was just a hippy girl trying to do her job," Lisa insisted.

"Maybe," Dean said.

Whether the girl was a witch or not, there was something about her that Dean didn't trust. Despite all the fru-fru stuff in the store, a real witch could stock up on some powerful stuff in there if they knew what they were doing.

Lisa, Ben, and Dean wound their way back to the inn. Dean hesitated when they got to the door.

"Hey, I'm going to continue to look around," Dean said.

"Really?" Lisa asked

"Yeah, I'll be back soon. Rest up." Dean waved away her concern. "I just want to check the place out."

"Okay, see you later," Lisa said, and she and Ben disappeared into the inn.

Dean quickly walked across the street and popped the trunk to the CRV. His close parking job made it difficult to get it open. Dean struggled, trying not to hit the hood of the car behind it. The Impala wouldn't have this problem.

He wanted to go back to the store and see what he could get out of the hippy chick, but something caught his attention. He looked up at the inn across the street and saw Ben in the window of their room. His eyes were as wide as saucers and he was beating on the window trying to get Dean's attention.

Dean grabbed his duffle, which was stuffed into the wheel well of the spare tire, slammed the door shut, then ran back across the street.

SCREEECH!

A car ground to a halt, its grill a mere three inches away from Dean's kneecaps.

Dean looked up again. Ben had disappeared from the window. He ran inside, startling Ingrid.

"Oh, Mr. Winchester, do you—" she called.

"No time, Bea Arthur," Dean yelled over his shoulder as

he took the stairs three at a time. He reached the landing and spun around, almost knocking Ben over.

"What's wrong?" Dean asked, grabbing Ben's arm and heading toward the door of their room.

"I don't know. I don't—" the boy stammered, he looked scared.

Inside, Lisa was curled on the bed, sweat dripping off her forehead. Her eyes were glassy and rolling up into their lids.

"Lis, Lis? can you hear me? Did you drink anything?" Dean shook her and frantically looked around the room. He picked up an open water bottle and smelled it. Nothing.

Lisa was shaking all over and her hands had palsied and curled up under her chin.

"What's wrong with her?" Ben asked, his eyes watering with fear.

"Ben, I need you to search around the room. See if you find anything like this," Dean said, taking the gris-gris bag out of his pocket. "Can you do that for me?"

"Yeah. Yeah," Ben said.

"Look underneath everything, inside everything," Dean directed. "Lisa, stay with me. What did you touch? Did you eat anything?"

Her body shook. Blood trickled from her mouth. She started coughing.

"Dean, what's happening?" she sputtered.

"Just stay with me," Dean said urgently.

"Dean?" Lisa choked. She reached into her mouth and tugged at something, a creature emerged from between her lips, wriggling in her grip. Staring at it in horror, she screamed and fainted. The lizard scampered away to the corner of the room.

"Mom!" Ben yelled.

"Okay, just stay calm. We have to find the bag," Dean instructed.

He took out his knife and sliced straight through the butter-colored wing-back chair in the corner. He flipped it over and dug through the springs with the blade. Nothing. He pulled all the covers off the other queen-sized bed, flipped the mattress, tore through the box spring. Nothing.

In the bathroom Dean poured out every lotion, tossed every towel onto the floor. Nothing.

He stomped back to the bedroom window and pulled down the curtains, kicking through the pleats.

Still unconscious, Lisa fell from the bed and was now writhing on the floor, but no more lizards appeared from her throat.

Then Dean saw it, a little bag sitting on the table underneath an aging, dried bouquet of magnolias. He picked it up and opened it. Inside was some dragon's blood, a black cat's bone, thyme, and, Dean guessed, a couple of different kinds of oil.

"What is it?" Ben asked.

"It's a hex bag and it's making your mom sick," Dean said as he took out his Zippo and lit it. The felt bag went up in flames and Dean dropped it into the trash can to smolder.

They gently lifted Lisa back onto the bed, and after a few moments she opened her eyes and rubbed her throat.

"What happened?" she asked.

"We had company. How do you feel?" Dean helped her sit up on the bed, gently brushing her hair away from her clammy forehead.

"I'm okay, I think. Who did this? What's going on?" Lisa gestured to the destroyed room.

"Don't worry, Ben and I had to find what was making you sick, but it's all right now. Or it will be—I'll fix it. I got to go out for a short while. Will you be okay here?" Dean didn't want to scare her, but he had to go and find whoever had done this. Maybe that little witch in the strange store could give him some answers.

"Where are you going?" Lisa looked at him, eyes wide and fearful.

"I won't be long," Dean said, leaning down and kissing her hot cheek. He then pulled his duffle onto his shoulder and looked at Ben. "Take care of your mom and stay here—okay?"

Ben nodded his head solemnly.

With a lowered voice Dean said, "Let's not tell your mom about what just happened if she doesn't remember. Okay?"

Ben nodded again, glancing at his mom with worried eyes. Dean reasoned he didn't need to tip Lisa off that there was something rotten in Salem—there was no reason to make her afraid and he could fix this.

Dean closed the door behind him, then turned and came face to face with a red-faced Ingrid.

"Sorry about the noise. Charades. So much fun. I'll pay for the damages," Dean said, brushing past them and heading down the stairs.

Dean kicked open the inn door and headed outside. He felt the outline of his gun in his duffle bag. He wasn't quite sure where he was going to go, but he knew one thing: There were witches in Salem.

TWELVE

"Pull over here," Samuel instructed.

Sam had pulled off Route 95 and into the area around Salem known as Danvers. He then pulled the van into a motel with a colonial theme. They unloaded their gear and Samuel checked them in under aliases.

Being in Salem at the same time as Dean posed a couple of problems. Sam would have to stay pretty much hidden, which would be difficult. His six-foot-four frame stood out anywhere. It might also cause some awkwardness if Dean caught sight of his long-dead grandfather.

To Sam it wasn't quite clear why they were here, but he had learned over the past couple of months to do what he was told. If Samuel had a reason to be here, so did he. If there were witches in Salem, Sam had plenty of experience with them and he knew that they were bad news.

Samuel and Sam walked side by side, lugging their gear towards their respective rooms.

"We can get a bead on Dean tomorrow," Samuel proposed. "Shouldn't be too hard, kid has the manners of a drunken ox."

"Actually, I think I'm going to go look around now," Sam said.

Samuel shrugged. "Fine. Just try to keep your big mug out of sight."

Sam nodded. After throwing his gear into his room, he made his way back to the van.

First he drove through the parking lots of every motel in the surrounding area, but he didn't spot Dean's car. Next, he decided to swing by the more touristy part of town. No sign of Dean. Then, as he turned a corner onto a smaller side street, he glanced into the narrow alley behind the buildings, and caught a glimpse of his brother as he ducked into a recess at the back of an old clapboard building.

Sam swung around front and parked his van on the street in front of a shop. He hopped out and peered in through the shop windows and clocked all the herbs in jars. He figured that Dean had come to the same conclusion he had—this place screamed witchcraft.

Daylight broke through the back of the store. It looked as though someone had just kicked in the back door. Wary of breaking Samuel's rules and encountering his brother, Sam decided to wait inside the van.

The store was closed from what Dean could see. The town seemed to be quickly closing down in the evening light. Around back he examined the door to the shop.

"No Ye Olde Alarm System?" he muttered to himself.

Dean's foot went clear through the rotting, wooden back door. His foot hit right near the lock, tearing it off its hinges so it hung lopsided, like a tongue hanging out of a dog's mouth.

Gun at the ready, Dean snuck into the back room of the store. Through the dim light he could see boxes and boxes of witch-themed items stacked on top of one another.

"Connie's Curios and Crap," Dean murmured.

He moved through to the main store. He figured that in his short time in Salem he had pissed someone off and while he, Lisa, and Ben were out, that someone had snuck into the hotel room and planted the bag. The hex put on Lisa had been strong. It took someone with a pretty potent knowledge of the black arts to put together a hex bag like that.

Dean moved through the shop, eyes peeled for anything suspicious. He poked around the counter near the register. Nothing of interest. To his right he noticed a steep staircase leading to the second floor.

Dean peeked through the narrow opening, up the twisting staircase. *Hobbit sized,* he thought. *Ugh.* Dean twisted around and pulled himself up the stairs, leading with his sawed-off. At the top was a pokey little hallway.

Floorboards creaked under Dean's weight. He winced.

WHAACK!

Dean felt the burning sensation radiate through the back of his head and down his spine as he fell forward onto his stomach. The sawed-off skittered across the wide-planked floor and came to rest under a heating unit. Above him, the hippy girl stood, a baseball bat emblazoned with a Red Sox emblem in her hands.

"Jesus Christ, Janice Joplin, take it easy," Dean said, rubbing the back of his head. He inspected a smudge of blood on his fingers.

"What're you doing here? Didn't you see the 'Closed' sign on the door? Or do you New York folks always just do what you want and walk in like you own the place?" she demanded.

"Whoa, hold it. First off, I'm not from New York. Secondly, I was in here an hour ago with my girlfriend—"

"That was your girlfriend? You look like her dad."

"What?" Dean put his hands up in a placatory gesture. "Okay, you can 'What to Wear' me a makeover later. The door downstairs was open."

"Open like falling open or unlocked? Because I'm pretty sure the hinges didn't shatter by themselves."

Dean shrugged, then pulled himself onto his feet.

"Can I finish? I'm here, then I go back to my hotel. Next thing I know my girlfriend's coughing up the GEICO gecko."

"Lizards? Who'd you piss off?" she asked.

"That's why I'm here. I came to find out."

"Not me. I don't do that revenge spell stuff." The girl went to sit by the small slanted windows. "That's more Connie's bag than mine."

"So you're not Connie?" Dean asked.

"No. I'm Sukie. Nice to meet you," she said dryly.

"Like Sukie Stackhouse?"

"God, no. Go back farther. Sukie Ridgemont, Michele

Pfeiffer's character in *Witches of Eastwick*? I was born the same year the movie came out. Thus the name."

"So where's Connie?" Dean asked.

"Connie's a strange bird. I don't see her much. I open and close the place most days. Occasionally I find a note from her telling me to wash the windows. That's about it. Why do you want to talk to her?"

"You have some really strong ingredients downstairs, stuff that could be used in some pretty powerful spells. Plus, you tried to sell my girlfriend a necklace with a black cat's bone on it."

"I did? I didn't know that."

"You didn't know there was a black cat's bone on something you sell?"

"No. I mean— Listen, I mostly do love spells, money spells, whatever. Just some herbs, a candle and a little chanting. I stay away from any hardcore stuff. Plus, Connie is the one that stocks all the shelves. Actually, she called this morning and told me to push the necklaces on anyone that came in. So I did. I really didn't know there was a cat's bone on it. She's the one with... umm... She dabbles in the darker stuff, if you know what I mean."

"Dabbles in witchcraft? How do you 'dabble' in witchcraft?" Dean asked.

"Okay, fine. She's like really, really into it. I try not to get in her way. Connie's like old school, been in town forever, way before the Skechers store and the yogurt shops started opening up."

"So, you're a good witch?" Dean raised an eyebrow.

"Just call me Glinda," Sukie said.

"Right, I get it. So where can I find this Connie? If she's pretty hooked in, I'd like to talk to her."

"Umm. I guess I can tell you where she lives." Sukie shrugged. "Her old family place, last name of Hennrick. Go north out of town, you can't miss it. What did you say your name was?"

"I didn't," Dean said.

"Weird, 'cause you look sorta familiar. You have family in town?"

"What's with the *Who Do You Think You Are?* genealogy questions?" Dean said, a little miffed.

"Wow, way to go for the Friday night TV. Were you under house arrest? No one watches that."

"Okay, Glinda, I'm out of here. And since you beaned me with a bat, I expect you're going to forget that your back door had an accident."

"Like I said, I have a wealth spell. I'm not worried," Sukie said.

Dean wanted to find Lisa's attacker, but was beginning to get the distinct feeling that there was more to Salem than he had first thought. He left by the broken back door.

At the front of the store, Sam got out of his truck and peeked through the window. He spotted a shopgirl and banged on the glass.

She looked up and mouthed, "We're closed."

"I just have a quick question," Sam yelled, indicating he needed her to open the door.

"Dude, come back tomorrow." She shook her head and went to the back of the store.

Sam cautiously doubled back to the alley where he had seen Dean. The coast was clear. Sam walked up the alley and peeked his head through the doorway. The girl stood there surveying the damage to the door.

"I just have a couple questions," Sam said.

"Listen Bigfoot, I'm already late, so if you don't mind, I'm just going to close this here door on your face and you can come back tomorrow to get your glow-in-the-dark witch mask."

"Okay Sabrina, cut the crap," Sam said, his patience at an end. "I'm going to ask you some questions and you're gonna flap those sweet hippy lips of yours. Get it?"

"Oh wow, the sensitivity training is doing wonders. You throw any puppies into rivers lately? Tell me, how do you feel?" The girl had lost her fresh-faced gaze, and she now looked decidedly mean. "Because I've seen corpses before, but never one walking and talking like you. Though you don't so much walk as lumber."

"What the hell are you on about?" Sam demanded. He hadn't met many people who could tell straight off that he was… unusual.

"Puh-lease, you can see your silly walk from a mile away."

"I meant about me," Sam growled.

"I'm a witch, lug-head. I got powers. I can feel things. You're off. Can't you feel that?"

Sam wasn't in an introspective mood.

"What'd you say to him?" He inclined his head down the

alley, in the direction Dean had presumably headed.

The girl smirked. "Who? The guy that just left? He your shower-buddy or something? You guys look similar—same Cro-Magnon brow."

"He's my… Forget it. What did he want?" Sam demanded.

"His girlfriend got sick. He thought someone like me or my boss might have hexed her. We carry a lot of shit here. I told him I didn't do anything. He and the chick seemed harmless. I might have mentioned that my boss was into heavier shit. But that's it. I sent him on his way. I don't need people up in my grill. I played it nice and sweet with him. You, I don't like too much."

"Well, glad I'm getting to see the real you. What about the other witch-bitches around here, know anything about what they're doing?"

"I don't hang with anyone else if that's what you mean. I live with my mom, who makes soap for a living. I work, I text my boyfriend, and occasionally I rearrange my Netflix queue. Like I told the other guy, not everyone with a gift hangs around together here. I know it's Salem, but we don't all put on witchy hats and ride around on brooms."

"And that guy just went away, you didn't tell him anything else?" Sam was skeptical this chick was telling the truth.

"Yawn. Yes, and no. Can I go now?"

"Yeah." Sam spun around on his heel and walked back down the alley.

"You're welcome," the girl shouted after him. "Dick."

THIRTEEN

A cool evening fog rolled in from the ocean. Dean walked back toward the inn. He took a shortcut through an old graveyard. Under normal circumstances Dean would end up digging and burning things when he was in a bone yard, but he found himself looking at the worn stone faces of various headstones. Lichen stuck to the weathered stones, making some of the names difficult to read. Nevertheless Dean found himself enthralled. These people had all been accused of witchcraft.

Dean knew a little about the history of the Salem witch trials. He supposed that maybe the people lying underfoot could actually have been witches, in that case, good riddance to them. But he also knew that envy and suspicion could cause a lot more harm than a couple of people doing spells so their crops didn't die.

Dean reached the inn, crossed the street and threw his duffle in the trunk of the car. He supposed that he should probably go up and see how Lisa and Ben were doing, he peered up at their bedroom window, the curtains were tightly drawn. But he really wanted to find this Connie woman. If she practiced the dark arts like her employee said, then she might be behind the attack on Lisa. She also might be powerful enough to be able to help him raise Sam. Either way, Dean needed to find out more information before he confronted Connie Hennrick.

Closing the trunk, Dean headed into the lobby of the inn. Ingrid smiled saltily from behind the counter. She waved Dean over. In front of her was an itemized bill of the damage to their room.

"I'm having the curtains and floor professionally cleaned. The fire you started in the waste basket smelled everything up. I've also moved you all to a different room."

Dean nodded and thanked her. He really didn't care. But now more than ever he wished they were staying in one of his usual crap-hole motels. He put on his sweetest smile.

"Ingrid, if I wanted to find out information about a family who's been in Salem for a while, where would I go? Is there a library in town or something?" Even in the age of the Internet, some information could only be culled from old-fashioned records.

"There's the Peabody Essex Museum. Not walking distance though. Lots of tourists go there to see if they were related to anyone in the Salem witch trials. My great, great, great, great grandmother lived in Boston and her husband came up to see the Court of Oyer and Terminer."

"The court of what?" Dean asked.

"It's the court that heard the testimony of all the girls accusing people of being witches. In any case, Peabody Museum. Look up your ancestor names. Though I never heard of Winchesters in Salem."

"Probably not. Thanks for the info," Dean said.

Dean made his way back out of the door again. After changing into a tweed jacket and khakis—his professor outfit—Dean followed his GPS to the museum.

An old woman in a beige pantsuit was just locking the door from the inside as Dean walked up. He rapped on the glass panel of the door and mustered his most academic-looking smile, pressing a Harvard ID up against the glass.

The old woman unlocked the door.

"Sorry, we're closed. Come back tomorrow," she said and went to close the door again.

Dean stuck his foot against it to stop her. He smiled winningly.

"Pardon my tardiness," he began, and cleared his throat. "I'm Doctor Jones from Harvard. I have a lecture tomorrow and I'm terribly behind on a crucial part of my research. Is there any way…?" Dean gestured with his hand.

The old woman looked him over. Dean beamed at her, turning up the charm another notch and keeping his foot in place against the door.

It must have worked as she smiled brightly back at him, nodded, opened the door and ushered Dean into a wood-paneled room.

"Now what family are you looking for, Doctor Jones?" she asked Dean, moving behind the counter.

"I'm actually looking for information on the Hennricks," Dean said.

"Humm, I'm not sure if we have much on that family. Let me see," she said, taking a list from a draw in the table.

Dean peered at it from upside down, it seemed to be a list of families starting from when Salem was first settled in 1628.

"Hmm. Abbey, Adams, Allen, Baily, Bayley, Bibber, Churchill, Campbell, Cory—"

"Wait," Dean said, taking the paper and flipping it so he could read it the right way round. "Campbell?"

"Yes, right here." She jabbed the paper. "Not much there though, if I remember correctly. I can get the box for you, if you want."

"Yes please," Dean said.

The old woman disappeared for a few minutes and then shuffled back holding a dusty box.

"This is all we have on the Campbells. Let me know if you need anything else," she said. "I have a few things to finish up so I can give you about half an hour."

Dean nodded and thanked her. She left him to it and he sat down at one of the dark-wood tables near by and opened up the box.

Inside was an old leather journal, imprinted in faded gold script "Nathaniel Campbell." Dean carefully opened the cottony, yellowed pages.

He had never heard of any Campbell relatives in Salem, Massachusetts. Though he didn't know about many relatives past his grandparents, Samuel and Deanna. But whoever this Nathaniel Campbell was, it seemed he was an avid journal writer.

Dean peered at the first page, it was dated 1664. A flowing brown script spread across the page. He began to read:

> I signed the homestead papers today with the honorable Cotton Mather. The price is three English pounds each year hence. The property starts around twenty meters from the old oak tree at the corner of the road to Ipswich. It runs around 500 meters wide and some 2,000 meters deep. On the west side it is bordered by a small brook, and on the south by the river that runs to Ipswich.

Dean stopped reading and flipped through a couple more pages. On a page dated "Feb. 1692" something caught his eye:

> A young girl's body was found north of the village today. Abigail Faulkner age 14 was found in the snow with her throat cut. I asked the village doctor, William Grigg, if I could see the body to give the poor girl her Last Rites. I got there before Reverend Parris—otherwise he surely would have raised a big fuss and then I would not have been able to examine her. The Widow Faulkner did not want to delay one minute, lest her daughter not rise up to Heaven. She gave me permission to administer them. I insisted on having a moment

or two alone with the body first in order to "make it right and proper" for the widow to see her daughter. In that short amount of time I came to a couple of clear conclusions that I am sure the good physician will not. Namely, the girl's neck was broken, even though it was sliced, the neck bones were pulverized, as if by a regular wood-chopping axe. But there was no bruising in the back of her neck. I fear the force might have come from something otherworldly. I am quite sure I exterminated the witches some years back, but perhaps more have fallen under the dark spell of Satan. I can only hope not.

But I fear that my sons may be correct: Witches are again in Salem.

Dean sat back and stared at the page. Could this be the journal of his ancestor? Could Nathaniel Campbell be a great, great, great grandfather on his mother's side? Dean shuddered. He had to read the rest of the journal.

Rising from his seat he peered out into the dark corridor beyond the wood-paneled room. The click, click, click of the docent's heels pierced the silence. Dean always carried his father's journal in his jacket pocket. With Sam gone, Dean really had nothing else to connect him to his family. He removed the leather cover of Nathaniel's journal with his pocket knife, then carefully wrapped it around John Winchester's. They were of a similar weight and size and surely no one else would be coming to look at an old

Campbell family journal. When Dean was finished he would return and switch them back.

"Did you find what you were looking for?" the old woman asked as Dean passed her on his way out.

"And more," Dean said.

Dean drove back to the bed and breakfast and was relieved to find Lisa and Ben watching TV and eating burgers they had ordered from the inn's kitchen—one waited for him as well.

Lisa said she was feeling better, but she still looked pale. She said she was going to rally in the morning so they could go see the clipper ships. Ben proceeded to speak in a pirate accent for the rest of the night.

Dean munched his burger and then sat back on the other bed and took out the pages of Nathaniel Campbell's journal.

"What's that?" Lisa asked.

"Just something I picked up from the library," Dean replied.

He started to read about a family of hunters named Campbell.

FOURTEEN

Caleb Campbell and his older brother by three years, Thomas, were walking back from the village when they saw a man and his cart emerge from a little-used road that ran to the northwest. He was wild-eyed and perspiring as he approached the boys.

"The Devil has been let out, boys. Get thee home and lock the door," the man yelled.

"Why sir?" Thomas asked.

"'Tis the Devil himself killed a poor little thing. Too gruesome for children like you to see."

The man indicated a wrapped bundle in the back of his simple horse cart. Two snow-covered shoes peeped out from beneath the burlap covering. It was a dead body, and from the size of the feet, and style of shoe, it was that of a young girl.

The man hastened his horses toward Salem Village.

Thomas and Caleb looked at one another.

"It's about time," Caleb said. "This village was putting me to sleep."

Even in the wintry light, Caleb's sandy-blond hair shone like a summer sun. He had dark eyes and a wide-set mouth. Though he was the younger of the two Campbell brothers, he was by far the better student.

Thomas was already acquiring his adolescent brawn. The breadth of his shoulders had outgrown his coat. His mother had tanned a couple of hides from the previous winter's hunt and sewn him a jacket. It was all deer hide, burnished to a walnut brown. She had pulled the collar up to cover most of Thomas's neck and sewn two large pockets for his mittens, which he would surely lose several times that winter. Thomas's coat didn't look like any of the other boys' clothes in town. But that was the way all the Campbells were—they didn't quite fit in.

The Campbell family had come from Europe with the wave of English-speaking settlers in the mid-1600s. No one knew exactly which country they had originated from. They traded a few of their crops in the village, but for the most part they kept to themselves. They did not attend church, which sparked the ire of many townspeople, in particular the new minister, Reverend Parris.

Nathaniel Campbell wasn't a religious man anyway, but he didn't trust Reverend Parris. He told his children never to trust a man so desperate for adoration and attention. "A man such as that can be dangerous," Nathaniel warned his family. It was for that reason Nathaniel told the clergyman that they would worship at home on Sundays and Thursdays, the days when people gathered in the tavern to talk about the Bible. Though in fact, rather than worshipping, Nathaniel made his three children study.

The Campbell children weren't learning the Bible—they already knew it back to front—instead they were studying Latin, herbs, and texts about monsters that their ancestors had written. The family business was hunting and it was very important to Nathaniel that his two sons and daughter continue the Campbell tradition.

Thomas looked at his brother.

"You go tell Father and I'll follow that man to town," he said.

"Why do you get to follow him? I want to follow him," Caleb objected.

"Because I'm older, and if I'm caught I'm better spoken," Thomas responded.

Caleb shook his head but started toward the family farm anyway, while his brother ran after the man and his cart.

Thomas was fast and caught up with the man's tired mare before it had reached Salem. In the village the visitor stopped and asked a local resident where to find the nearest doctor. He was directed toward the east end of town, and Thomas followed cautiously from a distance.

When they reached the doctor's, he waited a short way down the street, crouched down next to another cart, while the man stepped inside.

A couple of minutes later the portly physician emerged from the house and approached the cart. He scooped up the body of the young girl and hurried back inside.

Thomas ran to the window of the doctor's house and peered through the tiny glass pane. The men were laying the young girl's body on a table.

Thomas grew anxious. He knew that his father would want to find out what had killed the girl, and he could only do that by examining the body.

The ways Nathaniel could gain access to the bodies were many, but normally he would lie and dissemble. If they were in another town or county Nathaniel would dress up as a man of the church, or sometimes pose as a merchant or a judge. Nathaniel always kept a couple of changes of clothes in his sack for these exact occasions. He would insist that he needed to see the body before anyone else did. Once he had gained access, he was usually quick to identify the culprit.

Thomas knew that his father was used to seeing strange animal bites or scratches. He knew what kind of mark a wendigo made—his Indian friends had helped him identify the first one he had ever come across. But such things would have induced panic in the common colonist. Even though the Bible played the primary cultural role in Puritan communities, Christianity couldn't quash the inherent folk beliefs that people had brought over from Europe.

Many of the colonists were superstitious: the English spoke of baby-stealing fairies, the French of *loup-garou*, and German merchants of *Vampir*. So Nathaniel often hid evidence of those creatures, for the safety of the colony. Sometimes he would patch the wounds up on the victim's corpse before anyone else could see them—he carried a candle for just that purpose, to drip wax into the wounds to hide them.

Before Thomas could come up with a plan to gain access alone, his father and Caleb arrived at the doctor's in their rickety carriage. Thomas could make out the outline of the worn book of Latin spells inside his father's coat. He always carried it with him just in case the victim was demonically possessed.

Nathaniel jumped out of the carriage as Caleb tied the horse to a post. Nathaniel nodded to Thomas and entered the doctor's house.

Caleb left the horse and crossed the street toward his brother. The boys listened quietly at the window. They understood immediately that the men had identified the girl: Abigail Faulkner. She lived with her mother and two lame twin brothers just north of town on a small plot of land only big enough for a couple of pigs and a vegetable garden. Thomas and Caleb knew her only by sight.

Inside the house, the men decided that they had to tell Abigail's mother what had happened, and the doctor's servant girl was sent to fetch Widow Faulkner.

The widow arrived some twenty minutes later, already upset. Abigail hadn't returned home from a quilting circle she had attended at the Putnam household with a couple of other girls the previous evening. Her mother thought perhaps she had stayed the night with the girls and would return home today, but she had not.

Nathaniel gently explained to her what had happened

and showed the widow her daughter's body. Straight away she began to wail and weep. Nathaniel spoke to her in calm tones, telling her that he should administer the Last Rites immediately. Eventually she seemed to understand and nodded, allowing the doctor and the other man to help her into another room.

Nathaniel closed the door behind them then went to the window and opened it. His sons waited beneath.

"Hand me my bag. I haven't much time," Nathaniel directed.

They swiftly hoisted their father's large leather bag in through the window, and Nathaniel got to work. First he examined the girl's limbs looking for any strange bites or marks, besides the obvious cut through her throat. He found nothing. There was no smell of sulfur or scorching around the mouth, so no demons had been involved with her death.

Next Nathaniel took some herbs from his bag. He sprinkled them over the girl's body, lit a candle and chanted some Latin phrases. Nothing happened. Nathaniel looked at her palms and feet—nothing suspicious there either.

Finally he checked the back of her neck, and gently probing with his fingertips he realized something very strange—her neck was completely limp.

Nathaniel went briefly into the other room to speak to the widow, and thank the doctor and the man. He then took his leave.

When their father emerged from the house, Caleb and Thomas jumped onto the cart. Nathaniel reigned the horses in silence, and the boys knew better than to speak to their father when he was deep in thought.

Once they were near the edge of the village, Nathaniel spoke.

"Her neck was completely broken," he stated.

"Broken?" Caleb asked.

"Like a chicken's. But there wasn't any bruising. Usually, such as with a hanging, there would be bruising," Nathaniel mused darkly.

"How was it broken?" Thomas asked.

Nathaniel shook his head.

"There's one obvious way to break a neck without touching someone."

"Black magic?" Caleb hazarded.

"Exactly." His father nodded.

"Didn't her mother say that she was at a quilting circle at the Putnam household?" Thomas offered.

"Indeed," Nathaniel said. "You boys go round to the Putnam house. Take some eggs. Say you want to trade with them. Find out when exactly Abigail Faulkner was there last. Also, look for any signs of witchery."

"Yes, sir, right away," Thomas said. He grabbed his brother, climbing off the cart and pulling Caleb after him. They grabbed a basket of fresh eggs off the back of the cart. In their line of business it was wise to always carry something to trade.

The boys waved goodbye to their father and trudged through deep snow back toward the village.

The Putnam house was just off Old Meetinghouse Road.

When they reached the residence, they climbed the steps to the imposing front door and knocked determinedly. The echoing sound of their knocking was followed by a piercing scream from inside the building, then the heavy tromp of boots could be heard approaching the front door. There was another scream, and then a man with a long nose and a small birdlike bridge to his face opened the door.

It was Reverend Parris. His face was wracked with pain.

"What is it, boys?" Reverend Parris asked.

"We've come to trade some eggs and perhaps speak to Anne and Prudence? Is everything all right?" Thomas asked boldly, trying to peer around the figure of the clergyman to see what was happening inside.

Just then another scream came from inside the house and Anne Putnam, a small twelve-year-old girl, appeared behind Reverend Parris. She had a wild look in her eyes. She looked at Caleb, them being the same age, then grabbed his arm and tried to pull him into the house. Reverend Parris protested, grasping the girl's wrist and freeing Caleb.

Mr. Putnam, Anne's father, emerged into the hallway and the two men conferred briefly. Thomas and Caleb watched from the doorway.

"Come, come, you've come just in time," Ann cried to Caleb. "See, see them there? Look how they scream at me. There, there! Up in the rafters!" She pointed toward the ceiling. The boys stepped cautiously into the hallway but when they looked up, they could see nothing unusal.

Another young girl, Prudence, who the boys knew to be Anne's close friend, emerged from the shadows. She too seemed to be on the verge of hysteria. She cried out and fell on the ground, her body twisting into severe shapes and her tongue rolling out of her mouth.

As if suddenly noticing the boys' presence, the Reverend pushed them back out of the front door.

"We have no time for you, boys," he said. "Evil is upon us." Just as he shut the door they heard Reverend Parris say to Mr. Putnam, "The same affliction has come to my house. My daughter and servant girl too scream out. It's witches I tell you. Satan has come to Salem."

As the boys went back down the steps, Thomas turned toward his younger brother.

"I think Anne Putnam has taken a shine to you."

Caleb smirked at his brother's sense of humor.

"Are you saying only a girl afflicted by an unseen force would like me?"

"Yes," Thomas said matter-of-factly. "Let's go tell Father that it seems these girls are troubled by witches."

FIFTEEN

Nathaniel Campbell and his family sat around the rough-hewn dinner table in front of the large hearth. The family was in deep discussion about the current events. Rose Mary Campbell filled everyone's bowls with soup and a large crust of bread.

"I heard they've accused Parris's servant, Tituba, as well as Sarah Good and Sarah Osborne, of witchery," Hannah said. She was the eldest child, a well-mannered, quick-witted, fearless whip of a girl.

Though she was often left behind by Nathaniel and the boys on some of their more dangerous hunts, Hannah always made herself useful. She was fluent in four languages, including the local Indian dialect, which had helped her learn some of their religious practices. Her father relied on her to figure out many of the spells and books that they referenced.

"So we know that Abigail Faulkner and Reverend Parris's daughter attend a quilting circle with Anne Putnam and Prudence Lewis," Hannah continued.

"And all four of those girls are claiming to be afflicted by witches," Nathaniel said.

"Poor Sarah Good, Sarah Osborne, and Tituba. There will be a trial for those three I'm sure," Rose Mary said. "Nothing gets Reverend Parris in more of a tizzy than the talk of evil. It is strange though, I'm sure they are just old women."

"Are they witches, Father?" Thomas asked.

"I can't be sure. I'll try a marking spell on them, if I can get close to them at the trial. That should tell us for certain," Nathaniel replied.

"I can't imagine that those women are witches," Hannah said. "Tituba seems like such a simple woman when I see her in the village."

"Well then, who is afflicting the girls?" Caleb asked.

Hannah shrugged. "If I were a witch I wouldn't be caught so easily. Don't you think, Father?"

"The girls claim to be able to see the women afflicting them," Nathaniel observed.

"Well, I can say a lot of things. I can say I see a horse with a lilac coat on in front of me. That doesn't mean it's true," Hannah countered.

"I'll try a marking spell on the three women. Then we'll know for sure," Nathaniel repeated.

"Do you think those women killed Abigail Faulkner?" Thomas asked.

Nathaniel thought about it for a moment.

"I think we can be sure that whomever killed Abigail is also afflicting the girls."

* * *

A couple of days later, Reverend Parris's servant Tituba, a slave he had brought with him to Salem from his time in the West Indies, was taken to the meetinghouse, along with the elderly Sarah Good and Sarah Osborne.

A great crowd gathered outside. Whispers of gossip swept through the people: four innocent girls were afflicted with horrible visions and manipulations by the women. *They must be witches*, the people murmured.

In the colonies, witchcraft was punishable by hanging, though in the past when accusations of witchcraft had erupted, no one had been hanged. But a particular fear struck everyone in the late winter of 1692.

All of New England was undergoing social and political upheaval and Salem had undergone a series of severe strains: The English and their impositions; as well as the raids by King Philip, the leader of the Wampanoag Indians, and his men, already had everyone on edge; and a smallpox epidemic had swept through much of New England.

On top of that, it had been a particularly cold winter and the people of Salem were desperate to escape their small smoky houses. Salem was infused with gossip and dispute, the people were restless and volatile and ready to believe the worst of their neighbors.

Nathaniel and his children pushed their way through the throng of people outside and managed to find standing places in the back of the meetinghouse. The interior of the building was carefully designed to instill fear into those being tried.

Along the far back wall two severe and imposing male

figures, the judges, sat behind a long table. To the right of the table was a small platform with a banister, where the afflicted girls sat. The magistrates instructed the girls to face forward, toward them, but when the three accused women were brought in, the girls turned around and at the very sight of the women, started to writhe and scream. They pointed at the accused and cried that they had come to them as specters and asked them to sign the book of Satan. They claimed that when they refused, the women started to bewitch them.

Nathaniel, Hannah, Thomas, and Caleb carefully watched the young girls' theatrics and observed the fear in the eyes of the accused women. The four girls seemed to be completely caught up in their own game. If one of the old women bent down, all the girls bent down and screamed that they were being forced to bend against their will. If one of them turned her head, all the girls screamed and turned their heads at unnatural angles.

To the crowd in the meetinghouse, watching with gasps of horror and mutterings about Satan, this was proof enough that the older women were witches. But the Campbell clan wanted further proof.

Nathaniel bent low and slipped two bags of herbs and oils into Hannah and Caleb's hands.

"You're going to have to get close to the women," he murmured softly. "See if you can't push your way to the front of the crowd. Place the bags under their chairs. I will then try to get close enough to do the rest."

The children elbowed their way through the dense

crowd. When they neared the front, Caleb burrowed his way forward until he was directly behind Tituba's chair. He bent down as if to tie his shoelaces and quickly placed the bag in a corner of the chair spokes.

Being of slight build, Hannah managed to do the same for both Sarah Good and Sarah Osborne, with ease. She then slipped back through the crowd to her father's side.

As a fully-grown man, Nathaniel found it more difficult to get through the crowd. But eventually he reached the accused women. Trying to not to draw attention to himself, he began his chant, whispering just loudly enough for the marking spell to take effect.

"Nathaniel Campbell," a deep voice called out over the din of the crowd and screaming girls, "are you also possessed by witches?"

Nathaniel looked up and caught the eye of his questioner, John Hathorne, who was one of the judges, though he had no formal legal experience. The man's air was stately and his voice boomed over the packed meetinghouse.

"No sir," Nathaniel replied, his voice calm and clear. "I am praying for the girls that they will be freed from their bewitching."

This answer seemed to satisfy Hathorne and he nodded and turned back to the inquest. Nathaniel finished the chant. He then crouched down behind the women's chairs and peered at the palms of their hands. There were no marks.

Satisfied, Nathaniel retreated and signaled to his children to leave.

They returned home in their cart through the village,

which was semi-deserted since most of the people of Salem were still thronging around the meetinghouse.

"Those magistrates are idiots," Thomas declared. "Can't they see that those women aren't hurting the girls?"

"Then who is?" Caleb put in.

"Do you think they are putting on a show, Father?" Hannah asked.

"I'm not sure if they are faking or not," Nathaniel stated. "But I am sure that those three women aren't witches. There was no marking spot on any of their palms. Which means either those girls are making it up or it is someone or something else harassing them."

"But who would be doing that?" Thomas asked.

"I guess we will have to wait and see," Nathaniel replied.

SIXTEEN

Less than a week after the hearing, Thomas and Caleb were walking home from town. It was late in the day so they decided to take a shortcut in order to reach home before dark. The land they cut across belonged to Constance Ball, a tall, well-spoken haughty woman who was known to be very wealthy. Some in Salem said she had colluded with the French and the Dutch, and those associations had brought her great riches; other townspeople whispered that she had had much more sinister beginnings.

Constance Ball's land stretched for a couple of miles around the large and imposing house that she owned. The boys walked quickly and carefully around the tree line, wary, as they knew they were trespassing.

As they rounded the back of the property, the boys noticed the Ball family graveyard. Like many homesteads a graveyard was kept on the family land, but this one struck the Campbell boys as strange—they could see two unearthed graves on the small plot of land on the edge of the pasture. Knowing their father would want to learn more, the boys crept closer and saw two old headstones, each with a death date carved on it. Was someone digging up dead bodies?

Thomas and Caleb realized immediately that they had discovered something important. They ran the rest of the way home. When they arrived, Nathaniel was just taking his horse out.

"Father, we have something to tell you," Caleb said, hands on his knees as he caught his breath.

"Not now boys. Another body was found," Nathaniel said, pulling himself into his saddle. "I've got to go examine it and see if the neck is broken."

"We cut through Constance Ball's land and found two graves," Thomas said quickly. "The bodies had been unearthed. The ground was all dug up."

"Are you sure?" his father asked, leaning down from his saddle.

They nodded.

"Well then, that's something else to investigate," Nathaniel said.

"Can we come with you?" Thomas asked eagerly.

"Aren't you two chilled to the bone? I won't be back until long after dark."

"I'd rather go with you," Caleb said.

Nathaniel shrugged and hoisted Caleb up onto a small half-saddle that sat forward on the horse and moved off, Thomas jogged by their side.

When they arrived at Reverend Parris's parsonage,

Nathaniel sent the boys to the back of the house. He was going to try to convince Reverend Parris that he should be allowed to see the latest body, but if he could not, the boys would have to try and get a look at it another way.

Shivering in the cold and dark but eager to see the latest developments, Thomas and Caleb peeked through those windows they could reach.

Inside the house, Nathaniel spoke with Reverend Parris.

"Reverend, if I may, I'd like to see the latest body that was found."

"Absolutely not. Can't you see what disarray my house is in?" Reverend Parris threw his arms wide. Just then, a female screamed upstairs. "As you know, my daughter and servant girl are bewitched by those vile women."

"But the women are incarcerated—has this not stopped the affliction?" Nathaniel questioned.

Reverend Parris stared at Nathaniel.

"Satan does not rest in one place, Nathaniel. He can live anywhere, bewitch anyone. There are more witches in Salem and I aim to find them."

"And I would like to help you. But I can only do that if I see the body."

"The dead man was a transient. No one in town knows him. He is of no use to you," the clergyman said.

"How did Sarah Good and Sarah Osborne, and your own Tituba, kill this transient then? If they were not familiar with him, how would they have done such a thing? They've been in the Salem Town jail since the week before last."

* * *

Observing through the windows that their father was having little success in persuading the Reverend to let him view the body, Thomas and Caleb found their way into the root cellar beneath the house. There they found the dead body of the strange man lying on the straw floor. The cellar was dark and stuffed with cured meats and roots. A single candle illuminated the corpse.

"Feel his neck," Caleb commanded his older brother.

"You do it," Thomas said.

"You're always saying you should get to do more things because you're older. Now is your chance." Caleb smirked.

Thomas crept reluctantly toward the body and gingerly reached his hand behind the dead man's neck.

"He'll get stiff now," a small voice said from a dark corner of the cellar. "He's been dead over an hour."

Thomas stumbled back from the body. Caleb caught him by the arm before he crashed into a shelf of glass jars.

Prudence Lewis stepped out into the faint candlelight. She stared hard at the boys.

"You scared us," Thomas declared angrily.

"What are you doing in Reverend Parris's root cellar?" Caleb demanded.

"What are *you* doing?" Prudence shot back.

"We are here to examine the body," Thomas said, taking control of the situation. "Why are you here? Aren't you scared?"

Prudence shrugged.

"Are you still bewitched?" Thomas asked skeptically.

Prudence grinned. "Of course. Haven't you heard what Reverend Parris said? Satan has come to Salem and is using witches to do his bidding. I'm afflicted. Just not right now."

The boys left the strange girl in the cellar, climbed back outside and went around to the front of the house to meet their father. They waited pressed against the wall until Reverend Parris had shut the door on Nathaniel, then they approached him.

"Did you find anything?" their father asked.

"Yes. A dead body in the cellar and a strange girl," Thomas said. He went on to describe their encounter with Prudence Lewis and the dead man's broken neck.

"Well, I think we know who we need to try the marking spell on next," Nathaniel said.

"Who?" Caleb asked.

"Prudence, you dimwit." Thomas nudged his brother in the ribs as he spoke.

"What about the empty graves?" Caleb asked.

"We'll have to investigate further," Nathaniel said. "But we have to ask ourselves a question first."

"What?" Caleb asked.

"What do the witches want?" his father replied.

Dean set down the journal and looked over at Lisa sleeping in the other bed. He got up to check on Ben in the adjoining room. He had fallen asleep in front the television.

Dean was amazed. Not only were there Campbells in Salem during the witch trials, they were also hunters. Dean flipped through a couple more pages of the journal. In the margin Nathaniel had written the witch-marking spell:

Per is vox malum ero venalicium. Per is oil malum unus ero ostendo. Per is herb malum unus ero brought continuo. They mos haud diutius non exsisto notus.

Dean was sure that he could use the marking spell to identify a witch to help him. He wasn't much closer to finding a *Necronomicon*, but he was sure if he found a witch the book would follow.

SEVENTEEN

In the morning, Dean, Lisa, and Ben headed downstairs for breakfast. As Dean was finishing his coffee, Perry, the young girl from the clam shack, appeared at his elbow. Ben was visibly delighted. Dean, not so much.

"Hey there, Captain Morgan. How are you this morning?" Dean said with a good amount of snarkiness to his voice.

Perry cast a strange sideways glance at Dean.

"I'm great, Mr. Winchester. How are you?"

Dean frowned at the mention of his last name. Had Ben told her what it was? He didn't like strangers knowing it. Best to stay under the radar in such a small town.

Despite her earlier wariness, Lisa chatted amiably with Perry. She was warming up to the girl, Dean noted. He just nodded and pretended to read the paper. Then a little blurb under the local police blotter caught his eye:

Salem Police have found ten abandoned vehicles in the last two weeks.

All vehicles have been impounded at Salem's Lot and Tow.

Cars will be sold at State Auction at 11:30 a.m. today if they are not claimed.

Ten abandoned cars in two weeks is not unusual in a big city, but Salem was relatively suburban, despite its sprawl. Dean pushed himself away from the table. He really should be pursuing the *Necronomicon* and a witch to help him, but his hunter instincts were spiked. There was something not right about that many abandoned cars in a small town.

"Ready to go?" Lisa asked.

"Actually, I'm going to go check some things out. I'll meet you back here for lunch?" Dean said.

"Dean, we said we were going to go to the clipper ships together," Lisa said, a hint of frustration in her voice.

"I know. I know. Why don't we go later?"

"What are we supposed to do in the meantime?" Ben asked.

"I'll show you around," Perry piped up.

"Yeah sure, Perry must know the place pretty well. Let her show you the town. I'll be back soon," Dean said.

He kissed Lisa on the cheek and left the dining room in a rush.

He drove round the block and then stopped to change into a suit, before heading out into the morning traffic.

* * *

Three car lengths behind Dean, Sam pulled the white van into the same lane.

"This van sticks out like one of Heidi Montag's nipples. Couldn't we get something a little less conspicuous?" Sam asked.

"Stop complaining and follow your brother," Samuel growled. "We need to find out what he's up to."

"Because of these witches, right?" Sam said.

"Exactly, these witches are bad news, they're making monsters. Netting them will make me happy," Samuel said. "Any questions?"

Sam had plenty of questions but kept them to himself.

Dean pulled into Salem's Lot and Tow. A skinny kid appeared from a little shack perched on the side of the lot.

"Hey man," Dean greeted the kid, "my sister lost her car. We think it may have been stolen. Can I take a look in your lot?"

The kid shrugged.

"You'd have to prove registration and pay the fees to get it out."

"Or you sell it," Dean said.

"Well, not me, it goes to the police fund actually," the kid said.

Dean nodded. He hopped out of his car and headed toward the vehicles lined up in rows.

"What kind of car did she have?" the kid asked, falling into step beside Dean.

"I'll recognize it when I see it. Where are the ones that

were found the past couple weeks?"

The kid pointed out several cars off to one side. Dean walked over to them with purpose, as if he saw one he recognized.

The first vehicle was an old red Camry, a hand-me-down to a teenager type-thing. Dean made sure the kid had gone back into his hut, and then slid into the driver's seat. He flipped open the glove box hoping to find the registration, but it was empty. He looked underneath the seats, ran his hands over the door panels, peered under the mats, then finally noticed something shoved into the heating vent.

Popping the grate out threw a cloud of dust into the car. Inside was a small bag tied with a red string, very like the one that had made Lisa so sick. Dean cut it open with his knife and its contents fell into his lap. He identified withered herbs, a nasty bloody chicken feather and a chicken vertebra. Either the previous owner had been a witch, or a witch had put the bag in the car to keep it off the spiritual radar.

Dean heaved himself out of that car and checked the next one. Sure enough, inside was the exact same hex bag. Perhaps Dean wasn't going to have to look far to find a witch. But why all the abandoned cars? Dean decided to see if the police had any missing person reports.

"Duck!" Samuel shouted as he saw Dean pull his car out into traffic.

Sam and Samuel were parked right outside the lot—they hadn't expected Dean to pull out so soon. If he had turned his head to the right, he would have seen them.

Fortunately Dean never bothers to look both ways when pulling into traffic, Sam thought to himself.

"Where's he going now?" Samuel growled.

Sam gunned the engine and followed his brother into the traffic.

The Salem police station was a large freestanding brick affair. Sam and Samuel parked the van across the street, and watched as Dean mounted the steps to the door.

"It looks like he's working a case, not hunting witches," Sam observed.

"He's all ADHD. Believe me, he's tracking the witches," Samuel said.

"Why are you so sure?"

"I just know," Samuel replied tersely.

"Fine. Forget I asked," Sam muttered, watching the door of the police station.

Inside, Dean went to the desk clerk and asked to see the missing person reports.

"Well, most of thar ain't missing no more," the fat desk clerk said with a thick Massachusetts accent.

Dean nodded. "I totally get the whole Barney Frank thing now."

"Donch get yar mening." The clerk looked perplexed.

"Can I speak to your supervisor?" Dean asked.

The desk clerk eased himself out of his seat and led Dean to his captain, an older guy who sat behind a desk in a glass-fronted office. Dean was immediately struck by the captain's striking resemblance to Chief Wiggum in *The Simpsons. Sam would love this dude*, he thought.

Dean badged the Captain.

"Agent McBrain. Can I have a look at your local missing person reports?" Dean demanded in his best authoritative voice.

"Don't you guys up in DC have it in your computer?" the captain responded grumpily.

"Ah yes, the computer," Dean replied. "Well, we do, but I wanted to check for any recent ones that you hadn't filed yet. You've had ten abandoned cars found these past couple of weeks. Seems to me like you might have ten reports to go with them."

This seemed to perturb the captain.

"No need to make everyone crazy. A couple of abandoned cars don't seem like much trouble," he said.

Dean smirked—this guy was hiding something.

"It *is* a problem if those cars belong to missing people."

The Captain stood up and lumbered over to a cabinet. He pulled out a thick manila file and threw it onto his desk.

"Was goin' to wait till the summer was over."

Dean stared at him, incredulous.

"Really? You were going to wait until the summer was over to file the reports? Why?"

The captain shrugged.

"You can't have dead bodies coming up outta nowhere. Scares off the tourists."

"Wait! What dead bodies?" Dean grabbed the file from the captain's desk. He flipped through it quickly. Inside the folder were ten individual files, each with a crime scene photo attached. Nine of the ten victims were young women. "Wait a second, all these bodies you've found here, in Salem?" In every one of them the cause of death was listed as asphyxiation. "How did these people actually die?"

"Don't know. Still lookin' into it," the captain said.

Dean was pissed. He wasn't really a higher rank then this guy, but if he had been, he would have throttled him for sure.

"Have you reported this to the federal authorities?" Dean demanded.

"You're here now," the captain pointed out. "Besides, don't hurt no one. These here are transients." The captain pointed to the file. "Probably gangbangers from Boston."

"She's about as much a gangbanger as my grandmother," Dean said, holding up one of the crime scene pictures. It depicted a young girl with blonde hair, her face mottled with bruising. Around her neck was a peace pendant.

"Gangbangers? Really?" Dean spat. "Wait until Washington hears about this!"

He thrust the file under his arm and stomped out of the office.

As he walked away, he heard the captain again mumble something about scaring off the tourists.

Outside the police station, Dean tried to calm himself down. He needed to find out who or what had killed those people; they deserved some sort of justice.

Dean opened up his cell phone and dialed a number.

A business-like male voice answered, "FBI."

"Yeah, this is Agent McBrain from the Boston office.

You need to come down to Salem and see this shit. Ten girls dead, local police playing keep-away with the information," Dean said brusquely.

"What's your ID number, Agent?"

"Oh, sure, I'll give it to you. One moment. It's 1—" Dean hung up the phone. Hopefully, the little ruse would piqued the FBI's interest enough to get them to follow up and do all their CSI stuff running down the wrong people. But at least that way all the families would be notified.

Dean decided to go to the coroner's office too, even though he knew what he'd find: each cut would be exactly the same, the same depth in the neck for maximum bloodletting. It was ritualistic killing, sacrifices. The puzzle pieces still didn't jive though. Sacrificing usually meant that someone was trying to do a really powerful spell. But for what?

On some level Dean felt a buzz, like his brain was finally kicking into gear. He was hunting. He knew what to do. This was his world.

EIGHTEEN

Dean sliced through each of the small bags so their contents scattered onto the store counter and Sukie's bare feet.

"There are nine girls and one Justin Bieber-looking kid— all dead. All with these bags found in their cars. Why are you killing these people?" Dean growled.

As Sukie opened her mouth to speak, Dean grabbed a handful of her necklaces and pulled her close.

"And don't give me any of that 'I don't know nothing about being no witch' crap," he breathed and then let her go.

Sukie looked genuinely scared. She glanced furtively around the store as if someone might be watching.

"Listen, it's nothing to do with me, I'm not taking part in whatever they're doing. I just tell them what I see and I keep to myself," she stammered.

"So you told them about me?" Dean asked.

"Among others. I didn't know they were killing people, I swear I didn't. I just hear stuff. I knew something big was happening. But I don't know what."

"What are these bags supposed to do?" Dean asked, though he was pretty sure he knew the answer.

"They're like invisibility bags. You know, dissipates the psychic energy of the owner so a clairvoyant can't find them," Sukie said.

"Who's killing them?"

"I already told you, I don't know," Sukie said. "And I'm always here." She gestured at the store.

"So where else could someone get this stuff around here?"

"Nowhere, we're the only place. But I swear I didn't sell any of that stuff to anyone. I open and close this place every day of the week."

Sukie seemed to be telling the truth.

"Okay, so you're just Bush. Who's your Karl Rove?" Dean pressed. "Is there anyone else who could take this stuff and you wouldn't know?"

"No… I mean the only other people who have access are Connie and her girls."

"What are we talking, here? A witch brothel? Let me guess, everyone wears a lot of black lace, Fleetwood Mac-style?" Dean smirked.

"No, she just has girls that work for her."

"Are they all witches?" Dean asked.

"I don't know. How many times do I have to tell you? Do you mind if I clean up now? This stuff smells." Sukie gestured at the dust, bones, and crap before her. "If you want to know something, go ask Connie yourself."

"One more thing. What do you need for a marking spell?" Dean asked.

"Like what?"

"Something that marks a witch, a bad witch. Clearly not a witch-lite, like you," he said.

"I don't know. Do you have a spell?"

Dean took out Nathaniel Campbell's journal and pointed to the spell written in the margin of one of the pages.

"This looks old. What'd you do? Filch this from the Peabody?"

"Something like that. Just tell me what I need."

"Well, I don't know. I mean I can only guess. I can't tell you exactly. I've never seen this spell," Sukie said hesitantly.

"Guess then," Dean said.

"Well, I'd put a little Valerian root, some dragon's blood and I guess a little sulfur. Might work. I'm not making any guarantees." She moved round the store, gathering the stuff. She then wrapped it in a linen gris-gris bag. "You can try this."

"Thanks," Dean said.

"Hey, just so you know, I would never be involved with anyone that killed people. Connie is a Mean Girl, you know? I'm not like that."

Dean nodded and left the store.

It took all his self-control not to head straight to Connie's, crash through her front gates and rip her limb from limb. It seemed he was playing with a powerful witch, and he realized how close he had come to losing Lisa. Maybe he should call Lisa and check in, just in case…

This time he wasn't going to get caught without something

to hold over Connie. He was sure that she had something to do with the dead bodies, but he had no solid evidence. He could bring her to hunter justice—bind her up and smoke her like a Virginian ham—or turn her in to the authorities. He was going to have to get proof.

Back in his car, Dean opened the police file. He decided some old-fashioned shoe leather was called for.

NINETEEN

From their van parked down the street, Sam and Samuel spotted Dean walk out of the store.

"You wanna follow him?" Samuel asked.

"Nah, let's go talk to the little bitch inside," Sam proposed.

"I thought you said she didn't know anything," his grandfather said skeptically.

"Well, let's just see if she's changed her mind."

Samuel and Sam barged through the front door of the store to find it completely empty. The girl was gone.

Samuel gestured for Sam to go to the back while he would look upstairs. Sam headed behind the counter into the dark storage room. The back door had been fixed and it was so dark in the windowless room, he could barely see his hand in front of his face.

A floorboard creaked behind him. Sam spun around and came face to face with a strange woman with harsh features.

"I'm sorry, no returns," she said, her voice sharp and

grating. She flicked her wrist and Sam was thrown up against the opposite wall. "And no, I don't care if you're a Campbell."

He tried to fight the power that held him there, but the woman was too strong. He felt an unseen weight press against his chest. The women inched her hand up higher and Sam felt himself thrown up against the ceiling, he struggled to breathe as the invisible weight continued to press down on him.

"Especially without a receipt," she said.

"Some customer service!" Samuel growled, appearing in the doorway armed with a baseball bat. He swung high toward the woman.

"Please, you're going to use an instrument used in a game on me?" she sneered.

"No, I'm going to use this." Samuel pulled a salt-filled sawed-off from his hip and shot just shy of the woman's left shoulder.

"Salt? Really? You think I'm a demon?" She smirked, then stepped up to Samuel and took a large sniff. "You've been dead, old man." She pushed out her hand and Samuel started to gag. "You remember not being able to breathe? That's right, you do. And you were dead a while. So interesting… You and I will have to have a talk some time. Right now, however, I'm going to have a little—what do you call it?—barbecue."

With another wave of her hand, a fire started on the storeroom floor in the corner. The woman stepped to the doorway and spread a powder along the floor and the doorjamb.

"It was time I cleared out my inventory anyway."

And with that, she disappeared through the door.

Samuel struggled to move but seemed to be held fast in place in the doorway. Sam was still pinned to the ceiling, fighting for breath. The flames spread, catching on the boxes of merchandise and reaching higher.

"How is she keeping us here?" Sam choked.

"Look for a spot of blood. She got some on you somehow. Wash it off!" Samuel managed.

Sam struggled to move at all, much less look for a spot of blood. After a few seconds he managed to prise his left arm off the ceiling and found a dot of dark-red blood on the inside of his wrist.

"How am I supposed to get it off?" he called.

The fire had climbed the tower of boxes and now reached the ceiling. The flames were creeping toward his toes.

"Spit!" Samuel shouted.

Sam tried to muster saliva from his dry mouth. He spat on his wrist, and felt the invisible restraints loosen a little bit. Fighting to get his arm down by his side, he managed to wipe his wrist against his pants. He promptly fell face-first to the floor.

Without flinching, Sam sprang back onto his feet, and stamping on the spreading flames, he moved to his grandfather's side. He grasped his left wrist and wiped off the blood he found there.

Both free they staggered into the store, which was already filled with a thick acrid smoke.

On the floor by the front window they found the girl. Her neck lay at an unnatural angle. Sam bent over and checked her pulse anyway. She was dead.

They broke through the front door and out into the street. Still coughing, eyes streaming with the effects of the smoke, they dived into their van. Sam pulled away just as the fire trucks turned the corner.

"That was some powerful witchcraft. I've never seen a binding spell like that before," Sam observed.

"She must be the witch we want," Samuel said. "It needs someone that powerful to create something purely evil. She's strong, and I bet she's looking to get stronger."

"What do you mean?" Sam asked.

"Witches act like a magnet; the more witches that are around, the more power they have collectively. Someone who can cast that spell, and keep us there for that long, she's not playing around."

"What was the blood-binding spell? I've seen binding spells but never one where the person could leave the room and it still stayed in place. The only thing I know that can do that is a devil's trap," Sam said.

"Yeah, you probably don't want to see that spell again either," Samuel stated dryly.

"Why? What is it?" Sam asked.

"Witch menstrual blood," Samuel replied with just a hint of a smile.

"Agent McBrain," Dean introduced himself, leaning over the grimy desk of the county coroner. "I need to see all the bodies that have shown up in the past two weeks. You know, the ones killed by the same Salem serial killer that everyone here seems to want to ignore." He took back his badge and waved his hand toward the back of the basement office. "And I need to see them now."

The elderly white-haired man behind the desk scooted out of his chair without a word and led the way to the refrigerated section of the laboratory.

"Not very chatty, are ya?" Dean observed.

"Not much to say," the old man responded as he pulled out one of the body-sized stainless steel draws in the wall. "She was the first brought in. No identification on 'em 'cept a couple of tattoos."

Job done the old dude shuffled back to his chair.

Dean examined the first young girl. A slit ran from one side of her neck to the other: it was clean, not too deep, and brutally precise. He looked for any signs of witchcraft on the body. There were no charcoal smudges or flakes of herbs, and it didn't seem like she had been anointed for a sacrifice. But Dean noted she had defensive wounds on her hands and arms, as if she had tried to fend off her attacker.

This wasn't a clean ritual, this kid had put up a fight.

Dean bent down slightly to get a closer look at the neck wound. As he carefully adjusted the tilt of her head, he noticed something very weird. Not only had her throat been cut—her neck was completely broken.

"This wasn't in her report?" Dean called to the old man. The old grouch looked up, then came shuffling back toward Dean.

"What?" he asked.

"Her neck is broken. It wasn't in your report," Dean said. "You don't think that's an important thing to include?

She looks like a Raggedy Ann doll!"

The old man shrugged.

Looking back at the body, Dean noticed something on the girl's collarbone. It was a small "I Heart NYC" tattoo. Chief Wiggum was right about one thing—she was a transient. But what was she doing in Salem?

Dean checked all the other bodies. Every one of them had a broken neck. Dean sighed. Something rotten was in Salem. He had a bonafide case on his hands and that was the last thing he needed right now. All he wanted was a *Necronomicon* and a witch and to get his brother back—was that too much to ask? Now he had ten dead bodies, and—

His cell phone rang. Lisa's number flashed insistently at him on the tiny screen—one pissed-off girlfriend.

Dean answered, "Hi babe!"

"Hey Dean. Where have you been? Is everything okay?" Lisa's voice sounded worried.

"I've been, um, just around. Everything's fine—no need to stress," Dean said sheepishly. He really needed to come up with some good excuses for this sort of thing in advance. "How was the sightseeing?"

"It was great! I love hanging around with my pre-teen son and a girl who is coming on waaay too strong."

"So it's been good?" Dean said.

"No, not exactly. Are you done yet, I thought we were meeting back at the inn for lunch?"

"Okay, I just have one stop to make first," Dean said.

"Dean—what's this all about? Are you working a case?"

"Um, no. I don't think so. I mean, I didn't mean to—"

"You didn't mean to what?" Lisa's voice was worryingly calm.

"Nothing. Nothing," Dean retracted quickly, sensing this was not something to get into over the phone. Especially standing in a morgue surrounded by brutally murdered young women. "I'm coming back," he finished.

"Can you come back straight away, no stops," Lisa said. "Ben and I are waiting for you. He wants to see the clipper ships. Today."

"Great. Clipper ships!" Dean tried to infuse his voice with enthusiasm. "I'm on my way!" He clicked off his phone and with a last glance at the dead girls, headed for the exit. As he marched past, he noted the old coroner was paging through a Lands' End catalog.

"Hope ya find the people that are doing this. Last time they didn't catch anyone," the man observed, attention still apparently on the fleece jackets in front of him.

Dean stopped in his tracks.

"What do you mean 'last time'?"

"March of eighty-three, five dead girls. Was quite the hubbub." The old man looked up, meeting Dean's stare.

"March of eighty-three?" Dean repeated. Maybe it was only coincidental, but that was the same month and year that Sam was born.

Dean stepped out into the hot, hazy afternoon air. The atmosphere felt thick around him. He tried to put one foot in front of the other, but felt woozy. Both his knees failed to bend and he half-fell onto the hot cement steps. His cell phone rang again. Fumbling, Dean pulled the phone from his pocket. The screen read: SAM.

That couldn't be. Dean stared at the number and the flashing phone sign. He hit the answer button.

"Hey Dean, it's me, Sam. Remember? Your brother," a voice on the other end of the line came through. Dean knew he was hallucinating. He must be hallucinating.

He opened his mouth to speak but the phone kept ringing. Dean pulled the phone away and stared intently at the screen. It now read: LISA. He took a deep breath and accepted the call.

"You're on your way, right?" Lisa asked.

"Yeah, be there in a few." He hung up. That was weird. He'd had dreams, but never hallucinations. He stumbled to his car, got in, and drove off.

Across the street, Sam watched Dean pull away.
"He do that a lot?" Samuel asked. "Have girly dizzy spells like that?"

"Nope. I've never seen him do that before," Sam said, a slight look of recognition flickering across his face. There was a little something deep down there. A second later the grain of feeling, whatever it was, had disappeared again.

TWENTY

As Dean pulled up in the car he saw Lisa and Ben standing on the sidewalk, looking expectant. He tried to put on a poker face, but the phantom phone call from Sam had shaken him. However, he needn't have worried about Lisa picking up on his discomfort.

"Hi, remember us, the people you're on vacation with, *at your suggestion?*" she began. Not waiting for Dean to answer she pushed Ben toward the car. "Good, because you and Ben are going to go see the clipper ships together." Ben jumped into the passenger seat. "Do not feed him any crap."

"Do fried Twinkies constitute crap? How about beer dogs? I think I saw hotdogs fried in beer," Dean said, trying to lighten the mood.

"No and no. Have fun," Lisa said, kissing Ben and giving Dean a significant look over her son's head, as if to say, "Remember fun?"

Dean nodded. Fun wasn't really a concept he was

comfortable with right then. He drew a breath. For Ben he would have fun. What could go wrong?

A short while later they arrived at the clipper ship that was docked on the other side of the blue-green bay. As soon as the car stopped, Ben jumped out and ran ahead.

"Hey buddy, keep your cool in check," Dean called after him.

"Do you think there are pirates?" Ben asked as Dean caught up.

"Not sure there were pirates back in Puritan times," Dean said. He really didn't know—it was the kind of thing Sam would have known. "Let's go get tickets for the tour and we can find out." *Tours. Tickets. Jesus,* Dean thought, *this "fun" is turning into Mr. Rogers' nightmare.*

Dean noticed that there weren't a lot of other people walking up the gangplank to the ship. It seemed as though most people—even tourists—knew to stay away from such tacky crap. The ship wasn't even seaworthy; Dean noticed it was half-grounded on the pier. The thing wasn't going anywhere anytime soon. That was good, however. Dean wasn't too fond of the open water and he definitely wasn't fond of puking on his shoes. In high school he'd taken a boat trip on the Mississippi, and the unpleasant memory came back to him as soon as he set foot on the gangplank.

Ben handed him a ticket with a Jolly Roger skull and crossbones on it.

"This is going to be great," Ben said, leading the way to the gloomy anteroom which was the start of the tour. "And it looks like we have the whole tour to ourselves!"

"Are we late?" a voice said.

A pudgy old woman in a clinging powder-blue belted leisure suit, who clearly thought she was Super-Grandma, stepped into the room behind them. She held the hand of a little girl, about five years old, with a face like a mashed potato and a mouth rimmed with a red candy coating. The little girl's sticky-fingered other hand grasped at Dean's pant leg.

"Hands off the threads, Veruca Salt." Dean cringed and stepped away.

"Dakota darling, leave the man alone," Super-Gran said mildly.

"Ahoy there! Are ye all ready for a tour of the creakiest, creepiest ship to ever set sail the high seeeaass?" An old guy in a pirate costume leapt out from behind a plastic barrel.

"Ahhhh. Memaw!" The little girl screamed and pulled her grandmother back out toward the ticket counter.

"Guess not," Dean observed under his breath.

"We are," Ben said.

"Argh, grreaaat!" the old man said.

"That was a little more Tony the Tiger than Jack Sparrow," Dean noted.

The guide gave him the evil eye.

"You can be me grommet. Would ye like that?" he asked Ben.

"Totally!" Ben said. "Can we see the Gibbet first?"

"Ye know a lot about pirates, mate," the man said. "Just don't get too pushy. I got a system," he added, without the accent.

"We're going to start foreword on the ship at the forecastle," he continued, re-discovering the accent. "This is where the sayy-lors slept." The pirate guide led the way as they walked toward the front of the ship.

Ben turned to Dean and shrugged.

"There's a lot on the Internet. Pirates are cool," he said.

After walking through a narrow hallway they entered a small dusty room with bunkbeds attached to each wall.

"'Tis where the picaroons slept," the man said.

"Hey dude, you don't need to do the accent the whole time. I mean, we appreciate it and all, but, ya know, *not* necessary," Dean told the guy. The mock-pirate regarded him for a moment with tired eyes.

"Really? 'Cause this day sort of sucked," he admitted.

"Yeah. Relax. Just let us wander around," Ben said.

The guy nodded gratefully. "Okay. Just don't tell my boss. You guys seem cool, so how about I show you some of the places that the public doesn't get to see? I'm Teddy, by the way." He shook hands with each of them.

"Dean and Ben," Dean said. "Nice to meet you. Yeah, totally—show us the good stuff. Right, Ben?"

Ben nodded eagerly.

They followed Teddy to the main deck. Ben ran around pointing out where the swords were kept, and how the sails were steered. Teddy then led them down to the deck below, where the cannons were kept. It was a large nearly bow-to-stern open floor with imposing black cannons sticking out of a line of holes on each side of the ship.

"Do these work?" Ben asked, running toward one.

"Aw no," Teddy said smiling, "these cannons have all been cemented up for decades. They used to shoot twenty-four pound balls. Boys like you would run up and down bringing gunpowder from the bottom of the ship to set them off."

"You still have the cannonballs?" Ben asked.

"Gosh, no. They melted down whatever was found a long time ago."

"So what's this?" Ben asked, rolling a large cannonball across the floor.

Teddy looked surprised.

"That isn't supposed to be there—where did you find that?"

"Yeah, I suspect we shouldn't be here either," Dean said, pointing out of one of the cannon holes. Teddy ran to the hole and peered out.

They were in the middle of the open sea.

"How the holy hell did that happen?" Teddy cried.

"I think he might be able to tell us," Ben said, pointing to a tall, thin figure at the other end of the deck.

The figure limped toward them. As it moved closer, Dean could see it was a man. He appeared slightly translucent at first, but with each step he took, he became more and more solid, until he stood about twenty feet in front of them. He was dressed in a ruffled high-collar shirt with knee-high swashbuckler boots over tight trousers. A long silver sword hung from his belt.

He didn't look happy.

"Nice shirt," Dean observed.

The ghost turned his milky eyes toward them.

"Dean?" Ben had backed up against Dean, his eyes as wide as saucers.

"You know how you keep bugging me to teach you how to hunt?" Dean said calmly.

"Yeah," Ben said.

"Hunt? Hunt what?" Teddy was frozen to the spot, staring at the pirate.

"Pissed off pirate ghosts," Dean replied.

"What do you do first?" Ben asked, shuffling around behind Dean.

"Run!" Dean yelled as he pushed Ben and Teddy toward a door in the aft of the ship.

"Arrgh, ye scalliwags ain't going to gull me!" the pirate shouted. Dean looked back to see him limping after them.

"No one is gulling anything with kids in the room," Dean said, pulling an iron knife from his jacket and swinging at the pirate. His reach was too short, so he threw the knife at the apparition, but Captain Scalliwag was quicker than he looked and swiftly side-swiped it away with his sword.

"Through there. Now!" Dean directed Ben and Teddy toward the door.

"But ghosts aren't real!" Teddy screamed, tripping over the threshold.

Dean pushed Ben through after Teddy, then leapt through himself. He spun around and slammed the door behind him just as the pirate's sword blade cracked through the wood.

"Looks pretty damn real to me," Dean said, ushering them forward into the dark of the ship.

TWENTY-ONE

"How did that happen? And what do we do now?" Teddy cried as he led the way down some steps.

Dean shook his head. "I don't know. We could have passed through a portal of some sort. Could be a curse, a spell... Has anything like this ever happened before?"

"No, never," Teddy said, "and I've worked here since college."

Dean raised an eyebrow. Teddy was pushing fifty. Just then, a cacophony of harangues and the stomp of heavy boots on the deck above marched over their heads.

"Seems like there are more of them now," Ben said.

"Is there any salt on this ship?" Dean asked Teddy.

"Should be, we use it on the gangplank during the winter," Teddy said. "We usually keep large sacks of it in the galley."

"Okay, well, that's our second stop. First, where are the guns?"

"There aren't any! We don't keep guns on the ship."

"Well, I would say there aren't any pirates, but I'm pretty sure they're here. So where would they have stored guns on a working pirate ship?" Dean said.

Teddy shrugged.

"Gunpowder room?" Ben suggested.

Teddy nodded. "Right."

Dean punched Ben lightly on the shoulder and the boy straightened proudly.

Teddy took them down a long staircase to the very bottom of the boat.

"Through here," he said.

"You can't go in thar," said a voice behind them.

The trio swung around. A craggy old sea dog was shackled beneath the stairway.

"What are you going to do about it, Golem?" Dean challenged.

"If I wasn't chained up I would disembowel you," the old sailor retorted.

"You look like you could use a colonoscopy yourself," Dean said, bending down and taking out his pocket knife. He stuck it in the crevice between the floorboards and popped up one of the old planks.

"What are you doing?" Ben asked.

"Putting this poor cranky guy out of his misery," Dean said. He stuck his arm down the hole in the floor and pulled out a human skull.

"Wha'd'ye have there?" the sea dog asked.

"Hold it, Yorick." Sticking his hand back in the hole, Dean

pulled out a moldy burlap bag. Inside was a collection of bones. Dean put the skull into the bag, then produced a small tin box of salt from a pocket, which he poured onto the bag.

"RIP old man."

Dean lit his Zippo lighter and held the flame underneath the bag. It lit up instantly, burning bright. The old ghost started to scream.

Not waiting around to see what happened next, Dean pushed Ben through the door to the gunpowder room. Inside, the room was filled floor to ceiling with large barrels of gunpowder and an array of guns.

"This wasn't here before," Teddy said, amazed.

"Yeah, well, we don't want it to be either," Dean said. "The longer a supernatural force stays in this realm the more energy it gathers, and these ghosts are going to get all cozy in the present. So let's get them the hell out of here. Gather all the iron pistols you can."

"Even me?" Ben asked.

"Yeah, this *one* time, even you." Dean handed him a flintlock pistol that was as long as Ben's forearm.

"Pull back on this, aim, then pull the trigger," Dean instructed. "This hammer will create a spark, but it might take a second to fire."

"What about your *real* gun?" Ben asked.

"I didn't know there were going to be ghost pirates," Dean said, filling Ben's pockets with handfuls of iron pellets. "I left it in the car."

BANG!

The door rattled as buckshot hit the other side.

"They're trying to shoot their way in," Dean said. "Let's go."

The trio grabbed as many muskets and pistols as they could hold and climbed up the ladder at the far end of the room, emerging through a door into yet another part of the ship.

"This way!" Teddy cried, leading them through a small door.

"Um, Dean?" Ben stuttered.

"What?"

"How do I use this again? Because I think I'm gonna need to," Ben said, thumbing behind his shoulder. Dean looked down. The pirate ghosts had broken through the door and were now stomping through the artillery, gathering as they went. Now they climbing the ladder.

"Help me with these barrels!" Dean called to Teddy. They lifted three large barrels full of tar to the door, blocking it. More yells and shouts from the pirates echoed through the ship.

"Come on! We don't have much time," Dean said, urging the others on. "What's the highest point on the ship? We need to get an advantage."

"The poop deck! Follow me," Teddy said.

Dean shook his head in disbelief.

"Really?"

"Yes," Teddy said. "Let's go."

Ben, Teddy and Dean scampered up the deck. The ship was steadily making its way into the Atlantic; only a rim of land could be seen on the horizon. Peering into the open sea, Dean felt a momentary lurch of seasickness. He took a deep breath and tried to ignore the tilting of the deck beneath his feet.

The vessel had been completely transformed into its former, seaworthy glory. The deck was full of everything one would need for a long sea voyage: rope, tar, even animals.

"How did this stuff get here?" Teddy was aghast. "This is on the National Historical Registry. They can't bring livestock onto a national treasure," he said, pointing to a goat that bleated at them then scampered away.

Seconds later a slew of pirates appeared. Dean counted forty confused and pissed-off buccaneers gathered at the bow of the ship, then the pirate from the gun deck stepped forward.

"I'll not have mutiny on my ship, mate," he called.

Dean stepped forward.

"Well, I think we'll hang around. I think it's time you retired from raping and pillaging anyway. How about throwing in the towel? Go down to Boca. You know, relax."

"Why don't ye just get off?"

"Yeah dude, that means something different now. Okay," Dean said to Ben and Teddy, "when they advance, I want you to calmly—"

"Fire!" Teddy cried as he ineptly aimed his pistol at the ghosts.

Dean shrugged.

"Yeah, fire." He cocked an ancient pistol and fired into the crowd of oncoming surly sailors. An iron ball exploded out of the musket and hit a peg-legged pirate square in the eye, instantly vaporizing him.

"You got him!" Teddy said.

"He'll be back, and more pissed off. This is just to buy us some time," Dean said, letting off a two-handed barrage of gunfire. Another ghost vaporized, then a couple of seconds later re-materialized, stumbling, in the same place. "Ben, we need salt. Go find the galley!"

Ben scampered off as Teddy and Dean held the motley crew of pirates at bay. A few minutes later he returned, dragging a large sack of rock salt.

"Got it!" he called.

Dean cut open the sack and grabbed it at the base. He heaved a large semi-circle of salt around them. The ghost who seemed to be the captain of the motley crew charged the salt line but couldn't cross it.

"I'll get ye," he growled.

"Okay, Captain Crunch, keep your breeches on." Dean refilled his gun and shot him between the eyes. The ghost vaporized but then re-materialized. Teddy took a swing at him with a iron loading rod. It split the ghost in two. But just for a moment.

"Ah, Dean!" Ben cried.

A pirate had climbed up the outside of the ship and was now steadily forcing Ben to walk along the plank on the stern of the ship. Dean took aim at the pirate's back but Ben was directly behind him—he couldn't take a shot without hitting Ben too.

"Ben, stay calm. Aim your pistol at him and shoot!" Dean directed.

"It's jammed!" the boy called. Tears were streaming down Ben's cheeks.

"Throw it at him!" Dean yelled.

Ben hefted his gun at the ghost, but the grizzly pirate caught it deftly and instead aimed it at Ben.

"Duck!" Dean cried as he aimed and shot at the ghost. Ben hit the plank as the shot ripped through the ghost. Dean jumped to the plank and pulled Ben up and behind him.

The ghost quickly came back.

"Teddy! Shoot!" Dean screamed.

Teddy rotated a cannon, then lit the fuse. The ball rumbled out of the opening and arced toward the ghost. It obliterated the specter and punched through the stern of the boat.

"We have to turn this ship around. Teddy can you do that?" Dean asked.

"I can try," Teddy replied. He jumped over the salt line, caught a hanging rope and in a move that would have made Indiana Jones proud, swung to the other side of the deck, landing at the wheel.

"Ben, see that little dinghy right there?" Dean pointed. "Start lowering it down. When Teddy gets the ship turned around, you set it in the water and get in. You understand?"

"What are you going to do?" Ben asked.

"I'm going to make sure these pirates don't reach land," Dean said determinedly. He spotted a thick length of rope. Simultaneously shooting at ghosts, he dragged the rope over to a large barrel of tar, dunked in the entire rope, some two-hundred pounds' worth, then threw it over the side of the ship.

He called out to Ben, "Ben, grab the other end of the rope and don't let go. Okay?"

Ben waved as he fought to lower the dinghy on a pulley.

Meanwhile, Teddy pulled at the wheel and the ship began to turn in a big lazy curve.

The pirates all shot to one side of the deck, giving them temporary relief from attack.

Dean took the opportunity to throw salt mixed with gun powder in lines across the deck. Then he carefully lit each line. In moments an enormous crosshatch of fire spread across the surface of the ship.

Dean raced across the deck to help Teddy at the wheel. Perched on a turret, struggling against the ancient ring of wood, Teddy heroically stood fast and hung on, making sure the ship made a full turn. Dean kicked and shot at oncoming ghosts. A long-haired pirate attacked and Dean beheaded him with an iron sword. The pirate vaporized then reappeared just three feet away.

"Come closer, I want to rip your heart out an' eat it for me dinner," Hairy declared.

"Sorry, I'm not free for lunch, Long John Silver," Dean said, swinging the iron sword again and knocking the ghost clear onto the other side of a burning salt line. Dean turned back toward the turret just as another pirate climbed over a railing and snuck up behind Teddy.

"Teddy, watch out!" Dean shouted.

The pirate swung his sword.

It cut straight through Teddy's torso.

Teddy turned around and gasped. The ghost jumped

onto him and stuck his hand inside his chest. Teddy's eyes saucered wide, he clutched at his heart, then fell forward onto the wheel.

The ship pitched right, debris tumbled off the deck, a couple of ghosts plunged into the churning water. Dean raised his gun and shot at Teddy's killer. The pirate vaporized, then came back. Dean shot at him again and raced to Teddy's side. He was dead. *Crap, poor guy.* He glanced quickly over his shoulder to see if Ben had witnessed Teddy's violent end. *Better if the boy doesn't know what happened.*

Dean took another length of rope and tied the wheel of the ship so it was headed straight toward shore. He jumped onto the railing, shoved the gun in the waistband of his jeans, and pulled a hanging piece of rope close.

"Anything to do with Tarzan—always a bad idea," he muttered. He held on tight and heaved himself off the railing. The rope arced low over the length of the deck like a pendulum. Dean kicked and stabbed a couple of pirates as they clamored and grasped at his heels. At the top of the trajectory, Dean jumped off and pushed Ben into the dinghy.

"Tour's over."

Dean grabbed the tar-coated rope, and took a bag of gunpowder out of his pocket. He plastered it onto the end of the rope and lit it with his Zippo.

"Cut the rope!"

Ben produced a machete and cut the pulley rope. The dinghy swung out and hung for a second, then dropped harshly into the water.

The first explosion bloomed from the deck, rocketing flaming debris over the sides of the ship toward the dinghy.

"Row, row hard!" Dean urged.

Ben and Dean pulled at the oars, straining against the pull of the ship as it surged forward. They were caught in its wake. The two vessels were quickly approaching shore. But as furiously as Ben and Dean tried to row away from the ship, its thrust made it impossible to maneuver out of its grasp.

"Where's Teddy?" Ben shouted over the roar of the explosions.

"He's fine," Dean replied, looking sadly back at the ship. "Don't worry about him." Ben was too breathless from rowing to press him further.

The top deck caught fire as a series of smaller explosions ripped tank-sized holes in the side of the ship. Dean and Ben bobbed alongside the flaming fireball.

"We need to push ourselves away from the ship," Dean called.

Ben nodded. "We need a cannon or something."

Dean thought a moment. He looked around them, they were surrounded by debris bobbing in the churning water. What could he use?

"Help me get this thing in the boat," Dean instructed. He and Ben leaned over the side of the small craft, careful not to let it capsize, and pulled a cracked nine-foot-long piece of mast from the water.

Another explosion ripped through the back of the ship, shooting the cast-iron stove into the water. Seeing a solution,

Dean paddled and managed to get to the pipe which let out the smoke. He pried it off the sinking stove and grabbed a floating plank of wood.

"We need to nail this plank onto the bottom of this pipe. Find nails, whatever you can," Dean said.

As the ship sped toward the shore, Dean and Ben struggled to stay afloat as they fished pieces of debris out of the water and using the handle of Ben's machete managed to nail the plank onto the pipe. Dean shoved a bag of gunpowder down the end of the pipe and then, with difficulty, positioned the pipe against the bow of the dinghy and the plank that ran across as a second seat. They heaved the mast into the pipe, and turned the dinghy's bow toward the ship.

"Hold onto the stern, Ben. As soon as you feel the boat shoot forward—you kick!"

"Kick? Why?"

"'Cause this puppy is going to tear this thing apart like a chew toy," Dean warned. He lit a piece of tarred rope and dropped it into the pipe. "Hold tight!"

The pipe sizzled and cracked, then the gunpowder shot the mast out of the pipe. The mast was so long that it hit the ship while still in contact with the pipe. The dinghy shot forward, freeing itself from the wake of the ship. The explosion ripped the dinghy's stern off and Dean and Ben's legs dipped into the cold water. They both gasped.

"Kick!" Dean yelled.

They kicked the front half of the dinghy away from the ship. The sails were aflame, and the top of the ship was charring to black. The floating inferno narrowly missed a leisure tour boat. As the water calmed, closer to shore, the ship took a slow curve, as if it was trying to steer itself back to its old position. The flaming mass of wood and rope plowed into the old dock, throwing up debris onto the parking lot and a crowd of gaping tourists.

A fireball burst from the ship, instantly burning up the remaining ghosts on board. The inferno washed over the old wooden pier, setting alight a car which had the misfortune of being parked in the closest handicap space.

Fire trucks zoomed in from all corners of the parking lot. A crowd gathered behind them.

Dean and Ben continued to kick toward the shore. As the water became shallower, Dean pushed himself off the dinghy and pulled it onto the sandy beach. He paused for a moment, breathing deeply.

"Dean! Ben!" He heard Lisa scream from the rocks above the beach.

Dean helped Ben out of the water and the two of them climbed over the rocks; sandy, wet, and exhausted.

Lisa grasped Ben, hugging him despite the soaking, dirty state of him.

"What happened? You were supposed to go on a quiet boat tour—while docked!" Lisa said, looking incredulously at the damage.

"There were ghosts, Mom. Pirate ghosts," Ben said. "But we got them—we burned them and shot them. It was very cool."

Lisa looked at Dean.

"Did he touch a gun?"

"Lis, that's not the point. This was a 'three-hour tour' from hell," Dean responded. "Besides, he wasn't half bad with a flintlock." He ruffled Ben's hair.

"He touched a gun!" Lisa's eyes were wide and angry. "I said no guns. Ever."

"You know, Lisa, we could stand around here and talk this over, but I think maybe the police are going to want to… Maybe we should leave."

"Why does destruction follow you wherever you go?" she asked despairingly.

"This really wasn't my fault. Right, Ben?" Dean slung his arm around Ben's shoulder. "The pirates came after us first."

"Why would pirates come after you?" Lisa said. "What did you do to them?"

"They're ghosts, Lisa, it doesn't really work that way," Dean said, looking away toward the rapidly growing crowd of onlookers.

"Hey Dean, where's Teddy? Is he still on the ship?" Ben looked anxiously at the burned remains of the pirate vessel.

Dean ran a hand through his hair. No way could he tell the kid what had really happened. He'd been through enough that day already.

"He's all right. I think he's over there." Dean pointed vaguely across the parking lot.

Then he spotted her. Across the parking lot, a tall, tight-faced woman in a dark coat, staring straight at them.

"Well, how does it work?" Lisa said, trying to get Dean's attention. "Dean?"

The woman continued to stare at Dean over the commotion in the parking lot. He'd never seen her before, but there was something about her that was both familiar and threatening.

"Dean? Dean, I'm talking to you. Is there something I should know about? Are more ghosts going to come after us?"

Dean took hold of Lisa's shoulders and stared into her eyes.

"No. I promise. They won't," he said, firmly. "But you have to trust me and do what I tell you: Go back to the hotel and don't open the door to *anybody*. Okay?"

"Dean, you're scaring me. What is going on?" Lisa looked back at him, eyes wide.

"Can I be that guy and say I'll explain later?" Dean asked.

"You know in the movies that never works out," Lisa replied.

"I know. But you have to trust me on this. Everything is going to be fine. I came here for something, but I just think I stepped into something bigger."

"So unlike you." Lisa managed to crack a slight smile. "Go. We'll be fine."

Lisa hugged Ben close, as if reassuring herself that he was still with her and all in one piece. Dean nodded then swung around and beelined toward the crowd, but the woman was nowhere to be seen. He fumbled for his car keys in the pocket of his wet jeans. Miraculously, they were still there. He jumped into the car and sped off.

* * *

Fifteen minutes later Dean pulled up in front of the charred remains of Connie's Curios and Conversations. A policeman and a county coroner were pushing a white body bag into the back of a van.

Dean jumped out of the car and ran up to them.

"Hey dude, who is that?" he asked.

"Poor girl who worked there. Burned up like a crisp. Don't know why she didn't even try to get out," the county coroner replied, slamming the door shut.

Dean stared after the van as it chugged away. He got back in his car, flipped a bitch, and headed north to Connie Hennrick's place.

TWENTY-TWO

Dean was reeling from the death of Sukie. Apart from the incident with the baseball bat, the kid had been harmless enough. *I guess it proves you can't "dabble" in witchcraft. Dangerous shit like that always catches up with you eventually.* But Dean wished he'd been able to save Sukie. She hadn't deserved to die.

Sukie's death, combined with his *Titanic* moment and Teddy's death, sent Dean into an emotional spiral. He had certainly stumbled onto a case, something big which needed his attention. He still wanted to find a *Necronomicon* to raise Sam, but it was clear that the brutal killings, the hex bags, and the pirate ghosts, that something was going on and someone was trying to stop him from finding out what it was.

Dean headed north looking for the Hennrick farm, following signs to Ipswich Road. The road curved through woods. After a mile or two the trees bent over the blacktop, cutting out the gray sky. Dean slowed at a large iron gate with a decorative "H" mounted onto the face. He pulled up twenty meters further on and stopped. Dean took out Nathaniel's journal and started to read.

Nathaniel and his boys set out the next day to visit the Widow Faulkner. Nathaniel wanted to pay his respects as she'd lost a daughter. But his curiosity had also been piqued when Hannah mentioned that Abigail Faulkner was in a quilting circle with Reverend Parris's daughter, the girl who had been bewitched for two weeks. It seemed strange that almost to the day that the bewitching started, Abigail's body had been found. Did the two events have anything to do with one another?

Rose Mary wrapped up a loaf of freshly baked bread, and handed it to Nathaniel to put in his pack. It was widely known that since John Faulkner had died five years ago, his widow had struggled to feed her children and keep her small farm. Taking a little something for the family to eat was an appropriate gesture, especially after the loss of a child. At least that was Nathaniel's reasoning as he, Caleb, and Thomas set out.

What they reached the widow's homestead, they were surprised to find, rather than a rundown and poverty-stricken house, a prosperous little residence. The previously empty barn held two horses and two cows, quite a luxury in Salem.

Nathaniel rapped on the door. Widow Faulkner invited them into, not a cold unforgiving room, but a warm and cozy interior. There was food on the table and what smelled to Nathaniel like venison stew bubbling away on the hearth. That season had been particularly bad for hunting and someone would have had to be a very fortunate to bring home a catch of fresh deer.

Nathaniel formally introduced the boys to the widow. He passed on Rose Mary's condolences and added that he and the boys would be happy to do anything around the house if the family needed help. She declined politely, explaining that she was comfortable and had plenty of food for her and her two remaining children.

"And how are the twins? I seem to recall they have some difficulty walking," Nathaniel enquired.

"They are quite fine, thank you. Here they come now," the widow said, straightening in her chair.

Two identical boys about Caleb's age sprinted through the door and into the common room where the Campbells sat. Both looked healthy and ruddy, with not a sign of a limp between them. Whatever affliction had caused their lameness was completely gone.

Nathaniel wondered how a widow could go so quickly from abject poverty to living comfortably.

"Widow Faulkner, I'm so very sorry about the loss of your daughter," Nathaniel said earnestly, watching the woman's reaction.

"The Lord giveth and the Lord taketh away. Isn't that what Reverend Parris says?" she replied evenly.

"Indeed. You are correct. It seems that you want for nothing, however," Nathaniel said, gesturing at the evidence of comfort around them.

"Except my daughter. I would do anything to have my daughter back," the widow said.

"Of course. Tell me, did she have very many friends? Perhaps she was acquainted with Reverend Parris's daughter?" Nathaniel asked.

"No, not at all. On Sundays and Thursday evening prayers, perhaps they spoke. But they were by no means friends."

This was not the response Nathaniel had expected. He nodded solemnly, repeated his regrets, and indicated to Thomas and Caleb that it was time to leave.

Once outside, Nathaniel shook his head. He was confused. He had been sure the bewitched girls would have some link to Abigail's death.

As Nathaniel mounted his horse, the widow appeared at her door. She gestured to Nathaniel.

"Mr. Campbell, there is one more thing," she said.

"What's that?" asked Nathaniel.

"I loved my daughter, but I didn't agree with some of the company she kept."

"What do you mean?" Nathaniel asked.

The widow looked around nervously, even though no one was around.

"Like the Ball family," she said finally. With that she nodded politely and went back inside.

Nathaniel looked at his two boys.

"Feel like a visit to Constance Ball's house? This may be a link to those unearthed graves you saw on her property."

Caleb and Thomas nodded. Constance Ball's daughters were notorious throughout Salem Village. They never seemed to want to talk to anyone except each other, and they were also all strikingly beautiful.

The Ball residence was located not far from the Campbell family home, hence Thomas and Caleb occasionally cutting across their land, though they knew they shouldn't. The house was an impressive brick affair, its building material alone setting it apart from most of the nearby residences, which were clapboard. The one singular thing about the Balls everyone in Salem knew was that ever since anyone could remember, they had lived on that land, and in that house.

"Do you think Constance Ball has something to do with Abigail's death?" Thomas asked as he trotted alongside his father.

"I guess we will find out," Nathaniel said. "Do you know what to do once we are invited inside?"

The boys nodded. This was exactly the kind of situation Nathaniel had trained them for. They had sat up for long nights in freezing weather staking out potential vampire nests. They had seen their share of demon possessions. But Nathaniel also taught them how to be polite enough to be invited into a home, which was sometimes half the battle.

By the time the Campbells reached Constance Ball's house, a great wind had whipped up. Snow blew across the open fields, blinding them as they approached. Nathaniel tied up his horse and they ascended the steps. The door knocker was as big as Caleb's head. Thomas pried it from the door and let it fall against its brass base. Even over the wind the CLACK! could be heard echoing through the building.

A minute or two later a large man in black pants and jacket, the kind that buttoned all the way to the collar, opened the door, revealing a grand entranceway and a sweeping staircase. Nathaniel introduced himself and asked to be let in. The man led Nathaniel and the boys into a large living area to the right of the grand hallway.

Thomas and Caleb had never been in such a big house. Once inside, they found places next to the large roaring fire as they waited for the lady of the house. Nathaniel immediately recognized a couple of curious artifacts around the room, most notably a small worn-looking book perched on a podium. He peered at the first page—it was written entirely in Latin.

He heard the boys gasp as a long index finger suddenly closed the book in his face. Nathaniel looked up and found himself face to face with Constance Ball. She was a handsome woman, always well-coiffed, almost in a Renaissance style, but specifically overdressed for a colonial woman.

"May I help you?" she asked.

"Madam Ball, I'm Nathaniel Campbell and these are my sons, Caleb and Thomas." The boys bowed politely.

"I know who you are," she said. "Your property abuts mine. Is there a problem? Did one of my girls trespass?"

"No, not at all. Though perhaps you wouldn't mind if I spoke with your daughters?"

"What for?" Constance asked.

"I'd like to know if they were acquainted with Abigail Faulkner," Nathaniel said.

Constance affected a frown of deep thought.

"I'm quite sure I don't know the name," she said after a moment. She sat down in a straight-backed chair and glared coldly at Nathaniel.

"That's strange," Nathaniel said. "For her mother, Widow Faulkner, said that her daughter knew you and your girls."

"I'm not sure what you are aiming at," Constance said.

"You do know that little Abigail Faulkner is dead?" Nathaniel asked.

Constance paused before replying.

"No, I'm not sure that I did. Exactly what are you getting at, Mr. Campbell?"

During the exchange, Thomas and Caleb had crept behind Constance's chair. Caleb pulled a small bag from his pocket and tried to place it under her seat. Constance whirled around instantly, startling the boy.

"What are you doing down there, you little monkey?" she demanded.

Nathaniel stepped in.

"I'm sorry, he's a strange boy. Caleb, come here." Caleb did as he was told and took his place beside his father.

"Mr. Campbell, I've had just enough of your tomfoolery. You can leave now," Constance declared, rising from her chair.

"I don't think you understand," Nathaniel replied.

"Rathburn," she called. "Show these gentlemen out." The large man materialized in the doorway as though he had been listening behind it all along. He marched across the room and grasped Nathanial by the arm.

Nathaniel pulled his arm away from Rathburn's vice-like grip.

"*Per is vox malum ero venalicium. Per is oil malum unus ero ostendo.*" Nathaniel started to chant the Latin marking spell.

Constance smiled serenely.

"Mr. Campbell, if you wanted to know if I was a witch, why didn't you just ask?" With a casual flick of her wrist, Caleb went flying against the bookcases.

"Daadd!" Caleb's small body twisted up against the wall.

Nathaniel unsheathed the knife hidden beneath his coat.

"You think you can hurt me with that pig sticker? Mr. Campbell, you don't know me or what I'm capable of." She whirled her arm around and the room became filled with a gale as powerful as the one outside.

Constance turned to face Nathaniel. Another small hand gesture sent him flying across the room.

Thomas tried to tackle Constance, but she flipped him end over end into the corner.

"I'll not be attacked in my own home, you silly fool." Constance waved her hand again. The fire leaped out of the fireplace and began to swirl in a tornado up toward the ceiling. "*Eugae satan imus focales olle obligamus tu adque subsidium me clades mi trespassers,*" Constance shouted.

The fire burned closer and closer to Thomas, who lay in a heap on the floor, unconscious.

"Thomas! Wake up!" Caleb shouted.

"Oh, isn't that curious, your eldest seems to have lost his senses. Just like his father," Constance sneered. She stood regal as the fiery tornado swirled around her. "Tell me, Nathaniel, why would you bring your children here? Why put them in danger? Oh, I know why—you're a hunter.

All hunters are the same. Blow-hards who think they have the right to judge everyone but themselves. Let me tell you something," she leaned her face close to Nathaniel's, her breath was icy cold on his face, "we came here, same as you, for a new life. The New World is for everyone, not just those with their nose in a Bible."

"You killed Abigail Faulkner, an innocent young girl," Nathaniel spat back at her.

Constance shrugged and turned away from him.

"So what if I did. Sometimes the weak have to be punished for insubordination."

"Salem won't stand for this," Nathaniel yelled at her back.

"Please, Salem is doing a good job of extinguishing all rational thought. Don't you think, girls?" Constance turned to address five young women standing in the doorway. The flames reflected in their very dark eyes.

Constance turned back around and stared coldly at Nathaniel.

"Let's get one thing straight, Mr Campbell: I could kill you, it would be as easy as this." She clicked her fingers. "If you cross me again, your children will be orphans. I'll make sure of that." She raised her hand up, hovering near Nathaniel face. "And next time, I will not be so merciful."

Three large deep scratches appeared across Nathaniel's cheek, sending blood dribbling down his chin onto his coat.

"I can control many things," she hissed. "Nowhere in Salem is safe. Girls, show the Campbells the way out."

The five girls gathered in a circle, raised up their hands, and with a flick of their wrists Nathaniel, Thomas, and

Caleb blew through the glass-paned glass windows and landed on the snow outside. The gale wrapped around them. Thomas was still unconscious as Nathaniel lifted him onto the horse and they limped away.

Rose Mary opened the door as Nathaniel, Thomas, and Caleb approached the house.

"What on earth?" she cried. "Hannah, go get the herbs and oils."

Nathaniel gently laid Thomas on the table. Caleb tugged off his brother's boots, and Hannah pressed a warm compress of medicinal plants against Thomas's temple.

"What happened?" Rose Mary asked, leaning over her son.

"Constance Ball attacked us," Caleb replied.

"She's a full-fledged witch, she *and* her daughters," Nathaniel explained. "As Salem sends innocent old women to the gallows, the real witches are left alone."

"But why did they attack you?" Rose Mary asked.

"Because I asked her about Abigail Faulkner. Constance killed her. I just don't know why." Nathaniel sat down in a chair near the fire and kicked off his boots.

Thomas stirred and opened his eyes then sat up with a moan holding his head.

"I'm sure that woman is up to no good," Nathaniel continued. "She has a Latin spell book. I think it's a *Necronomicon.*"

"What would she be doing with that?" Hannah asked.

"I've only seen one once. It's filled with all sorts of ways for binding demons." Nathaniel indicated his cheek. "The book has many powerful spells. All of them dangerous and all of them evil."

"Like what?" Caleb said.

"Unless I can read it, I have no way of knowing," Nathaniel said. "But take great care in everything you do now, in town or wherever someone can see you. Constance is up to something and the atmosphere in town is like a dam about to break."

"What about the graves?" Caleb asked. "What do those have to do with it?"

Nathaniel shook his head with frustration. He wasn't sure what Constance's plan was, but he knew that it must tie in with Abigail Faulkner's death, and the unearthed graves.

TWENTY-THREE

Dean closed Nathaniel's journal. He was slowly putting it together. Connie and Constance, the old house off Ipswich Road. Could they be one and the same? Could she still be alive, hundreds of years later?

From the back of the car, he pulled out one of the machetes hidden in the spare tire wheel well and cut down some of the low hanging branches from nearby trees. He piled those on top of the car for cover and then walked back toward the heavily padlocked gate.

In the distance behind the gate a large brick house loomed tall, surrounded by empty expanses of field on both sides. A high stone wall extended all around the property.

"Guess I'm not going to be invited in," Dean said to himself as he hoisted himself onto the flat part of the wall.

Dean felt something give under his hand. He looked down. Stuck into a crevice in the rock and mortar was a weathered-looking hex bag wrapped in red string—a protection gris-gris bag. He was in the right place.

Dean jumped down the other side of the wall, feeling the soft earth sink under his shoes. It was going to be difficult to sneak up on the house with all that open space around it. Dean surveyed the area and decided to enter from the back. He snuck around the perimeter of the fields, keeping hidden in the tree line.

Once he was behind the house, he made his way up the slope and hid behind a barn. From what he could see, five young girls were working on the farm. One was pulling weeds in a what looked like a kitchen garden, another was leading a cow across a pasture. It looked idyllic, if not really old-fashioned.

Dean heard the titter of voices coming from within the barn and peeked in through the wavy glass panes to see two women grooming a horse.

This is either going to turn into the hottest Puritan porn I've ever seen, or these bitches are witches, he thought.

He turned his head and—

WHACKKK!

He was twisted round and thrown up against the solid wooden surface of the barn. A heavy weight pressed up against his chest, but the brawny field hand in front of him wasn't even touching him.

"Hey, sorry, man. Lost my way? Do you give pony rides here?" Dean said.

The man didn't answer. Instead, he flicked his wrist and Dean dropped to the ground. Silently, he gestured that Dean should walk toward the house.

Once inside, Dean was pushed into a chair next to a large stone fireplace. Heavy curtains were drawn across floor-to-ceiling windows; so it was impossible to see outside.

Moments later a middle-aged woman walked into the room. Dean immediately recognized the woman who had been staring at him in the parking lot. Closer up, Dean could see she had a high-browed forehead and a face set with a wide mouth.

"Do you often trespass on private property?" she asked in a crackling, accented voice with a slight European lilt to it.

"Angela Lansbury. Wow, I'm a big fan," Dean said sarcastically, springing from his seat.

The big guy in the corner flicked his wrist again and Dean was thrown back into his chair.

"Don't worry big guy, I'm not going anywhere. You and I can go out back and milk a cow together. Would you like that?" Dean grinned.

"What do you want?" the woman asked. She lowered herself into a seat opposite Dean and stared coldly into his eyes.

"Well, Constance—I'm assuming you're Constance Hennrick, Connie of Connie's Curios. Can I call you Connie? Under normal circumstances, Connie, I would cut your throat with a silver knife, chant a little bit then make sure you were buried well and good in four different places. Considering you tried to kill my girlfriend and drown me and her kid, I think that would be letting you off easy," Dean said. "Though I might have spared a couple of those hotties you have outside if they behaved themselves. It's hard to find good help these days."

"Effective salutation," Connie said. "Sadly, I've lost patience."

She got up and gestured to the heavy in the corner.

"Wait," Dean said. "About this afternoon, you don't deny it, so I assume it was you. You have to be pretty powerful to resurrect an entire ship's worth of pirates."

Constance simply shrugged.

"Then you are exactly the person I've been searching for," Dean said.

"And why is that?" she said.

"Because I need your help."

"I really don't have time for little piglets like you." She gestured again, and the heavy strode over and pulled Dean from his chair.

"Wait, wait. Listen," Dean said, "I need a *Necronomicon*. I need to raise someone who is caught in a very powerful cage."

"You wouldn't know what to do with a *Necronomicon* if you had one," she said.

"No, you're right. That's why I need you," Dean said.

"It's an impossibility. A book like that has powers beyond your paltry imagination. I am quite sure you don't have the stomach for it."

"So you have one?" Dean persisted.

"If I did, I wouldn't let you anywhere near it. Besides, what on earth makes you think I would help you?" she asked.

"Not a thing. Only that I am pleading with someone that under normal circumstances I would gank in an instant," Dean replied.

"Sorry, I don't work for peasants, much less the likes of *you* and *your kind*," Connie said.

With that she left the room and the brawny guy dragged Dean out of the chair by his collar, pulled him through the house, out of the front door and down the driveway.

"Hey, Paul Bunyan, lay off the jacket!" Dean said, gasping for breath.

The guy opened the gate and threw Dean out into the road. He landed on a double yellow line, some twenty feet away from the driveway entrance. It was quite a throw.

Dean got up and dusted himself off. Things were not going well.

He limped back to his car, bruised and battered and still a bit damp from his pirate adventure.

On the passenger seat the case files he had taken from Chief Wiggum had been jostled by the drive, fanning out all the pictures. Dean picked up a particularly brutal photo of a girl in a BU sweatshirt. He was torn. There was a case here.

All the gris-gris bags in the victims' cars were certainly the work of witches, probably that of Connie and her girls.

Dean shook his head at his bad luck. He was just kidding himself. There was no other explanation—Connie had to be the Constance from Nathaniel's journal. And to make matters worse she was up to something very, very bad. Again.

It figures that the one person I need help from could have killed ten people. Dean shook it off and decided to go back to the hotel. He should make sure Lisa and Ben were okay.

Just then two large black Escalades slid out of Connie's driveway and turned south. Dean's car was still camouflaged by tree branches so he was pretty sure they didn't see him. Dean waited until they had disappeared from view, then he turned his car around and followed.

TWENTY-FOUR

Sam and his grandfather sat in the parked van on the side of the road hidden around a curve.

"We're going to lose them," Sam said.

"Just wait," Samuel responded sternly. They sat silently for a few moments. "Okay, now go. Just hang back a little bit."

"Not my first rodeo, gramps," Sam muttered as he started the vehicle.

As they made their way into the glowing suburban traffic outside Salem, they watched the two Escalades ahead of them pull into a shopping mall parking lot with Dean's CRV not far behind. It was about nine p.m. and there were very few cars left in the lot, only a few stragglers, laden with shopping bags, were making their way out of the mall. A large megalith sign, 'Books 'n' Novels,' clung to the stucco side of the mall. Inside Sam could make out the employees shutting off the lights and locking the doors. The Escalades were parked in the two spaces closest to the bookstore doors.

Dean parked on the outskirts of the lot, away from the lights. He reached for his flask. The Jack Daniels went down easy and took the edge off the crazy day. Dean wasn't quite sure why Connie and the girls would need to make a bookstore run at nine at night. Chances were it wasn't because they were after the next *Twilight* novel.

Sam and Samuel waited in the white van on the other side of the lot, far away from the store.

"What do you think they're doing?" Sam asked.

"No idea, but I don't think it's to pick up Ad Hoc," his grandfather replied.

Sam raised an eyebrow.

"Thomas Keller's new... Forget it. I'm a fan is all," Samuel said.

"You're a fan of celebrity chefs?" Sam asked.

"Do you know how hard it is to get a restaurant up and running?" Samuel asked with sincerity. "He's a genius."

The last bank of lights in the store was shut off. Dean watched as a mousy-looking girl emerged from the double glass doors holding a large key ring. She shoved the key in the lock and fiddled with it, twisting and turning it in an increasingly desperate attempt to lock up the store.

A figure slipped out of the back door of one of the Escalades and approached her. Dean perked up as he clocked the gorgeous blonde girl in boots and a short jean skirt.

"Need some help?" she asked the mouse, who was beginning to visibly panic. The parking lot was silent as a grave. When he wound down his window, Dean was just about able to hear the exchange.

"No, thanks," the other girl replied, without looking up. "It's just these stupid keys. My manager needed to leave early and—"

In an instant the blonde elbowed her in the face. A look of surprise and hurt washed over the mousey girl's features, and a line of blood dribbled out the corner of her mouth. She tried to raise her hand in a futile attempt to block another parry, but she was far too slow. The other girl punched her in the stomach. She dropped the keys and doubled over, then stumbled, losing her balance. Her assailant was behind her in an instant, effortlessly catching her by the underarms.

Several other girls all dressed in dark hoodies jumped out of the Escalades and circled around the glass doors. Dean recognized them from Connie's farm; he counted seven of them in total.

One of them retrieved the keys from the ground and pushed open the door, then the entire group walked into the store, the first girl dragging the passed-out employee. The girl with the keys expertly pried open the face of the burglar alarm and neatly disarmed it.

A few moments later, Connie herself slipped out of one of the cars and slid across the parking lot and into the bookstore.

* * *

Back in the van Samuel and Sam waited.

"We can't go in if Dean's here," Samuel said. His voice tinged with frustration.

"Well, if they're witches let's catch them in the act. Either we will or Dean will."

"They're most likely going to hurt that girl," Samuel pointed out.

"So how are they doing it, do you think?" Sam asked. "If they're creating monsters they have to be using some sort of power for the spells, right? They must be using human sacrifices. Only way to really get a lot of juice for a spell big enough to change people into monsters."

Samuel closed his mouth. There were no monsters, he just had to keep up the ruse to trick Sam into believing they were in Salem for a reason other than to make sure Dean didn't try to raise Lucifer with a *Necronomicon*. Maybe he had taken the lie too far.

It seemed to him that since he had arrived back on Earth, he found himself doing things he never would have done before Mary's death. Like being in business with a demon—the "King of Hell" no less. Samuel slowly shook his head. Where had his moral compass disappeared to?

They watched through the giant glass windows of the bookstore as the group headed toward the central area and started moving entire sections of books, apparently clearing out a space.

"Come on, Dean. Make a move," Samuel murmured under his breath.

* * *

Inside his car Dean was furiously loading his sawed-off with real bullets—those girls weren't ghosts, that was for sure. He was going to need real firepower.

From the glove compartment, he pulled out a ski mask. The good thing about Lisa was that she packed for every eventuality; even if it was the middle of summer she brought winter clothing just in case they got caught in a blizzard.

Dean pulled the ski mask over his head. Connie was inside and Dean didn't want to get ID'd by her—after all he still might have to use her.

Dean considered how to approach the store. Since the entire facade was plate-glass windows, he might have to create a distraction first. He zipped open a pocket on his duffle bag and pulled out four small blocks of C4.

"Bobby, you're a life saver," he said to himself.

Bobby has a near limitless of suppliers that could get them just about anything, even highly illegal C4.

Dean pushed a series of wires into the clay-like blocks. He got out of the car and pulled Ben's skateboard from the back seat. He then crept along the side of the building.

At the front corner he put the skateboard down, got down on his stomach and glided past the windows, low enough to remain unseen by occupants of the building. As he steered himself past the windows, Dean pushed the blocks of C4 against the glass, until every twenty feet of window had a charge attached to it. Dean then grasped his duffle and ran around the side of the building.

Halfway down the long side of the building a ladder ran up the wall to the roof. Dean clambered onto a nearby dumpster and, leaning precariously, managed to catch the bottom rung. He hoisted himself onto the ladder, scrambled up and then made his way cautiously across the roof.

Inside, Connie's girls were clearly doing some construction of their own; a large rumbling echoed from below. Dean unscrewed an air-conditioning vent and climbed in. He could hear several voices chanting in Latin from inside the store. Crawling through the ducts, he tried to get closer to the source of the chanting.

Dean approximated that he was in the middle of the store, when he saw light filtering through a large square vent. He peeked through the slats and counted seven young girls and Connie standing in a circle. In the center, the Books 'n' Novels employee knelt, whimpering.

"Please, I'll do anything. I'll empty all the registers. I know the code to the safe in back—I dated one of the day managers." Tears streamed down her cheeks, but her pleas were ignored as the girls continued to chant.

Dean focused his gaze on Connie. In her hands she held a small, ancient-looking book.

The *Necronomicon*.

He froze. Could it be the one mentioned in Nathaniel's diary?

Connie stepped forward into the circle. She held up a long silver knife and approached the blubbering captive.

"Finally, sisters, the time has come when we can raise him," she began, her voice cold and clear. "He will be

our husband and our leader. Lift up your voices to him."
Connie started to speak in Latin.

Dean slipped the small remote out of his coat pocket.

"Sorry Connie, your body count is going to stop here,"
Dean murmured. He pressed the button.

Nothing happened.

He tried again.

Nothing.

I'm too far in the duct for it to work. There's too much interference,
Dean realized. *Crap.*

Connie held the knife over the girl as the chant
continued.

Dean frantically pressed the button over and over. Still
nothing. He was left with only one option.

He turned around awkwardly in the tight space, and with
all his weight stomped onto the duct cover. The chanting
stopped abruptly. Dean continued to bash his foot against
the air-conditioning cover.

He heard Connie's powerful voice echo through the
store.

"You're not going to stop me, Campbell."

There was a crash as Dean finally broke through the vent
cover, he reached his upper body into the store, holding
onto the edge of the vent with one hand.

Connie flicked her hand and Dean watched horror-
stricken as the employee's head spun around 180 degrees.
The girl's eyes grew wide, then lifeless. Connie caught her
with one hand by the nape of her floppy neck. With the
other she sliced the blade across her throat. Blood dribbled

out onto the floor, pooling over the linoleum and the industrial-grade beige rug.

The girls began chanting again.

Reaching his arm as far as he could into the store, Dean pressed the button on the remote.

Almost immediately, percussive explosions ripped through the building. Shattered glass blew everywhere. Books flew off the shelves and shredded magazines confettied everyone inside.

Dean hung from the ceiling and having replaced the remote with his sawed-off shotgun started firing. The girls took cover behind the bookshelves, but Connie remained where she was and continued chanting. Each bullet Dean fired at her ricocheted away—she had a seriously heavy duty protection spell on her.

Right beneath Dean the linoleum floor started to fracture, then heave upwards as if it was taking deep breaths. Great chunks lifted up then toppled over. The exposed earth underneath fell away, and a pair of grimy hands broke through the soil, pushing away the rocks and stone.

Connie's chanting had ceased. She looked up at Dean. With a flick of her hand he was pulled out of the vent and thrown against the back wall.

"Out of my way, worm," she hissed.

Connie then knelt down and gently pulled a figure out of the ground. Dust and dirt fell off of the body, like a mummy coming to life, and the figure twitched and creaked from hundreds of years of confinement. The girls gathered round in deference.

Must be a long buried witch, Dean realized. *So that's what she's up to, sacrificing young girls to resurrect her long-dead buddies. Nice.*

Out on the highway, Dean heard sirens scream. The girls deftly picked up the earth-encrusted figure and moved rapidly out of the store.

Dean abruptly fell from the wall down onto the maternity section. He pulled himself out of a crushed shelf display of books on breast-feeding. He limped to the front of the store and out of a gap where one of the windows had been.

So much for creating a diversion.

The Escalades were long gone. He got in his car and peeled out of the parking lot just as a long line of emergency vehicles popped over the curbs and surrounded the store.

Sam and Samuel pulled the van away.

"Guess we know what they're doing now: resurrecting people. Didn't look like a monster to me though," Sam said, weaving in and out of traffic.

"I could be wrong," Samuel said.

"Or you could be lying," his grandson said angrily.

Suddenly he pulled the emergency brake and skidded to a stop on the side of the busy highway.

"What the hell is going on, Samuel? I trusted you! I don't think we're here because those witches are creating monsters. So either you bring me up to speed or I am more than happy to leave you here. You'd make a great Red Sox fan, since they always seem to lose lately. And this certainly is a losing game. *Tell me what's going on.*" Sam stared at his grandfather.

Samuel shrugged his shoulders, recognizing that he was beaten.

"Dean is trying to get his hands on a *Necronomicon*," he admitted.

"Why?"

"I'm assuming so he can raise you from the dead. Get you out of Hell."

"Dean shouldn't put himself in so much danger," Sam said matter-of-factly.

"That's it?"

"It would be bad if Dean tried to raise Lucifer mistakenly. But this is a case," Sam said. "Those witches are up to something. You don't start resurrecting old friends for the hell of it. "

Samuel shook his head, he couldn't tell Sam about his deal with Crowley. He needed to make sure Dean didn't raise Lucifer. *Such a stupid boy,* thought Samuel. He couldn't leave Sam to watch Dean and go on this wild goose chase with witches. Whatever they were up to.

"Sam, I have things to do. I have to get back to herding Alphas. You know that," Samuel said. "And I need your help."

"Sorry Samuel. Innocent people are getting killed. This is a case. You can go back. But I'm staying."

Samuel nodded. "Okay, fine."

Sam leaned over Samuel and opened the passenger door.

"I'll see you later."

Samuel stared incredulously at his grandson.

"You want me to get out here?"

Sam shrugged.

"I want to follow Dean. He's on that old witch's tail. I don't want to lose him."

Samuel got out of the van. A light drizzle twinkled in the headlights of the few cars on the road at this hour.

Sam nodded, pulled the door closed, then continued to follow his brother.

Dean snuck into the hotel room just past midnight. Lisa was asleep on the bed, but as soon as Dean sat down to take off his shoes, she stirred.

"What's that smell?" she asked.

"Cordite," Dean said.

Lisa sat up and peered at Dean.

"Why were you firing a gun?"

"Shooting practice," Dean said, lying down on the bed beside her. "You still mad at me?"

"Yes," Lisa answered.

"Okay. Can we talk about it in the morning?" Dean asked.

Lisa nodded and turned her back on Dean. He shrugged; that was as good as he was going to get tonight.

He tried to close his eyes but exhausted as his body was, sleep wasn't on the cards. He had set out to find someone to help him to raise his brother, and he had. It just hadn't turned out like he thought it would. He had found a *Necronomicon*, and he had found a powerful witch who could use it. Everything would be perfect if it weren't for the fact that she was killing young girls, and bringing old witches back from the dead.

Once again he opened up Nathaniel's journal.

TWENTY-FIVE

A couple of weeks later all of Salem Village was in a frenzy. Tituba, Reverend Parris's servant, had admitted to practicing witchcraft. She said that four figures had come to her in her sleep and told her to "sign a book" to swear allegiance to Satan. The magistrates, now four men, insisted on knowing the names of the people who had forced Tituba to hurt the girls.

More names were called and more innocent people were brought before the magistrates and accused of witchcraft. As each accused person was brought into the meetinghouse, the afflicted girls would scream and writhe in pain.

Nathaniel, Hannah, Caleb, and Thomas watched the proceedings from the back of the meetinghouse. As each day passed the theatrics of the court worried Nathaniel more and more. The town was clearly being whipped into a frenzy over witches. But since Constance and her daughters were absent from the proceedings, the question remained as to who in the court was a real witch.

From his position at the back of the room, Nathaniel had a clear view of Prudence Lewis. Day after day she stood closest to the accused, always in the same place, with the rest of the girls lined up to her right. After watching her carefully for many hours on end, Nathaniel noted that it seemed whenever the girls went into a fit, Prudence Lewis was the one they all followed. If Prudence started to scream, they all started to scream. This happened time and time again as more and more accused witches were brought in.

Nathaniel could not believe that the people being accused were all witches. One woman in particular, Martha Cory, he knew to be a pious woman who attended church every Sunday as well as Thursday scripture services. She could not be a witch.

But what was at work? It seemed as if the afflicted girls were being harassed in some way. But by what? Scrapes and scars showed up on their faces and wrists. If they weren't doing it themselves, someone or something must be doing it to them. This behavior, coupled with the strange encounter Caleb and Thomas had had with Prudence Lewis in the cellar, made Nathaniel suspect that Prudence was somehow influencing the other girls.

"Boys, I want you to follow Prudence Lewis," Nathaniel said. "I want to know where she goes tonight, when and with whom."

Caleb and Thomas nodded.

That afternoon, as the winter sunlight waned and most

of Salem trudged home through the snow, Caleb and Thomas waited for Prudence to leave the meetinghouse. She emerged escorted by Reverend Parris and John Hathorne and together they walked to Parris's home. Once there, the men went inside but Prudence remained outside.

After a few moments she stepped out onto the road, and peered both ways as though to check for spies. The boys crouched behind a hedge on the other side of the road, and held their breath.

Apparently satisfied that she was alone, Prudence started walking up the road away from the village, before taking a sharp right to cut across a field. Caleb and Thomas followed a good distance behind her. They could barely see her figure in the waning light as she disappeared into the tree line.

"Is she going toward Constance Ball's?" Caleb whispered. His shoes crunched on the firm snow as he followed in his brother's footsteps.

"Looks like it," Thomas replied.

"Should we tell Father?" Caleb asked.

"Let's see what happens first," his brother said.

When Thomas turned back around he suddenly stopped in his tracks. Prudence was nowhere to be seen.

"Where did she go?"

"She was right there," Caleb said.

They squinted at the tree line fifty yards in front of them. Prudence had definitely disappeared. The brothers looked at each other—this wasn't what was supposed to happen. They started walking again, still keeping quiet. Thomas drew out a silver blade from his jacket. Caleb took out a wooden bat.

They hadn't any shotguns with them.

"Don't make a sound," Thomas murmured.

"I'm trying not to. You don't make a sound," Caleb hissed back.

They crept into the woods at the very spot where they had last seen Prudence. On the ground there was a circle of small footsteps, but they didn't lead in any direction, they just stopped as if someone had scooped her up off the ground. Thomas and Caleb peered into the dark canopy above them. Shadowy, sinewy trees poked upward, their frozen branches creaking in the wind.

"Does she fly?" Caleb whispered.

"Shush," Thomas said. His blade at the ready. "She has to be around here somewhere."

"Thoma—" Caleb screamed.

Thomas spun around to find Caleb five feet in the air, pinned up against a tree. Prudence Lewis stood three feet away. An unseen force held Caleb up. His eyes bulged in fear.

"Thomas, I can't breathe," Caleb croaked.

"Let my brother down," Thomas commanded.

"Aw, if it isn't the Campbell boys. Did your daddy tell you to follow me?" Prudence hissed.

"Let Caleb down and maybe I won't kill you!" Thomas threatened.

"Oh please, you can't kill me. I'm so much more powerful than you silly boys can imagine," Prudence said. "Not only can I do this," she flicked her wrist and Caleb's ears started to bleed, "but right now it seems like I can get anyone in Salem to believe anything I say!"

"You're the one afflicting the girls," Thomas declared. "None of those people are witches. You are!"

"Maybe, maybe not."

"Why are you sending innocent people to jail?" Thomas demanded.

"If I tell you that I might have to kill you. Though, I might kill you anyway," she said with a smile.

Thomas lunged at her with his knife.

Prudence took an enormous leap and landed on a low tree branch fifteen feet behind him. The distance gave Thomas ample room to run to Caleb. He jumped and hung onto Caleb's feet, but his brother didn't budge, and he was quickly turning blue.

"Let him down! Or I swear to God I will burn down this entire forest with you in it."

"I'd like to see you try!" Prudence taunted.

Thomas pulled a couple of bags of herbs from his coat. He spread them on the ground and started chanting in Latin.

"*Ego vocamus upon bonitas of life, ad concertamus tergus hic malum. Imus circa me conditi annulus of ardor. Imus circa me loco custodia.*" A small flame of fire sprang up in Thomas's hand, which he threw at the base of the tree. The fire quickly spread to form a ring around the tree and the two boys.

Prudence dropped elegantly back on the ground, standing outside the ring of fire.

"Looks like you're stuck," she observed maliciously.

"Or you are," Thomas said. He chanted a little more Latin. The fire rose and crackled, until it reached eight feet high. Then Thomas gave one last command in Latin.

The fire exploded over the woods. Prudence covered her face as the percussion threw her onto her back twenty feet away. Caleb dropped to the ground and Thomas ran to his brother's side. As quickly as it had started, the fire died down to embers around them.

"How did you do that?" Prudence demanded. "You're not a witch!"

"No, but we are not without our own tricks," Thomas replied.

Thomas pulled Caleb up from the ground and turned back to Prudence.

"I know what you are, and you're not going to get away with tricking the entire town into thinking those people are witches."

"Oh really? And what are you going to do about it, Thomas Campbell? Tell your father? Tell the magistrates? I have them wrapped around my finger like a string. I'll make sure that they know what you are." Prudence turned on her heel and in an instant was gone.

Thomas grabbed Caleb's shoulder and the brothers retreated back across the frozen field toward home.

"Well, one thing's for sure," Caleb said.

"What?" Thomas asked.

"Prudence is definitely not as pretty as she used to be." Caleb smirked.

TWENTY-SIX

Dean woke up at gone nine a.m, alone. He pulled himself out of bed and headed downstairs, hoping to grab a cup of coffee. Lisa was sitting at a table drinking hers, and when she looked up as he walked in, a little scowl crossed her face. Clearly, she still wasn't happy with Dean about yesterday. The fact that he had come home past midnight probably hadn't helped.

Dean pulled up a chair and sat down across the table from her. He fingered the lace tablecloth. He anticipated that Lisa was going to go after him, but didn't want to be the one to speak first. This obviously wasn't turning out to be the vacation Lisa had hoped for.

He took a deep breath; someone had to break the stalemate.

"So. I thought we could go to the beach today," Dean began cautiously.

Lisa raised an eyebrow.

"Haven't you had enough of the water? Any second I'm expecting the police to come through the door and arrest you for causing millions of dollars of damage."

"That wasn't specifically my fault," Dean countered. "Anyway, you don't have to worry about the police, I had Ingrid change our name in the registry."

Lisa shook her head.

"You just think of everything don't you?"

Dean had to admit that he did.

"Where's Ben?" he asked.

"Perry came to pick him up. I think they went sightseeing and then to watch a movie," Lisa said.

Dean furrowed his brow.

"To a movie or to watch a movie?"

"I'm not sure. She's a nice girl, Dean," Lisa said. "I've spent more time with her than I have with you in the past couple of days. I'm thinking about taking her home instead of you."

"But you don't know anything about her," Dean objected.

"So? She's a girl, Dean. A regular girl. Not everything is a conspiracy."

"Lisa, I'm not some wack-a-doodle who thinks we didn't go to the moon. Though I still would like to know why we haven't gone back." Dean shook his head, he was getting off topic. "The point is, I've seen things and there are monsters everywhere. Do you know what's *really* hiding in the sewers of New York? You don't want to know.

"But I would like to get to know the girl a little more before sending Ben off on his own with her."

Lisa got up from the table.

"He's *my* son and if I think it's okay for him to go see a movie with a girl, then it's okay."

Dean threw up his hands. He hated this "blended family" shit. At least with his father you always knew whose word to go by.

Dean followed Lisa out of the dining room and through the lobby area of the inn. Ingrid stood in her regular gnomish way behind the registration counter.

"Mr. and Mrs. Winchester!" she called. "Oh sorry. I meant Mr. and Mrs. Newsted. Would you like to schedule that ghost tour now? It's ten percent off for all guests."

"Ingrid, I hate to break it to you, but you don't have any ghosts," Dean said.

Ingrid gasped.

"Look," Dean said pulling out his EMF meter. "See, nothing. No ghosts. If there were ghosts in this place believe me, I would know."

A touristy-looking couple in Bermuda shorts and T-shirts printed with "I believe in ghosts" stared at Dean. They looked crushed.

Dean turned around.

"Sorry. Just couldn't keep my mouth shut any longer."

Lisa apologized to a despondent Ingrid and dragged Dean out of the inn and onto the brick sidewalk.

"Really? You had to do that didn't you?" Lisa looked at him, incredulous.

"Lisa, I really don't want to get into a fight about this. Where is Ben? I'm going to go pick him up."

"There's no talking sense into you," Lisa said, taking out her phone. "You can call him and ask."

"You don't even know where he is?"

"He's with Perry, Dean. Get over it."

Dean pointed to her phone.

"Get him on the phone, now."

"Why are you doing this, Dean? What aren't you telling me?"

Dean pursed his lips. For a moment, he thought about blurting it all out, the *Necronomicon*, the witches, the horrible murders. But he imagined her terrified face and just couldn't do it. The truth hurts and Lisa was the last person he wanted to cause any pain.

"Can you just trust me?" he said gently.

"We aren't here *just* for a vacation, are we Dean? Is Ben in some kind of trouble?" Lisa persisted.

"I don't know that he's in trouble. I'm just playing it safe. I want us three to spend time together and I would rather he not discover *Love Story, Part Two: The Salem Years*. Just call him. Please."

Lisa pressed some buttons on her phone, then put it to her ear. After a few moments, she spoke into it.

"Ben, it's Mom. You're supposed to always keep your phone on, we talked about this. Call me as soon as you get this. Dean and I are going to come pick you up." Lisa hung up and looked back at Dean. "Should I be worried?"

"No, he's just watching a movie with a strange girl in a strange town with some very strange things going on in it."

"What does that mean?" Lisa asked.

"It means that, yes, there is something happening in this town. But I swear I didn't know about it until we got here," Dean said. It was, strictly, the truth.

"I knew it. Why couldn't you tell me?"

"It's complicated."

"Now what are you doing?"

Dean had opened the car, which he had parked in front of the inn. He had pulled out his laptop and was furiously hacking into Lisa's cell phone site.

"Wait a minute, how do you know my password?" Lisa asked, looking over his shoulder.

"You have a GPS on the phone right?" Dean said. "I'm just activating it so we can see where he is."

"You still haven't answered my question: How do you know my password?"

"Lisa, please. Favorite Show: *Gilmore Girls*. Town you grew up in: Cicero. Name of first pet: Snowball."

"When did I tell you about my guinea pig?" Lisa asked.

Dean looked at her.

"Hello! First date. I learned many things. Including how bendy you are," Dean said with a smirk.

"I can't believe you're breaking into my private account and trying to charm me at the same time."

"Please, it's not the first time," Dean said. "Okay, got it." He brought up the tracking map of Ben's cell phone. The little blip said he was somewhere on a street called Harpers Circle.

"Where is that? Is it far?" Lisa asked. "They were supposed to go to the *movie theater*."

"No, you assumed seeing a movie meant going to a movie theater. You can't assume that with boys. Believe me, I know," Dean said as he put the address into his phone. "Let's go and get him, before this becomes a Thora Birch Lifetime movie."

Lisa looked at him as they climbed into the car.

"You know, some of your pop culture references are seriously obscure."

Dean nodded. He did know that. They pulled out into traffic. Dean was really hoping he was overreacting and everything was fine, but he had learned a long time ago that you can't be too careful in a town when things are going ass-over-elbows.

TWENTY-SEVEN

Following the GPS, Dean and Lisa drove out of town and onto a double-lane freeway. A short while later, they turned onto a side street. Even though it was mid-morning, the streetlights were slowly flickering in response to a bank of dark clouds pushing in from the shore.

The road swung around in a large circle. On one side a deep thicket of trees ran along the edge; on the other a series of modern apartment buildings were set at different angles around the grounds. Suddenly, the landscape opened up, revealing a long brick building topped with spires and gothic-looking windows, that stood in stark contrast to the modern buildings that surrounded it.

Dean surveyed the scene. He had omitted to tell Lisa what else he had found out during his brief foray on the Internet. This wasn't some ideal planned community that had popped up out of nowhere. The complex had been built on the grounds of the old state insane asylum.

They parked the car at the leasing office and walked in. Behind the counter a kid, who looked scarcely older than Ben, was sitting watching a baseball game on his computer.

"Are the Sox up?" Dean asked the kid, who hadn't even glanced up as they walked in.

"Bottom of the eighth. Two runners on. Ortiz is up."

"Great. Can you tell me what apartment Perry—" Dean looked at Lisa. "What's her last name?"

Lisa shook her head.

"I don't know."

"Can you just look up Perry, then?" Dean said to the kid.

The kid had finally peeled his eyes away from the screen. He was regarding Dean doubtfully. "No can do, bro. I can't give out residents' apartment numbers."

Dean took a twenty from his wallet.

"How about now?"

The kid eyed the money.

"Yeah, I mean, I'd have to get some sort of—"

Another twenty joined the first.

The kid smiled, clearly he was going to try to milk this for all it was worth.

"It really puts my job on the line, man."

Unfortunately for the kid, he had overplayed his hand. With one arm Dean pushed the kid away from the desk, with the other he spun the computer screen around.

"Hey, you can't do that. That's private property," the kid whined.

"Well, now it's public," Dean said, typing a search for Perry's name into the computer. He drummed his fingers impatiently as the computer creaked into action. Finally it produced an answer: "Kirkbride Building, apartment twelve," he read.

Dean swiped back his twenties and Lisa and he left. Dean swung the car back around and they parked in front of the large brick building.

"Well, at least this is nice," Lisa said.

"Yeah, about that..." Dean pulled a pair of sawed-offs out from under his seat.

"What the hell are those for?" Lisa squealed.

"Relax, mine has real bullets, yours has salt. You might have the advantage here," he said.

"I thought you said there was nothing to worry about?"

Dean nodded. "There isn't. Prophylactic measure. No pun intended."

Lisa rolled her eyes. They walked up to the entrance and rang the buzzer to Perry's apartment. After about thirty seconds with no response, Dean began to methodically ring each of the apartment buzzers in turn. Eventually someone carelessly buzzed them in.

Apartment twelve was on the first floor. Noise filtered from each of the doors as they passed. At apartment twelve Dean knocked on the door and gestured for Lisa to talk.

"Ben? Ben Braeden? You come out here this instant," Lisa called.

"Could you sound like more of a mom?" Dean asked.

"You try it, smart ass," she countered.

"Fine. Give me your phone." Dean took the phone from her and called Ben's number. From inside the apartment they heard his phone ring. "Okay, so we know he's in there or was there and someone hit 'ignore' when you called before."

"He knows not to do that," Lisa said.

"Maybe it wasn't him. Hold on," Dean said. He took his lock pick from his jacket pocket and fiddled with the lock. Seconds later, it clicked open. He turned to Lisa with a serious look in his eye. "Okay, so no matter what we find in here you're going to stay calm, right?"

"I don't like the sound of that. What aren't you telling me?"

"Probably no need to worry, but this building was an insane asylum up until 1992, and in my experience, not always, but usually there are some very angry, delusional ghosts in places like these."

"That's crazy, Dean. It's an apartment building now."

"Just follow my lead," Dean said, opening the door and walking into the apartment with his sawed-off at the ready. "Perry? Ben? Time to go home." They moved through the apartment, checking each room in turn but the place was clearly empty. Lisa retrieved Ben's phone from the living room sofa.

"Is that definitely his?" Dean asked.

Lisa nodded.

Dean peaked around a corner into what looked like a young girl's bedroom. A feeling of relief washed over him when he saw that the bed was neatly made.

When he opened the doors of the built-in closet the uneasy feeling returned. Set into the plaster wall at the back was an old oak door.

"Wasn't quite the walk-in closet I was expecting," Dean said.

Lisa looked over his shoulder.

"That's strange."

'Okay, so here's the deal: I go first. You don't shoot unless I tell you to. Clear?"

"Who are we shooting at? Is Ben in there?" Lisa sounded panicky.

Dean pulled open the door. A musty blast of cool air hit them as they descended a steep spiral staircase.

"Somehow I don't think this is on the rental brochure," Dean said.

At the bottom of the staircase was a vaulted hallway which disappeared into gloom in both directions.

"These must have been used by the doctors and nurses to go between the buildings in the winter," Dean explained.

"They couldn't have made it a little more cozy?" Lisa said, shivering in her T-shirt.

Dean walked first into the pitch black of the tunnel. A cold chill ran through him. He took out the EMF again—the needle pinged to the max.

"That's not good," he said.

"What? What isn't good?' Lisa rushed forward to Dean, but something stopped her. "Ah, Dean?"

Dean glanced in her direction, then quickly pulled her behind him. He lifted the salt-filled shotgun out of her hands and pointed it into the darkness behind them.

BLAMMM! The gunshot echoed through the tunnels.

Out of the gloom a figure appeared. It was the ghost of

an old woman in a stained robe. She continued to advance on them.

"Time for your treatment," she wailed.

Dean shot at her again. But the specter quickly flicked to standing six inches away from Dean's face. He backed against the wall with Lisa still behind him.

"No exceptions! Every day!" The ghost howled and held her head.

"Move," Dean hissed urgently.

But it was too late. The ghost shot her hand out, hitting Dean square in the chest. Both guns fell from his hands and he clutched at the collar of his T-shirt, dropping to his knees.

"Can't... can't breathe," he choked. His heart was quickly becoming solid, freezing over.

"Shoot her!" Dean gasped.

Lisa reached for the salt-filled sawed-off and fumbled as she tried to aim it at the ghost.

"Now, please," Dean croaked as his lips quickly turned blue.

Lisa pulled off a shot. The bullet hit the ghost, dissipating her in an instant.

"I got her!" she said proudly.

"Only for a second," Dean said getting off his knees and rubbing his chest. He took a canister of salt from his jacket and poured a line across the tunnel. "Let's go." Dean grabbed Lisa's hand and pulled her down the tunnel.

"Ben! Ben! Where are you?" Lisa called.

Two more disgruntled ghosts of mental patients swarmed

at them. Dean quickly let off a couple of shots, then poured another salt barrier.

"Mom!" Ben's small voice echoed faintly through the tunnel.

"Ben?" Lisa called, running forward into the darkness.

Dean yanked free an iron rod that was serving as a railing on the wall. He used it to obliterate each ghost they encountered as they moved quickly forward. Further down the tunnel the low ceilings opened up into a kind of catacomb. Light seeped out from underneath an iron door. Ben called from the other side.

"Hold on, Ben. We're here," Dean responded.

"I'm so glad you've come to join us," a voice said.

Lisa and Dean turned. A decidedly older-looking Perry stood behind them. Far from fifteen, she now looked like she was in her early twenties.

"What concerned parents you are," she mused. "I find it touching. Really, I do. You don't see that much these days, what with all the divorce. But you two seem to really make it work." Perry sauntered up to Dean. She was inches away from his face. "Oh, but wait, Ben isn't your child, is he Dean? But yet, here you are. Still attached. That's okay though. I don't mind. I was hoping I could be your baby mama, as they say these days." Perry laughed.

"In this light you look a little older, Perry. So what are you pushing," Dean spat at her, "one hundred? Two hundred?"

She eyed him. "If we're going to have a child together, I might as well be honest. Let's say somewhere around three hundred-eighteen. But age doesn't matter when you have a lust like ours. Right, Dean?" Perry pawed at Dean's chest.

"Lay off, you old slut," Lisa growled.

"Oh look, mama grizzly made an appearance. Let me tell you something," Perry turned toward Lisa, "a boy like Ben... Well, you really should be more careful. You wouldn't want him ending up on Dateline."

Lisa pulled back and punched Perry in the mouth. A line of blood trickled from her nose. Perry eyed her with shock.

"You have more spunk than I thought."

"And you have a little mark," Lisa said indicating Perry's nose.

"Bitch!" Perry flung her arm aside and Lisa flew across the hallway. She collapsed to the ground, out cold.

Dean faced down Perry.

"So what's the endgame here, Perry? You part of the killings?"

"You think I have to answer to you? You have no idea how long we've waited for this exact moment in time. It's all happening, and let me tell you, none of us are going to let you stand in our way." Perry advanced on Dean.

Dean swung the iron rod. Perry stopped it easily with one hand. Dean swung his gun around and aimed it at her, but she knocked the gun away with merely a finger. Dean was empty handed.

Perry shot out her arm and caught Dean by the collar, and then spun around and threw him against the wall. Dean crumpled to the floor, trying to catch his breath.

"You should know that being this old has a lot of advantages. If you're really nice, I'll let you in on the little magic secret. Forget all those animals that you hunt—vampires and all. Disgusting. Witchcraft is the real power. Who knew that a little spell and fifty human sacrifices could bring you immortality? But here I am. Living proof."

"I wouldn't call what you are 'living'," Dean said.

"Of course you would. And it's something that's bothered you from the get-go. Dean, you know you have a code of ethics. Are you really going to kill me? After all, I'm human. You don't want to kill a human. I'm not a monster, after all."

"We'll see about that," Dean said, as he leapt for the iron rod on the floor and swung it at her.

"Tsk. This is grounds for some serious relationship counseling." Perry grabbed Dean by the throat and pushed him into a corner. "I think we should start this romance on the right foot, don't you, honey?" Perry swiped the iron rod from Dean and bashed it down on his left foot.

Dean howled in pain.

"There we go. Now I know you can't run. Just stay here for a little while. I want to get to know my new stepson better."

Perry flicked her hand and Dean's wrists magically bound together. She then disappeared into the room beyond the oak door. For an instant Dean caught a glimpse of Ben tied to an old electrical shock chair, then the door slammed shut. Dean struggled against his invisible bonds.

TWENTY-EIGHT

Lisa stirred. She slowly opened her eyes and saw Dean on the opposite side of the hallway near the door. Her head ached

"Dean? Dean, where's Ben?" she said.

Dean shushed her. She watched him squirm on the floor. He was trying to empty out his pockets with his hands bound behind his back by an invisible force. A couple of packets of herbs fell out of his jacket. He kicked off a boot and with his big toe drew a series of sigils on the dirt-covered floor. He chanted a couple of words in Latin, then awkwardly flung his lit Zippo into the center of the circle. The herbs caught fire. Dean pulled his hands apart.

"Nothing like a little white magic to counteract the black," he murmured.

He got up and gently pulled Lisa to her feet.

"Are you okay?" he asked.

She nodded and rubbed her head where she had hit the wall.

"I think so."

Dean handed her the gun with the bullets.

"You're going to need this," he said.

"I'm not sure if I can shoot her," Lisa said nervously.

"You're going to feel differently in a second," Dean replied ominously.

He swiftly loaded the other gun with real shotgun shells, then kicked open the oak door.

Inside, Ben was strapped to an electroshock chair in a dark, tiled room that must have been used for electroshock therapy. He looked scared but otherwise unharmed.

Perry sat nearby on a Victorian-era stretcher.

"Mummy and Daddy come to take their little boy home? I don't think so," she said.

She jumped off the stretcher and with a flick of her wrist the gurney flew across the room. Dean pulled Lisa to the ground, the speeding bed narrowly missing their heads. It struck the door blocking their exit.

Dean and Lisa peeled themselves off the floor.

Dean cocked his gun at Perry.

"Let him go and maybe I'll let you live to see your three-hundred and nineteenth birthday," he growled.

"Oh Dean, you and I are going to have such fun together. Imagine wiling away the years, just you and me," Perry said. "But not yet. Still have a lot of business to do here."

Perry walked toward Ben and took out a sharp blade.

"This is what you don't understand Dean: All my powerful friends passed away a long, long time ago, so now we are just trying to get the old gang back together. We have a big gig coming up. But to do that, we need nice innocent young things like Ben here. You'd be sacrificing him to a good cause."

Dean pointed his gun at Perry.

"Get away from him, bitch."

"Dean, that's no way to speak to your betrothed," Perry said. She put the knife to Ben's throat and ran it up and down the muscles of his neck. "You're not in control of this situation. I am. And it would behoove you to learn some old-fashioned manners!"

Perry sliced the knife across Ben's cheek for emphasis.

Lisa screamed and pulled the trigger on the gun she was holding. The bullet zinged toward Perry. She stepped out of the way, and the bullet grazed her shoulder. The wound cauterized immediately, like she wasn't made of human flesh at all. Perry looked down at where the bullet had touched her. There was a rip in her shirt.

"This is my favorite shirt. Now look what you did to it!" She clenched her hand and Ben started choking. "This will be cleaner anyway."

Ben's eyes rolled back into his head as his face turned blue. His hands clenched and unclenched, straining at the wrist straps.

Dean stepped forward and leveled his gun at Perry.

"You're way too old for him." He pulled the trigger.

The bullet blasted through her right wrist, detaching it so that the five-finger stump of her hand hung loosely from a couple of tendons attached to her arm.

Seizing the moment, Dean sped across the room and

knocked the witch to the floor. Recovering quickly, Perry scissor-kicked Dean. He ducked and landed on top of Perry, grabbed her round the neck with both hands and squeezed. She struggled against him but Dean's whole body weight was pinning her down. He held on until she looked as though she had passed out. He then released her throat and pulled her up so he could hold her arms tight behind her back.

"Let's tie her up," he said.

Lisa walked over to Perry and kicked her with a well-placed sandal heel under the ribs. She used the rope that Perry had used to secure Ben to tie Perry firmly to the base of the electric chair, while Dean kept hold of her, just in case.

Dean then picked Ben up off the chair and heaved him onto his shoulder.

Ben's eyes slowly fluttered open.

"What happened? Where am I?"

"All I can say is no more dates for you, buddy," Dean said gently.

Perry quickly came round and struggled against her bonds.

"You can't take him!" she cried and shut her eyes, mustering her powers once again.

Lisa, and Dean with Ben over his shoulder, didn't wait to see what would happen next. They exited the room, Dean indicating to Lisa that she should grab the discarded iron bar, then ran back down the hallway. As they crossed over the salt lines more asylum ghosts swarmed around them.

Dean remembered he had taken the salt shells out of the sawed-off.

"Ben, grab those shells in my pocket and load them into this gun," Dean said, holding the sawed-off over his shoulder.

Ben grabbed it, and refilled it while still being carried over Dean's shoulder. Lisa swung at the ghosts with the iron bar as best she could, clearing a path for Dean and Ben. Ben handed the gun back to Dean and then took the other and filled it in turn with salt shells. Dean then set him down and started shooting, protecting their sides and rear as they leapt forward down the dark tunnel.

"Almost there," Lisa called from ahead. They reached the spiral staircase and raced upward. Once in the bedroom, Dean pulled the heavy dresser in front of the doorway.

"That's not going to hold her for long," Dean said as they left the apartment and ran down the hallway.

Outside, they piled into the car. Dean started the engine and they squealed out around the long oval loop surrounding the planned community. The car jumped off the curb and peeled into traffic.

Two miles down the highway Dean spotted a used-car dealership. He pulled the CRV around back.

"What are we doing?" Lisa asked.

"We need a new car—Perry knows this one," Dean said, hopping out of the vehicle and approaching a grubby salesman.

Minutes later Dean came back. "Okay, everyone out."

"Dean, I love this car. I'm still making payments on it," Lisa protested.

"You aren't now. Now you're making payments on this."
He gestured to an old Ford 100 truck which looked as
if it had been through a war. "Actually, I'm kidding. No
payments." Dean handed Lisa a stack of one hundred dollar
bills. "We can buy a newer model when we get back."

"Yeah, exactly when is that going to be, Dean? I think
I've had enough of this vacation," Lisa said as they climbed
into the truck with Ben between them.

"Soon, Lisa. Soon," Dean replied.

He pulled the truck back into traffic and headed north.
Dean knew he couldn't go home now. There was too much
at stake. This had come to be about much more than getting
Sam back—these witches were up to something. Something
big and horrible.

"Just a little bit longer," Dean said.

He pulled the truck into a rundown motel and jumped
out.

"Why are we stopping here?" Lisa asked.

"New digs. I'll be back in a second."

Dean left them in the car and headed into the New
England colonial-themed lobby, complete with a Paul
Revere statue.

This is more like it, he thought.

TWENTY-NINE

Sam sat on the bar stool staring into space, but when the hot blonde, twenty-something in the tight jeans and the Old Clappy's Clam Shacky T-shirt walked in—he noticed. Her right hand was bandaged up to the elbow but she still held herself with much more poise than was usual for someone her age. She looked around the bar and sat down a couple of stools away from Sam.

"Whiskey, water back please," she called to the bartender.

The bartender, a grizzled old Red Sox fan, peered at her through the gloom.

"Gonna have to see some ID, young lady," he said, lumbering toward her.

The girl dug her hand into her pocket but came out empty. She leaned over the bar, smiled and gently touched the man's hand.

"I don't have it. But I'm good, right?"

The man blinked a couple of times, as if he had forgotten

the question he had asked two seconds earlier.

"Sure, sweetheart. No problem," he said.

He returned with her drink a few moments later.

"It's on him." The bartender nodded toward Sam at the end of the bar.

Sam raised his drink in the girl's direction.

"You're persuasive. I like that in a woman," Sam said.

The girl eyed him. Then she slipped off her stool and took the seat next to him.

"I'm glad. Not many men do. Usually they're scared of me."

"I don't see why," Sam said, "you seem perfectly sweet to me."

"I do? Well, thanks. I'm Prudence, by the way." The girl leaned over and stuck out her hand.

"Sam. Nice to meet you. Prudence? Interesting name."

"Old family name," she said. "I used to hate it, but over the years I've gotten used to it. Cheers," she said, raising her glass to clink with Sam's.

Sam looked at the girl. She was definitely do-able.

"Why don't you come back to my room? I have a six-pack and another one in the fridge. We could get to know one another better." Sam ran his hand down his stomach, indicating one of the six-packs.

"Does that work on all the girls?" Prudence asked.

"Pretty much, yeah," Sam said.

"Guess it's working now too," she said, throwing back her whiskey. "Let's go."

They headed toward the door. Sam walked behind the girl

to admire the view. She was cute, very cute.

Back at the motel, Sam popped open two beer bottles. He held one out to Prudence, then hesitated.

"You're over twenty-one right? I wouldn't want to be accused of corrupting a minor."

"Way over. But thanks for your concern," Prudence said, taking the bottle. She strolled around the colonial-themed hotel room. "Nice place. I remember when this was just a field, not a parking lot and a chintzy motel."

"Really?" Sam stepped behind her and pushed his hand down her shirt. Prudence turned around and looked into Sam's eyes.

"There's something you should know about me," she said.

"What's that?"

"I'm more experienced than I look." Prudence smiled and started undressing.

Sam did the same and dropped onto the bed. Prudence approached him, took off the rest of her clothes and started to ravenously kiss him. Sam pulled her small body onto his.

"What happened to your hand?" Sam asked.

"Misunderstanding. I got greedy. Took something before I should have. Patience is key. I forget that sometimes."

"I'm having trouble being patient right now," Sam said, angling himself under her.

Sam reached to shut off the light. He glanced at the little notepad neatly placed underneath the Paul Revere-like lantern lamp. On the heading it said: "YE OLDE COLONIAL INN est. 1919."

"You remember this place when it was just a field?" he asked casually.

Prudence continued to nibble on his ear.

"Yeah, why?" she said as she straddled him. "You remind me of a horse I once had."

"Giddy-up," Sam said.

A little while later, Sam got up from the bed. He pulled on his jeans.

"Where are you going? I was just getting ready for more." Prudence patted the bed beside her.

"Just looking for something I think you'll like," Sam said, digging into his duffle bag. "Here it is."

Sam swung around and pointed his sawed-off shotgun at her.

Prudence looked up at him.

"Whatever," she said, laying back down on the pillows. "Second time today, no big deal. When are you people going to get it into your heads that I can't be killed... Not like that, anyway."

Sam advanced on her.

"So what are you? A shapeshifter? Werewolf? What?"

Prudence ignored the gun and instead climbed off the bed and grabbed her T-shirt.

"I'm a witch, ya big ox. And an old one at that. But I still need to get out and let loose. It's been a very stressful summer."

A cord of rope hit her in the back as she pulled on her jeans. Sam stood closer now, still aiming the gun at her.

"Sit down and tie your feet."

"You really think something like this is going to hold me?" Prudence asked over her shoulder.

"Take a closer look," Sam said.

Prudence held the rope up and noticed a weave of different herbs braided into the cord and a smelly paste rubbed into the crevices.

"Think of it as my own lasso of truth," he said.

Prudence sat mechanically in the straight-backed chair next to the bed and tied her feet to its legs.

"What are you going to do to me, Sam? You know, I would have let you tie me up if you'd asked."

"Stop yapping. I'm going to ask you questions and you're going to answer them. Get it?"

Setting aside the sawed-off, he pulled the ropes tightly around Prudence's lithe wrists, conscious of securing them as tight as possible around her bandaged one. He then left her and went into the bathroom. Pipes creaked and there was the sound of water rushing into the bathtub. Back in the room, he grabbed another chair, swung it around, sat down and crossed his arms over the back, resting his chin on his wrists. He stared at Prudence.

"So let's play 'What the hell are the witches doing?' shall we? First question: Why are you resurrecting bodies? Whose are they?"

Prudence's lips broke into a smile, her tiny, pearl-white teeth gnashed together.

"Oh games? I love games. But you have to play by the rules. One question at a time. But I'll answer both for you. None of your freaking business. And screw off."

"Wrong," Sam said.

He stood up and spun the chair around. He grabbed the back of Prudence's chair with one hand and his chair with the other and dragged both into the bathroom. He set the empty chair sideways next to the bathtub so that the legs pointed parallel to the side of the tub. Next he hefted Prudence's chair so that her head hung halfway into the filled tub.

"So this is what we are going to do," he began "Again. I hate to repeat myself. You're going to answer my questions and if you don't, you get dunked." To demonstrate, Sam lifted the legs of Prudence's chair and her head dipped into the water. Sam then righted the chair. "See? It's a lot of fun."

"Whatever, Sam, I took swimming lessons in the thirties. Eighteen thirties. That's not going to do anything to me."

"Oh, I forgot something," Sam said. From his back pocket he pulled out a polyester pillowcase. He thrust it over her head and re-dunked her. "Now, officially, this isn't happening. Just remember that if you ever go up in front of Congress."

He pulled her back up. Prudence strained to catch her breath. But with each breath the wet material caught in her mouth, making it impossible to take in air.

Sam stood back and watched her panic.

Then he dunked her back into the water, *One Mississippi, two Mississippi...* and brought her back up.

"Let's try that again," he said. "Why are you resurrecting bodies?"

Prudence gasped and flailed her head from one side to the other.

"It's a process," she gasped. "A means to an end."

"What's the end?"

Prudence stayed silent. Sam tipped the chair back again.

"Okay, okay. We need the power, for a larger purpose. We're resurrecting the most powerful witches of all time, most from back when we first came to this country."

"Why?" Sam asked. "Keep talking."

"I can't breathe. Take the hood off. Please," Prudence whined.

Sam whipped the pillowcase off her head and she gulped air.

"Keep talking," Sam directed.

"Let me catch my breath," Prudence wheezed.

Sam sat on the toilet, impatient.

Prudence looked at him. A smile crossed her face.

"What are you smiling at?" he growled.

"Oh nothing. Just you. Men. Big, stupid babies with no ability to understand cause and effect."

"What the hell does that mean?" Sam said.

"You forgot what water does, asshole," Prudence said.

Sam glanced into the tub and saw that the dark paste that he had rubbed on the rope had come off during the dunkings. Prudence's long hair cascaded down her back, soaking both her shirt and the ties that bound her. In an instant, she tore apart the rope that bound her wrists, threw out her hand and Sam flew out of the bathroom and landed on his back in the middle of the bedroom.

"Give a lady her privacy, will you?" Prudence slammed the bathroom door behind her.

Sam got up and staggered toward the door. He pounded on it.

The door flew open. Prudence was completely free of her bonds and it seemed she wasn't in the mood for talking. With a flick of her wrist she threw Sam against the motel room door. He slumped down, trying to not to lose consciousness.

"What is it with you Campbells? Why can't you stay out of the way?"

"How do you know I'm a Campbell?" Sam demanded.

Prudence stomped over to Sam, picked him up by the collar and bent down until they were face to face.

"Because I can smell it on you," she spat. "You're always the goody goody do-gooders who come to rescue everyone. When it's really *you people* who need rescuing. The funny thing is you've been doing it for hundreds of years and you still haven't learned."

"You know, I see your yapper moving, but I really don't care."

Prudence swung her leg over Sam's lap and straddled him.

"You of all people should care, Sam Winchester. Because even though little you is up *here*, the real man-of-the-hour is below. And now that he's out of that pesky cage, with all those super seals broken, he can be freed again."

"How do you know about that?" Sam struggled to move, but her legs held him tightly in place. *Who the hell is this little bitch?* he wondered.

"Really, you're going to ask me that? Do you have any

idea how powerful I am? How powerful my family is? I know everything about you. Besides word gets around in certain circles.

"I'm sort of pleased to meet you actually. It's a bit of an honor. Lucifer's vessel. Too bad he still isn't in it. That would have been one hell of a honeymoon."

"You want to spring Lucifer? That's ridiculous. That's suicide," Sam said.

"For a human like you. For powerful witches, not so much. Still difficult. No one aces their SATs on the first try. We didn't in 1692, but we didn't have all the facts. We didn't know about the seals. But compared to his previous prison, Lucifer is in a bed and breakfast. And we're going to get him out."

"You can't put a collar around his neck. He's not going to do what you tell him. Believe me, we've tried," Sam said.

"Oh yes he will. We have a little book that we've been using for ages. It's not an Oprah pick—the human sacrifices alone would make that a no-go for her. But it's very powerful and it's going to take Lucifer and wrap him around all our little fingers. After we raise him, he'll do exactly what we tell him to do."

"It will never work," Sam said.

"Third time's the charm. You know, we tried again when you were born, thinking maybe the seals were broken when you popped out. But no such luck. But now. Thanks to you. Well, we can't lose.

"I must say I'm glad this body got saved though." She ran her finger down his chest. "Because it is a specimen. See, I have a little theory: You're up here, Lucifer is down there, but you guys were specially made for one another. I think if this works, he's gonna pop into you like a hand into a glove. Hmm. Somehow that turns me on a little." Prudence ran her tongue up Sam's cheek. "Yummy. Anyway, I would love to stay and chat but we have three more sacrifices to make before the big day. We will be seeing a lot of one another. Very soon."

"You can't do that. You can't raise him," Sam said.

"Oh Sammy, don't tell me what I can and cannot do. Besides we are raising *all* the Princes of Hell. So, don't worry, Lucifer won't be lonely. He's going to have all his brothers with him. Unlike you. Got to run. Bye now." Prudence leaned down and gave Sam one last salty kiss on the mouth. Then she left.

Sam pulled himself up and headed for the mini-fridge. He took out a bottle of beer and sat on the bed mulling over the night's events. Going after Prudence would prove futile at this point He'd have to wait and catch them in the act. And what would happen if the witches actually succeeded in raising Lucifer again? Would he come after him? Sam shook his head. He wasn't scared, he actually felt very little. Revenge was the only thing he could feel; he only cared about getting those witches. It was a need. Not even a rational thought. It was the only thing he could concentrate on.

Sam stood up, grabbed his duffle and left the motel room. He walked down the cement sidewalk that ringed the motel rooms, passing room five. Then got into the van and left.

* * *

Ten feet away inside room five, Dean thumbed frantically through Nathaniel's journal. He needed to know what Perry was talking about. If she was three-hundred-and-eighteen years old, as she said she was, then she had to have been involved in the Salem witch trials. Which meant she had to have a connection to Constance. Killing young people, resurrecting bodies--what were the witches up to?

"What did you give him?" Lisa asked.

She sat propped up on the other bed. Ben slumbered beside her. Dean had figured the kid would need a good night's rest, what with his encounter with Perry and the events of the day, and as being tied up could have adverse affects on a child, and maybe a clear head and a good breakfast would make the experience a little more manageable for him...

"Just a little something. Don't worry. It's prescription," Dean said.

"That's what I'm worried about."

Dean turned back to Nathaniel's journal. He wondered if there was a way to raise Sam and stop Connie in the process. He came across a passage and started reading.

THIRTY

Nathaniel and the boys set off for town the next morning. They knew Constance was a witch, and the boys' encounter with Prudence proved that she was too. Nathaniel warned Caleb and Thomas to be extra careful. They didn't know what the witch's next move would be. Nathaniel suspected that it had to do with the unearthed graves, but he had no proof. The one thing he was keenly aware of was that he had to stop the witch trials. Innocent people were being sent to jail and soon the hangings would begin.

Nathaniel and his sons reached the meetinghouse a little late. Every day the building would be so packed full of people that a crowd would form outside the door, spilling onto the street. The Campbells pushed their way into the room and found places at the very back in a corner. Three new people had been accused of witchcraft, and they were brought up to the stand and questioned. In most cases, the accused were so frightened that they weren't able to answer the magistrates' questions clearly, which only made things worse.

After an hour or so of futile questioning, two men appeared in the doorway dragging a woman between them. As they pushed their way through the crowd, Nathaniel recognized the woman as Bridget Bishop, who twelve years before had been accused of witchcraft, though at the time no proof had been found. As she was pushed before the magistrates, the crowd started to spit accusations.

The afflicted girls took one look at her and started to scream. Bridget covered her ears with her hands and the girls did the same. Everything Bridget did, the girls pantomimed, contorting themselves as if their movements were being painfully forced from their bodies.

The judges called for calm.

Judge William Stoughton, who had been appointed by the governor, spoke first. He asked Bridget if she knew why she had been brought in front of the court. She said she didn't know. Stoughton told her that she was accused of hurting the girls through witchcraft. He pointed to the afflicted girls, including Prudence Lewis, in the corner. Bridget replied that she didn't know the girls.

As she spoke, Prudence started to wail and writhe around. The other girls followed suit. The crowd rumbled with fear and anger, convinced that Bridget was hurting the girls before their very eyes. Bridget started to cry.

Anger rose inside Nathaniel until he could stand it no more.

"Your honors, I'd like to speak if I may," he called. Nathaniel raised his hand and pressed forward through the crowd. All heads turned to look at him as he moved. A murmur swelled from the crowd and passed like a wave out into the street. *Nathaniel Campbell has something to say.* The magistrates lifted their eyes at this new interruption.

Nathaniel reached the front of the room and addressed the judges. His voice rang loud and clear and the crowd hushed so they could hear his words.

"Magistrates, I'd like to speak on behalf of the accused," he began. "By my count you have some sixty-two people in jail for witchcraft at the present."

William Stoughton responded, "Mr. Campbell, you do realize that this court has recently been appointed as a court of Oyer and Terminer by the governor of Massachusetts?"

"I do know that, yes. But that doesn't change the fact that you have imprisoned a large number of people. And the proof that they are witches, well…" Nathaniel paused, then continued, "Your proof, sirs, is like smoke."

"What do you mean?" Stoughton asked.

"If I set a fire right here—" Nathaniel began.

"Surely you wouldn't do that," Stoughton said.

"You're right. But this is an example. If I set a fire with you on one side of the smoke and me on the other, you would see the smoke one way and I would see it another way."

"I don't understand your meaning," Stoughton said.

"We would both see smoke, but it would look different to you than it would to me because of the different places we are standing, you over there, and me here. As the smoke twists and turns it looks even more different. If we both had to describe the smoke, you would not recognize what

I described and I would not recognize what you described, even though we were looking at the same fire."

"What is your point, Mr. Campbell?" Stoughton asked. "We are running short on time."

"I would think that when lives are at stake accuracy is as important as expediency," Nathaniel said.

Stoughton's face tightened.

"I'd like you to arrive at your argument, Mr. Campbell."

"Judge Stoughton, the afflicted girls are describing what smoke looks like from where they are seated. And others are describing what smoke looks like from where they are. Both are correct, but perhaps that means that neither is more right than the other."

"Are you wasting our time, Mr. Campbell?" Stoughton asked. His patience was clearly running out.

Nathaniel took a deep breath. He had to make the judges see what was clear as day to him.

"Perhaps what this woman did isn't being perceived correctly by those young women over there," he said, keeping his voice clear and steady. "Perhaps they are feeling hurt, but it isn't coming from this woman."

"Are you accusing these young girls of lying, Mr. Campbell?" the judge's voice was steely.

"I'm not saying they are lying," Nathaniel replied, "only that perhaps they are mistaken."

Prudence stopped her hysterics for a second and stared at Nathaniel. She then started to scream and point at him.

"Stop! Stop, you evil man!" she yelled. "I've done nothing to you and you are pinching and scraping me!"

The judges looked at Prudence as she writhed in pain, red welts swelling on cheeks. Then they turned back toward Nathaniel.

"Mr. Campbell, why are you hurting this innocent girl?" Stoughton demanded.

"I'm not," Nathaniel replied firmly. "I am but standing here."

"But she says you are hurting her. Look how she writhes in pain."

Prudence continued to scream and cry.

"Seize him!" Stoughton declared and gestured that the two men standing closest to Nathaniel should restrain him. The men immediately grasped hold of Nathaniel, holding him tightly so that he had no hope of escape. "Nathaniel Campbell you are charged with witchcraft. Take him to the jail."

Nathaniel was marched forcefully through the crowd and out into the cold morning air.

Panicked, Caleb and Thomas pushed through the other onlookers to follow their father. They stumbled out of the building to see the men drag Nathaniel to a cart and throw him into the back. He recovered quickly and turned around, frantically scanning the crowd, searching for his children.

"Father!" the boys shouted, racing toward him.

"Boys! Go tell your mother. Don't worry about me. Watch Prudence, she's dangerous. Find out what she and Constance are doing!" Nathaniel called as the cart pulled away.

The two brothers looked at one another, realizing they were on their own. They stealthily returned to the packed meetinghouse. As they walked in, Thomas looked over at Prudence. She stared back at him with a small smirk on her face.

"You stay here," Thomas whispered to Caleb. "I'm going to go tell Mother."

Caleb nodded and Thomas crept out of the meetinghouse. He took his father's horse from the post and rode home quickly over the same field where Prudence had attacked them.

When he reached the Campbell homestead, his mother was outside feeding the pigs. Thomas leapt from the horse and quickly explained what had happened.

Rose Mary called for Hannah. They would visit Nathaniel in jail.

The women quickly got ready. Hannah took a couple of silver pieces from an old box. She also packed a basket full of food, since many prisoners didn't get fed at all in jail.

Back outside, the three said goodbye and agreed that they would meet back at home that evening to exchange news.

THIRTY-ONE

The snow and the freeze had melted in only a couple of weeks and the damp smell of spring was making the village all the more jumpy. Now that the weather was better, it had been decided that the hangings should begin. The crowd buzzed around the meetinghouse like angry bees waiting for the next victim. As soon as the last paper was signed the accused were taken out of the meetinghouse and loaded onto a wooden cart.

The entire village would then follow the creaking cart into Salem Town as it made its way off the main road and up the grassy hill. In each instance, Prudence Lewis followed behind the crowd, supported by her uncle and Reverend Parris. She among all the girls insisted on witnessing the deaths of those she had accused.

Bridget Bishop had been the first to be hanged. The entire village had come out to see her undoing.

After the first hanging it seemed as if the town could not

wait for more. Another hanging was scheduled for two days later, and after that it seemed as if the hangings didn't stop. Day after day, women and men were brought from the jail to the hill and hung until they were dead. Some protested their innocence even up to the last moment, as their heads were pushed through the noose. Others stayed silent.

Thomas and Caleb watched the proceedings from a grassy field, far from the eyes of the townspeople. Since Nathaniel's arrest and imprisonment, they had kept out of sight. Their mother was the only one that went into town. The children stayed home. While Nathaniel was in jail, they didn't want to provoke the witches.

Day after day they went over the question of what exactly the witches were up to. Accusations of witchcraft had become rampant in Salem, with any strange behavior leading to accusations between friends and neighbours. However, the Campbells' only real concern was Constance and Prudence. Both were powerful, dangerous witches. But proving that to the judges seemed impossible. It was clear that Prudence was puppeting the trials, but why?

There were over a hundred accused people, many of them held in the same jail as Nathaniel. With each passing day, the family feared that Nathaniel would be the next to be called up by the magistrates and hanged.

After witnessing a particularly brutal hanging early one morning, Thomas and Caleb made their way home through the woods and fields. They followed their usual route which took them far from Salem Village, out of the range of the prying eyes of any hysterical villagers or vengeful witches.

As they entered a clutch of trees, they came across a small hill they normally didn't pay much attention to, hidden as it was from the view of the main path. Today, they both paused and stared as the knoll was dotted with dirt mounds. Someone had clearly tried to hide freshly dug earth under piles of branches spiked with furry new leaves. Curious, the boys cleared away the branches.

"You first," Thomas said.

"Why me?" Caleb sighed.

"Because you're the youngest," Thomas insisted.

Caleb knew what he had to do. He knelt down and started scooping the earth away with both hands. The dirt came apart easily, and soon body parts started to appear like gruesome spring flowers. Thomas knelt down to help his brother.

They uncovered five bodies in all, each with their throat cut, just like they had seen on the dead bodies of Abigail Faulkner and the transient. They didn't recognize any of the corpses. Clearly, the witches had got smart and decided that murdering travelers and hiding the bodies was a more efficient way of operating.

"What should we do?" Caleb asked.

"We need to tell Father," Thomas said.

"How can we do that? They won't let us in to see him," Caleb pointed out.

"I guess we need to handle this by ourselves then," Thomas said. The boys slid down the hill and headed toward home.

* * *

That night Caleb, Thomas, and Hannah dressed in dark clothing and stealthily rode toward the jail in Salem Town, Hannah on her mother's horse and the boys riding their father's. Unlike Salem Village, the town was heavily populated as it crowded around a couple of inlets with the bay stretching beyond to the sea.

The children dismounted a couple of blocks from the jail and tied the horses up behind an old barn. The jail was an imposing red stone building set on a grassy plain, which meant approaching would be difficult without the guards noticing. Pulling out his pocketknife, Thomas cut down branches and grass and draped them over himself and his siblings for camouflage.

Moving slowly and silently, they crawled toward the building.

Once they had reached the safety of its dark shadows, they shed the branches and Thomas took from his pack a long rope with an iron hook on the end. He whipped the rope up with practiced ease and caught the hook on the stone balustrade at the top of the building.

Caleb then grasped the rope and started walking up the wall. His goal was a narrow barred window some thirty feet up. Hannah had visited the jail with her mother on several occasions so she knew roughly where the cells were and which hallways led where. She was confident that this particular window led to a small hallway that should be deserted at night. Nathaniel was being kept two floors below.

Halfway up the side of the building, Caleb lost his footing and he smacked against the stone wall with a thud.

Hannah gasped, and she and Thomas dived for cover under their discarded camouflage branches.

There was a loud clang as the guard opened the gate and peeked around the side of the building from which Caleb dangled. Fortunately, he didn't look up, and in the faint moonlight failed to spot Thomas and Hannah holding their breath beneath the branches.

After a few moments, the guard went back to the front of the building, but it was clear he didn't immediately go back inside. The smell of a pipe stuffed with English tobacco wafted around the corner.

Time was running short. Shaking off the branches, Hannah gestured frantically for Caleb to continue climbing. When he reached the window he slid one leg in, then the other, and disappeared from view.

Inside the building, Caleb dropped four feet to the ground, and there was a faint splash as his boots hit the wet stone floor. The inside of the jail was cold and dark, and the stench of human waste was almost overpowering. Caleb could hear someone groaning in one of the cells closest to him. He shivered, feeling a tingle of fear go down his spine.

Pushing the thought aside he got out the rough sketch Hannah had supplied him with. He examined the piece of paper by the faint light from the window, then inched forward into the darkness. A staircase in the back corner of the building should lead him down to his father's cell.

"Who's there?" a female voice whispered out of the darkness. "Please, sir. Please help me."

Knowing he couldn't afford a moment's distraction, Caleb stopped and hoped that the woman would think he was gone.

"Please sir, come closer," the voice said.

Caleb crept over to a small three-foot-by-two-foot cell. He could see the faint outline of a woman huddled in the corner.

"Sir, Dorcas Good, Sarah Good's daughter, is over in the cell beyond. Please see if she's well. Her mother was hanged and no one has spoken or seen to her in weeks."

"I will," Caleb whispered.

"Is that you, Caleb?" the woman crawled toward him. Caleb could now see it was Marium Teller. An old woman who used to sell apples on the street.

"Yes, ma'am. It is me," Caleb replied.

"What a good boy you are. Are you helping your father this fine day in your fields?"

Caleb eyed the poor old woman, she had clearly lost her mind. In his jacket pocket he had stuffed a couple of loaves of bread. Caleb took one out and slid it between the bars for the old woman. He then continued down the hallway, moving as softly as he could.

In an even tinier, damper cell, chained to the wall, was four-year-old Dorcas Good. Her mother had been one of the first to be accused of witchcraft and she had been second to be hanged after Bridget Bishop. Dorcas was filthy and covered in dirt and her own feces, Caleb struggled not to recoil from the smell. The tiny girl looked at him with wild, untamed eyes. Caleb pushed his last loaf of bread toward her. She grabbed it and started to tear into it with her teeth like an animal. The sight tore at Caleb's heartstrings. Despite her being such a tiny child, Dorcas had been accused of witchcraft. How the magistrates could think such a thing was impossible to know.

In the faint moonlight, Caleb found the staircase and made his way carefully down two flights of stairs and onto another corridor of cells. He passed Marshall Lewis, a man who was accused of witchcraft because his neighbor's horse went lame after they had an argument.

"Hey you boy!" Marshall called out. "Whatcha doin' here?"

"Shushh," Caleb said.

"Hey guards. Guards! What's this boy doin?"

Caleb frantically looked for a place to hide, he noticed two bars of one cell were a little more spread apart then the rest. He squeezed through them and found himself in a cell with a sleeping woman.

A minute or so later, he heard the guards march heavily along the corridor coming to investigate the commotion.

"There's a boy in here. There's a boy in here," Marshall cried.

"Shut up, ye old coot," a guard said, spitting on him.

"But he's there, he's over there!"

The guard undid the lock on the man's cell and gave him a slap with a bully bat. Marshall huddled in the corner until the guard tired of beating him and left.

Caleb waited until the coast was clear and then climbed out from between the bars. He pitied the man, who was clearly crazy, but his second close encounter with the guards only made him want to escape this terrible place even more quickly.

He crept on and a few minutes later, to his relief, he found Nathaniel's cell.

"Father?" Caleb whispered.

"Caleb. Dear boy." Nathaniel reached through the bars and grasped his son's shoulder affectionately. "How on Earth did you get in here, and how do you think we're going to get out?"

"Thomas thought of something. Don't worry," Caleb replied with a smile.

Reaching into his jacket for his tools, Caleb deftly picked the lock on the cell just like his father had taught him.

The two Campbells moved swiftly and silently down the corridor, they turned a corner and paused. The guards were close by. Caleb gestured for his father to wait.

At that moment, they heard a terrible wail of pain coming from outside the jail.

It was followed quickly by a sudden commotion as the guards rushed outside to see what was going on. Nathaniel and Caleb crept cautiously down the stairs and toward the entrance to the building. The guards had all fled outside, bar one, who Nathaniel swiftly took care of with a carefully placed blow to the head.

From the gate of the jail in the distance, Nathaniel and Caleb could see a bonfire surrounded by robed figures. It looked like a gathering of witches but in actuality, as Caleb explained briefly to his father, it was a series of sticks clothed in Hannah's old dresses. The guards crept closer, convinced by the firelight casting strange shadows that they were about to surprise a witchy gathering.

Meanwhile, Nathaniel and Caleb slipped away. As they ran, Nathaniel looked to his youngest son.

"Well done, Caleb," Nathaniel said. "Are you okay?"

"All those poor people in jail. They're not witches, Father."

"I know. We're going to take care of this, I promise."

They hurried to find Hannah and Thomas.

THIRTY-TWO

Dean flipped the pages and noticed a note written in different handwriting in the top right-hand corner of the journal:

This is the last journal entry by Nathaniel Campbell.

Fall 1692
Much joy and pain I feel tonight. As I write this, night falls around my cozy house. A home filled with my family and love like nothing else. But it is tonight that I must go out and fight perhaps the most hideous evil I have seen in my many days as a hunter.

For posterity now seems to be the perfect time to recount my induction into the profession of being a hunter.

It was very fortunate that my family and Rose Mary's met on the treacherous voyage to the New World. As it turned out, there would be two families of the same profession in this New World, hers and mine. Of course, this was before we both were born. My father and Rose Mary's father fostered a strong friendship and created a pact to protect each other's families. With that pact they also promised to pass along the family profession. Sadly, Rose Mary's mother died in childbirth in 1650. This brought our two families even closer. My father had married a hunter, and my mother's mother was a hunter too.

Because of her mother's passing Rose Mary and I were very close, and she would often visit my parents' homestead. In fact our parents were close until the day Rose Mary's family perished in a wendigo attack, and only she survived. My father never forgave himself for being unable to save his friend and his family.

When we came of age at ten years old, my father took us both out to the woods. I must recount that both Rose Mary and I were most afraid of what my father was about to do. Until this time we didn't know about hunting, we thought our parents were simple farmers. But, of course, that was not the case. My father took us a mile from the house into the darkest recesses of the woods and I will never forget the sight before me. Tied to a tree, chained with iron shackles, was a naked man shivering in the cool night air. Rose Mary squealed, but then held her tongue. I, however, knew that my father wouldn't have shown us this strange sight unless there was a lesson to be learned. He handed Rose Mary and I a flintlock musket each. The weapons felt heavy and unwieldy in our small hands.

"What are we to do with this?" I asked.

"Just wait and watch," my father replied sternly.

As the moon rose full over the woods, slowly the man

before us started to snarl. Then he began to arch his body, howling in pain as silver hair sprouted over his entire body. Eventually what stood before us was a man no longer, but rather a most uncommon beast—a wolf.

So hideous and frightening was the sight that Rose Mary cowered and I wanted to turn away, but my father insisted we keep our eyes on the creature. Still shackled to the tree, the wolf paced and gnashed his awful teeth. He lunged at us as if there wasn't a man inside him at all.

"See the animal before you," my father said, "he was once a man. A good man. But he has been unfortunately cursed. He was bitten by a creature, much like the creature you see before you now. It's in his nature to roam these woods and hunt and eat humans. The man inside him would surely be appalled by such acts. But the animal, it's his instinct. What do you think the man would feel if tomorrow he woke up and remembered all the awful things his animal self had done in the night?"

Rose Mary piped up, "He would surely feel most awful."

"Exactly Rose Mary, he would hate himself. He would be ashamed, and he might even turn his rage upon himself. But he won't stop. He can't stop, because this animal is inside him. The one blessing is that he won't remember his actions as a beast once he turns back into a man. But he will kill. So what do you think this man would ask us to do?"

"He would surely ask us to kill him to save the people he might kill," I offered. "If he was a good man he would."

"You are exactly right, Nathaniel. You are such a smart boy. He would ask us to kill him. So the question is. Who will help this man tonight?"

Rose Mary and I looked at one another. Neither of us had ever held a gun, much less thought of killing a man. But it was without question the right thing to do. The animal that paced and growled before us would do much harm. Harm that the man inside of would be horrified at.

Rose Mary and I agreed to level our muskets at the same moment, thus neither of us could singularly feel guilty for killing the creature. And that is what we did. Father told us that only a silver bullet would kill the animal. As much as I was saddened about our act, it was the right thing to do.

I recall that story because that animal was a man beneath. And it is always an awful thing to kill a man. But there is a greater good to be served. As I go into the fight tonight with my own two sons by my side I will tell them that story, because it's with a heavy heart that I know there will be lives lost. We must kill the witches, or we ourselves will be killed. Though they are most undoubtedly human, they are evil. And we must eradicate them.

I consider myself a most lucky man for having lived the life I have. I found a most loving and wonderful wife early in my life and my three children are my ultimate joy. This hard and sometimes lonely life of hunting would be intolerable if it wasn't for them.

Dear family, if you are reading this, I've either lost my facilities or come to my end. Please remember that I love you all. I will meet you in heaven most surely.

Your father,

Nathaniel Campbell.

THIRTY-THREE

In loving memory of Nathaniel Campbell and Rose Mary Campbell, loving parents to Thomas, Caleb and Hannah.

My siblings and I thought it appropriate to close my father's journal with the last entry relating his death. Perhaps later generations will be able to draw wisdom from his sacrifice. The remaining pages have been written by Thomas Campbell, age fifteen, Fall 1692.

The night that my brother Caleb and I broke my father out of jail, the village of Salem had turned to chaos. After my father confronted the magistrates and unveiled Prudence as a witch, most of residents went into hiding. Rightly so, for they had sat within a few feet of her for weeks, under her spell and believing every accusation she made. Upon discovery, Prudence fled. The night that followed would be the last night my father and mother spent in this corporeal realm. This is what happened.

Later that night, we retreated to our home. When we

opened the door we realized that the witches had been there before us. Our mother had disappeared. She had set out our secret signal that something had gone wrong, so we knew that she had been either forcibly taken or was already dead. Our parents made up this signal for us when we were small children and they would go out hunting. If something bad happened, Father told us to turn over a tea cup and leave it on the kitchen table. That is what we saw when we entered the silent house. It was our mother's sign to us.

My father was weakened from exhaustion and lack of food in prison but he wouldn't stop to rest. He immediately pulled up the hidden door set underneath our kitchen table—built into the floor we had an arsenal for emergency use. Now was such an emergency.

We armed ourselves and forced my father to drink a warm cup of broth, then we set out for Constance's property. We knew that Constance and Prudence were close to accomplishing a most evil task. So evil of a task that my brother and I hardly wanted to think of it. Raising the devil wasn't something father had trained us against. Raising the devil would essentially make Hell on Earth. Both my brother and I knew that we must defeat the witches or risk losing the entire New World to evil.

Hannah made sure we were all warmly wrapped up and we left her behind, well armed, to guard our home. Father kissed her on the forehead before leaving.

"My dear girl," he said, "you are the strongest, smartest young woman to walk the face of God's great Earth. Do not ever change."

A single tear streaked down Hannah's cheek as though she already knew what was in store for my father.

"Don't behave as though you will never see me again," she said. "I'll make sure there is a home for you to come back to."

We took my father's horse, our most sure-footed and silent. We would tie him up away from the fight in case one of us needed to flee or fetch help. Though I think we all knew there was no more help to get.

As we approached Constance's residence, the lights of a hundred witches' lanterns showed through the trees. Most of the figures were obscured behind a small knoll, so we could not see where our mother was. Father gave us the signal to wait. We sorted out our weapons on the damp ground. After a few minutes, the congregation of witches began to chant, their horrible voices building in strength and power as they continued.

Then a sound echoed through the woods which will be forever burned into my soul: my mother's screams.

We grabbed our guns and crawled up the hill on our stomachs. Down below was a most horrific sight. A hundred witches chanted in unison, most no more than resurrected bodies of rotting flesh and bone. These putrid, wretched beings were now animated living things once again. Their voices were pitched low and threatening, and the noise continued to build, until our heads felt full of the horrible sound.

The witches moved around a great fire built in the shape of a ring. Inside the ring a hole was filled with perfectly round rocks. In front of the fire a large platform had been erected. This is where my poor mother kneeled. I knew she was scared. As proficient a hunter as she may be, no one could face down a hundred witches and not fear for her life.

Terror washed over my father's face. There were many more witches than we had previously thought, the resurrections more numerous than we could ever have imagined. There must have been many more murders than we had discovered. All those people, including poor Abigail Faulkner, had been used as sacrifices for these resurrections.

I thought about the innocent people that the magistrates had sent to the gallows. They were not among the witches. The accused were all good, God-fearing, innocent members of the church, yet they had been put to death.

At that moment, two more witches appeared out of the woods dragging the body of a man. He seemed to be alive. Closer inspection revealed it to be Reverend Parris. The witches brought him to face a witch who was dressed in ceremonial garb. As she turned her head, I saw with a shiver that it was Prudence. She shot out her arm and lifted his petrified face to hers. The chanting halted and her sneering voice carried to our ears through the still night air.

"Why Reverend, why are you so scared? It is I, innocent little Prudence. Perhaps my station takes you as a bit of surprise. But you didn't really think all those innocent people were really witches did you? Well I suppose you did. But it had to be done. You would surely have paid much too much attention to the dead bodies popping up around Salem Village if we hadn't created another antagonist for you to concentrate your foolish beliefs. You sir, and I say this having known my fair share of men of God, are a pitiful, greedy human being. The kind of man who doesn't deserve the respect of anyone."

Reverend Parris cried out like an infant.

"Why have you brought me here? I am not one of your evil clan."

Prudence smiled. "But you are, Reverend. You blindly followed a group of hysterical children, and you used them to do your bidding. One by one you eradicated your enemies."

"I don't know what you speak of," the Reverend moaned.

"Tsk, tsk, Reverend. Of course you do. Don't you remember the nights you spent with your sweet little niece by the fire? Where you would placidly recount who you thought might be practicing witchcraft? What impressionable young woman wouldn't want to please you. Especially one so easily swayed. That is how you made sure everyone in the village with whom you had a disagreement was jailed or hanged."

"That's not true! I'm not what you say," the Reverend cried.

"Don't try to deny it, Reverend. Make your peace with God, this will be your last night on Earth. You'll be meeting Him soon enough."

With that she flicked her hand and the Reverend flew up in the air. He landed on the ground some distance away with his leg at a most unnatural angle. He cried out in pain. But Prudence ignored him, turning her attention instead to our mother. Mother was silent, but I knew she was afraid.

My father turned to Caleb and I.

"Boys, we will surely be outnumbered. We are but three against a hundred powerful wtiches. You must go ask for King Philip's help. We need more men. Unfortunately we didn't part on good terms last we spoke but try to convince him of our need. If we don't stop the witches, our world as well as Philip's tribe and way of life will be endangered. The *Necronomicon* could destroy the entire world. Please get him and his men. They *must* come."

Caleb and I nodded. We knew the Wampanoag Indians were fierce warriors, they had killed many colonists from Boston to the territories north. Caleb and I had never traveled east to their land; moreover, we had never gone such a distance alone. King Philip had fostered a friendship with Father and he had always come to our house. The thought of a long, hurried journey on horseback through the night was daunting but the moonlight would light our way.

We said goodbye to Father, slid back down the hill and silently slipped away. We led the horse for a mile over the meadow so our retreat wouldn't be heard by the witches. Riding tandem, we escaped east.

We rode hard, crossing dark fields and still darker woodlands. We crossed over a series of streams and soon came to a cliff that led down to a river. Beyond the water lay the woods that bordered King Philip's territory.

We crossed the river at a shallow point, keeping our legs raised clear of the rushing water. By necessity we made a disturbance, and as soon as we got to the other side we knew that one of Philip's scouts had seen us. Within a mile, we came to a clearing and found ourselves surrounded by

Wampanoag Indians. These men were fierce, proud people and when they moved you could see their power and skill. We dismounted and waited, soothing our agitated horse and soon King Philip came forward.

I approached him respectfully.

"Please accept our humble apologies for arriving without invitation. But my father, your friend, Nathaniel Campbell, urgently needs your help and that of your men."

King Philip was a most handsome man, tall, powerful. He ran his nation deftly and had the skills of any colonist negotiator. I didn't know whether I would be able to convince him to help. Any fifteen-year-old would have been nervous, and I was shaking in my boots.

"Why should I put my men at risk? Your father is a most kind and learned man, but I cannot lead my men into a battle which doesn't concern them," he said.

I thought for a moment. I wasn't sure what my response should be. He was right, of course—why should he put his men in danger? I knew I had to be cunning without being defensive or impolite.

"Gracious King, there are witches in Salem who are conspiring to open up the gates to Hell—they are trying to summon the devil. If they succeed, the evil will spread past the boundaries of our colony to you and your people. Your men would be drawn into a fight with the creatures of Hell. The witches will not heed the river which is a barrier between your nation and our colony."

"Your Christian gods do not frighten us, we have our own protector spirits," King Philip replied.

"I'm very respectful of them," I said, "as is my father. However, the evil that will unfurl over this land will be too great for even your most powerful protectors. I understand caution. My father speaks of it often. But in this is not the time for prudence, this is a time for action. I beg of you to lend us some of your men."

"You do not require my presence?" King Philip asked.

"We would like nothing more, for you are a powerful warrior, but my father wouldn't think of asking you to put yourself at risk. You have a great nation to run."

King Philip thought for a moment.

"I always appreciate a courteous word from a colonist, but I must refuse your plea. My nation and its safety is the most important thing and I cannot lead them into peril."

I nodded respectfully. What else could I do? Caleb opened his mouth to protest, but I shot him a look to silence him. We bowed and received a gift of fresh water in a skin from King Philip's wife, and then we left. Once we were out of earshot, Caleb began to weep.

"Stop that," I said. "We will find a way to defeat the witches. But not if you have such soft resolve."

Caleb wiped away his tears and we dug our heels into the horse's sides to push it forward and back into the river. That's when we heard the pounding of hooves from behind us. King Philip had allowed his men to fight. They came in full warrior regalia. Caleb and I were filled with hope and we gave them our thanks. They followed us back across the river.

It was another hour at full gallop to reach the village and then ten minutes to get to the edge of Constance's lands.

We dismounted a mile away and led the horses closer. The Indian horses were well trained and didn't make a sound as we approached.

My father saw us coming and came to meet us. He greeted the men's leader, who was King Philip's brother, and together through gestures—for the brother did not speak English—they made plans. The Indians would circle the witches while my father created a diversion, and with guns drawn Caleb and I would free our mother.

The Indians moved off silently to take their places.

When I peeked back over the knoll a most unsettling sight lay before me. My mother had been led down to the ring of fire, and the witches encircled her, their voices louder than ever. Constance led the crescendo of chanting, calling upon the four Princes of Hell to rise.

The first she called forth was Belial.

Seeing the dire situation before us, my father started the attack with swift signal to King Philip's men.

Moments later, the Indians emerged from the woods. The orange firelight illuminated their painted brown-skinned bodies and they looked like other-worldly warriors. In an explosion of action, they attacked the witches, their large sticks and spears impaling and beheading the enemy in turn. Muskets were drawn and bullets flew.

Seizing our moment, in the midst of the chaos, Caleb and I ran down the hill, stumbling and tripping toward the fire. It seemed the resurrected witches were easily brought down with a musket shot to the head or a quick stab through the heart.

However, Prudence and Constance proved to be much harder to defeat.

When Caleb and I reached the bottom of the hill, Prudence attacked us from the left. Caleb pulled back his musket to shoot, but she grabbed it and flung it into the fire. It landed on the rocks with a clatter. She flew at Caleb and caught him by the neck. He was thrown down with such force that his body made a mark in the earth.

Grasping a burning log from the fire, I swung it at Prudence's head from behind. She flipped over to face me, somehow unhurt, and flinging the log from my hands, she encircled my neck with her fingers. I fought to breathe, realizing as I choked that my adversary must be weaker than she had been, since she was using physical force for her attack rather than spells or the black arts. It seemed most of her energy had been sucked away by the resurrection still taking place a few feet from our fight.

From the corner of my eye I could see my mother struggling against Constance's powerful grip as she held her over a large brass bowl. The fire glinted off a large knife that the tall witch brandished in her other hand. Just as she raised her arm to strike, my father attacked Constance from behind. Constance let go of Mother and she fell into the edge of the fire. She rolled away but was unable to get up, as her hands and feet were tied. I struggled harder against Prudence, desperate to warn my mother of the approaching danger, but the witch was still too strong and I watched in horror as another old woman caught my mother by the nape of the neck.

This new woman seemed more powerful than the other resurrected witches. She slung my mother over her shoulder with ease. She took Mother back to the brass bowl, and again held her over it.

With a wrench I momentarily freed myself from Prudence and managed a croaked scream, but Prudence gained footing and hit me on the side of the head, my vision blurred for a few seconds and she caught hold of me again.

Still battling Constance, my father reached out to my mother, but it was too late. The strong old witch picked up a knife. The *Necronomicon* lay open at her side. She started to chant. I desperately fought Prudence but her grip only intensified. Caleb was surrounded by three witches and was unable to get off a shot. Another witch bore down on him and knocked him off balance. He swerved, catching his foot in one of the stones near the fire.

The old witch continued to chant from the book then she held the knife across my poor mother's neck and slit the life out of her. My mother's blood drained into the brass bowl and at that moment a deep rumbling echoed through the woods.

My father threw Constance off him and kneeled at my mother's side. Her head slid to one side and my father pressed his face to her breast, the life drained from her dear, pure heart. My father grabbed the book from the old woman with one hand, with the other he drew his pistol and shot her between the eyes.

Constance was embroiled in a fight with one of the fierce Indian warriors, so with the *Necronomicon* in hand, Father

moved away into the shadows. I knew that the *Necronomicon*
held powerful spells, but it also held their reversals.

Suddenly the stones in the center of the ring of fire
started to drop as if a deep hole had opened up beneath
them. The rumbling grew louder, and the earth beneath our
feet became warm. A blast of heat, far surpassing the sun
on the hottest of any June day, emanated from the hole. The
fire ring almost doused itself; the heat coming forth from
the hole seemed hotter than fire.

I tried to roll away from Prudence but she held me fast.

King Philip's Indian warriors, men of great resolve,
stopped their fighting and stared at the hole. It hurt to look
in the direction of the fiery pit, but no one could draw their
eyes away from the figure that was slowly rising up from
the earth.

Constance shook off her adversary.

"Belial, I call you forth," she shouted. "I have raised you,
I am your Queen, I am your bind to this earth." She repeated
the chant over and over, her voice louder and louder. While
the creature, with great horns, gradually dissolved into the
shape of a man.

Constance caught one of her young farm hands by the
arm, pulled him close, and, grabbing the knife, started to
chant once again. I realized she was trying to raise the
second Prince of Hell, whose name I knew to be Leviathan.

My father reappeared from the shadows. He was
holding the *Necronomicon* and had his own buck knife in
his other hand.

"Evil, vile creature," he cried out to Constance. His

voice steady and true. "You will not succeed in creating Hell on Earth."

Then he started to chant from the *Necronomicon*.

"Oh god of dark and god of light. You are summoned no more. Hide your evilness in the cage from which you came, you are not wanted on this mortal plain. I forbade *vos of atrum pergo huic regnum. Vos es inconcessus ut ingredior inter lux lucis. Vos es inconcessus ut futurus in is terra. Vado tergum qua vos venit. Vado tergum ut vestri cage. Vos es non volo. Per vox of lux lucis quod filiolus of Olympus quod bonus verto tergum ut atrum.*"

And with that my dear father took the knife and sliced his own neck. He fell into a heap, his blood mixed with my mother's in the bowl.

An inhuman scream echoed forth from the creature in the middle of the fire. Frigid air pushed forth from all corners of the wood, extinguishing the fire, and the figure disappeared back into the hellish fire at its feet. The earth closed up and rocks tumbled back into their place, imprisoning the Prince of Hell back in his fiery domain.

With the beast's disappearance the resurrected witches started to visibly lose energy, making them a lot easier to kill. Caleb extracted himself and beheaded a slew of the old bags of bones. I wrestled from Prudence's now much weaker grasp and swung around ready to attack Constance, but she and Prudence retreated swiftly into the woods, disappearing from view. Two of the Indian warriors went after them, but they came back minutes later. The women had evaporated.

We rapidly executed the rest of the witches, and threw their bodies into the middle of the ring. We piled wood on top of them and re-set the fire. Leaving the bodies for others to find would serve no purpose except to frighten them. We had what we needed to end the frenzy within the village.

I approached the quivering figure of Reverend Parris. He attempted to stand but was unable. I helped him up, supported him back to one of the horses, then helped him mount. As he tried to walk away I held the reigns.

"Reverend Parris? What say you to what you saw this evening?" I asked.

"Young man, I can hardly believe my eyes. I must return home and pray about it," he replied avoiding my direct gaze.

"That is not what I meant," I said. "You will call off the witch trials now. You will petition for the release of every jailed innocent. Will you not?"

He nodded, still not looking at me.

"Let me hear you say it," I said.

"I will do everything in my power to release the innocent and I will tell the magistrates that the afflicted girls have been healed by the hand of God. Salem Village no longer harbors Satan."

"Very well, have a safe ride home," I said. "You never know what might lurk in the shadows."

A look of panic crossed the Reverend's face. He rode unsteadily off across the meadow.

By this time the early morning light was illuminating the carnage before us. Caleb leaned over the bodies of our poor parents as he recited the Lord's Prayer. I stood beside him and joined in. The Indians had made a litter from logs and pine boughs. We laid Mother and Father on it and covered them with a torn coat.

The warriors promised to tell King Philip of Nathaniel's bravery. I thanked them for their fight. Without them we surely would have been defeated. The Indians then galloped off quickly, they didn't want to be caught on colony land during daylight. And with that Caleb and I headed toward home carrying our deceased parents.

As we approached home, Hannah appeared at the door and came to meet us. As she neared us her face was stricken with both relief at our survival and grief for our parents. We brought them inside and prepared their bodies for burial. We wanted them to be interred on our homestead and not in the village cemetery.

Our hearts were heavy that night. But one thing was clear. Our father would want us to continue hunting the evil in this world. In the early dawn light Caleb and I spoke about it. We debated when and how to tell our sister who was asleep in the next room. I knew after I recounted this story she would understand why we had to leave Salem and seek out others in need of our help. Though I feared she would be lonely I knew it was essential for her to stay in Salem and see the Reverend kept all his promises.

I left her the following letter.

Dearest Hannah

When you wake, Caleb and I will be gone. I hope you understand that after tonight saying goodbye to you would too hard. But knowing your strength and wisdom you will understand why we needed to leave. After the fight with the Salem witches, Caleb and I realized that all the country villages and towns are being abused and attacked by the kinds of evil we know how to fight. It would be lovely and comfortable to stay with you here, to see you marry and have a family. It would be lovely and comfortable for Caleb and I to do the same. But we feel that would be wrong and selfish. The world outside Salem needs us.

Please understand that our choice was not an easy one. And leaving you alone perhaps was not what Mother and Father would have wanted. But I know you'll agree that there is a greater good at work.

We hope that God grants you a long and happy life. If ever we come by this way again, please leave the light on for us. You will forever be in our hearts and prayers. Keep up on your Latin, you are the best scholar in the family.

God bless.

Your loving brothers,

Thomas and Caleb.

THIRTY-FOUR

Dean closed Nathaniel's journal, there were no more entries. Constance was Connie, Dean was certain of that, and could Perry be Prudence, or was that taking things too far? Though there wasn't an exact map in the journal, Dean was pretty sure Constance had occupied the same house all these years. He guessed that she must stay hidden for a couple of generations and every now and then, after a while had passed, she would return to public life. That way no one could grow suspicious of her longevity. It was sort of the perfect way to exist forever.

Now, after all this time, Connie once again had the opportunity to raise Lucifer and as much as it hurt him, Dean now saw that he couldn't let her do it. Sam would be forever bound to a coven of witches and Dean could not unleash that evil upon the world. He had to find a way to stop them.

He watched Lisa and Ben sleeping soundly, both had dropped off fully clothed on the other bed. Dean had explained that now was not the time to get cushy. Hunters slept in their clothes as you never knew what might wake you up in the morning. The TV blared out late night infomercials. Dean got up and checked his wallet, a couple of towns over there was a twenty-four-hour hardware store. He would need some rope, more salt, just in case, and, of course, knives. Buying ammo was going to be a tad harder at this hour of the night, but he could figure that out later.

Dean left the motel room quietly, careful not to wake Lisa and Ben. He got into the truck, noting that the motel parking lot was empty except for a white van parked in the far corner. Dean started the ignition and pulled away.

Sam watched Dean pull away in that nasty truck from inside the white van. He could have followed his brother, but he knew he didn't have to take care of him. The thing that he wanted to take care of was the fact that Prudence had a tail on him. On his way here a small two-door hatchback had made every turn Sam did, and was now parked across the street from the motel.

It wasn't Prudence herself behind the wheel, but Sam was pretty sure he recognized the girl as one of the ones from the bookstore break-in. She was probably put in charge of tallying Sam's every move to make sure he didn't get in the way of the remaining resurrections.

The only thing on Sam's mind was how to take the witches down. Whether they were human or not didn't matter to him. He didn't know where the witches were planning this resurrection. And he had to find out. He could waste a lot of shoe leather. Or he could deliver two of the last resurrections to the witches on a plate. Pulling transients over and killing them couldn't be easy. Perhaps he would just force the witches' hand.

Sam pulled a mask on over his head, took out his sawed-off and loaded it with just one bullet. He wouldn't need to call Prudence; the girl across the street would do that for him. He got out of the van and braced himself in front of the motel door to Lisa and Ben's room.

CRACKKK!

Sam's foot splintered the door off the jamb. Inside the room, Lisa sat up quickly, eyes bulging with fear, but Sam slapped her across the face before she could start screaming. She rolled over the bottom of the bed. Ben stirred in his sleep, but stayed unconscious—Sam guessed that Dean had given him a sleeping pill.

Lisa crawled across the ground toward one of Dean's bags. Sam, staying silent lest he give his identity away, pulled the bag out of her reach. He roughly flipped her over onto her stomach and tied her hands and feet together with zip lines.

"Wh-why are you doing this?" she cried. "Please, just take me, leave my son!"

Sam didn't answer. He grabbed a balled-up T-shirt of Dean's and stuffed it into her mouth. Next he rolled Ben onto his stomach and tied both his hands and feet together. Ben snored loudly, unaware that his de facto uncle was setting him up for a kidnapping.

Lisa continued to try to scream through her gag, but the noise was muffled and ineffective.

Sam's entire set-up had taken less than two minutes. He headed back outside and closed the door behind him. He looked at the car across the street. The girl's faint outline could be seen through the dark windows of her crappy car. She was peering at him as he emerged from the motel. Sam smiled. There was no way she wouldn't be curious.

Sam got into his van, took off his mask and pulled out of the parking lot. He raced up the highway until he was out of sight of the girl's car. Then he made a rapid U-turn, came back around, and parked in a donut shop parking lot facing the street.

About half a mile down the road, Sam spotted a figure racing across the four-lane highway and into the parking lot of the motel. It took about a minute for the girl to return. She ran back across the road and slid back into her car and pulled it around into the motel parking lot. Being a witch, Sam surmised that she would be strong enough to carry Lisa and Ben out of their motel room and into her hatchback.

Sam waited until he saw the car pull out. It headed toward him, north up the highway. He crouched down, but the van was indistinct enough among all the other vans in the donut shop car park that the girl drove past without noticing. A few seconds later, Sam pulled out and followed her, a safe ten car-lengths behind.

Sam guessed that the girl probably didn't have time to ask her superiors about whether or not to bring the two victims home. She had acted on instinct and that was to Sam's advantage. She would lead him right to the resurrection sight. He hoped he would be able to deal with the witches without getting Dean involved. Meanwhile Sam wouldn't actually let the witches harm Lisa and Ben. That wasn't the plan. The plan was to stop the witches and systematically kill them all. Sam glanced into the back of the van. It was chock full of enough explosives to rip a hole in the Lincoln Tunnel, except Sam was going to use it to stop a different kind of destruction.

Sam continued following the car as it turned onto Route 128 and headed north.

Dean got out of the van balancing a bag of donuts, two coffees for him and Lisa, and a hot chocolate for Ben. He thought they could have a quick breakfast and maybe then he would put them on a train back to Cicero. It would be easier and safer to wrap this up without them. He had already put them through enough.

Dean had no idea how he was going to stop the witches, he would make it up on the spot, like usual. The only thing he was hoping for was that the witches hadn't picked up anymore transients. But he had taken care of that by calling Officer Wiggims and putting out an ABP on both Perry's car, which he had seen earlier in the week, and whatever caravan of cars Connie owned. At least then Connie would find it a little more difficult to get around town.

The motel door was cracked open. Dean immediately put down his provisions and took out his gun.

"Lisa? Ben?" Dean called.

He kicked open what remained of the door, and through the dim light he could see that both beds were empty. A quick scan of the room told him that someone had been pulled off the bed, the coverlet was on the floor at the foot. And there was a little piece of plastic, the kind that sometimes pops off a plastic zip tie. Most police officers use them, but Dean didn't believe they had been arrested.

Dean grabbed his duffle bag, noticing that it wasn't where he left it. Instead it had been thrown into a corner, out of reach. On the table, a paper cup was turned upside down.

Months ago, when Dean and Lisa were talking about Dean's childhood, he had shared the signal John Winchester had taught him when he and Sam were young. "If the shit goes down, try to turn a cup over on the table. It won't look out of place to anyone but us," John had said. Dean knew someone had taken Lisa and Ben. He ran out the door and into the motel lobby, but the bored young woman behind the counter hadn't seen anything.

In the truck, Dean popped open his laptop, it seemed that Lisa's cell phone had been disarmed. The last time it pinged off a cell phone tower was nineteen miles north of Salem, toward the shore. After that, someone had turned off the GPS in the town of Gloucester. He decided to start there.

Dean peeled into traffic. He desperately wanted to call Bobby for a little help, maybe he could do more legwork on tracking down the cell phone, but he didn't have time. As he pulled onto Route 128 he noticed in his rear-view a black Escalade barreling down on him. Dean pushed the pedal to the floor, but the old truck only belched out a trickle more horsepower.

"Should've taken the Impala," Dean muttered to himself.

The Escalade pulled out from behind him and into the adjacent lane of the highway. The large car then swerved deliberately into Dean's driver's side. Dean's truck swerved onto the sandy side of the road, and fishtailed. Dean fought the heavy vehicle to regain control and then he righted himself back onto the road. But there was no way to outrun the newer vehicle.

The Escalade pulled in behind the truck and hit its bumper with a CRAAASSHH, jolting Dean into the steering wheel. Dean willed the truck forward and steeled himself for another hit. The Escalade came full force and lifted the truck's back wheels off the road.

Seconds later, it crashed back down, the shocks gave way and Dean's back absorbed a good amount of the jolt from the old bench truck seat.

Dean tried to swerve to escape another hit, but the Escalade was too quick, it rammed into the rear bumper of the truck and it spun around into oncoming traffic. Dean cut the wheel and bumped roughly back into the correct lane.

The Escalade came back again and surged forward, passing Dean. He craned his neck to get a look into the car, but couldn't see past the tinted windows.

The black car cut him off again. Dean slowed down and desperately reached beside him for his duffle which had slid onto the floor. Keeping his eyes on the road, and one hand on the wheel, Dean felt for the strap, grasped it, and pulled the bag into his lap. He fished out his sawed-off and leaned out of the side window, aiming the gun at the back window of the Escalade. The driver hit the brakes, sending the car skidding to a stop. Dean jammed on his brakes in turn, and the old mechanism squealed in response.

He couldn't stop in time and the truck hit the large car with such force that Dean's chin almost reached the windshield. The truck teetered on the front two wheels, then crashed back down. It gave one last sputter and the radiator exploded.

Satisfied, the Escalade sped off.

Dean grabbed his duffle bag and got out of the truck, ignoring the other drivers honking at his sudden halt. He was battered and bruised and now more desperate than ever to find Lisa and Ben.

He knew he needed to keep heading north. On his right side he could feel the cool wind of a storm pushing in from the sea. He assumed if he kept walking forward eventually he'd come to a town. Just then, a large sixteen-wheeler slowed and stopped in front of him. Dean climbed onto the runner. The driver rolled down his window. He was a wizened old guy in a trucker's cap, and bore a strong resemblance to Bobby.

"You need a lift?" he asked.

"Yeah, if you wouldn't mind. Going to Gloucester," Dean said.

"It's not too far. Get in," the truck driver groused.

A mile down the road Dean realized that he had left his laptop in the truck. He desperately tried to look up the address of the last ping of Lisa's cell phone on his phone.

But the site just indicated that the cell had somehow passed through town.

"What's past Gloucester? Anything?" Dean asked.

"Well, there's Rockport. It's a little hoity-toity for the likes of you though," the trucker replied.

"Actually, I think that might do," Dean said.

"Suit yourself," the driver said. "Mind if I put on the radio?"

The driver hit the AM button. A traffic report blared through. Then a serious-sounding newscaster repeated a warning that an Amber alert had been issued for a teenage girl last seen getting into a black Escalade. Dean realized that the witches, in a desperate attempt to get hold of a couple more bodies, had not only take Ben and Lisa but also a poor girl just out for a walk by the beach.

They pulled through Gloucester and after a few miles on the seafront road came to Rockport.

"Gotta let you off here," the driver said.

Dean thanked him and hopped out of the truck cab. Rockport was a quaint small town pressing up against the rocky shore on the Atlantic Ocean. Dean looked around. Even though it was summer, with a storm coming in, there wasn't much of a crowd. Off in the distance, dark clouds hugged the horizon and lightning illuminated large patches of water miles out to sea.

Dean pulled up his collar, made sure that Nathaniel's journal was snug inside his jacket, and started walking. Around a bend in the road, he saw in the distance several large houses clinging to the side of the shore. Further past them, an enormous house perched on top of a hill. One side of the property was ringed with long rocky boulders that stretched into the sea.

Dean pulled out his binoculars and trained them on the property. Panning around the area, he noticed a dust cloud which was being kicked up by a black Escalade as it wound its way up the road to the house. Taking a deep breath, he resisted the urge to kick the road in frustration. Even if the witches were hiding out in that grand house on the hill, he still had to find a way to stop them. He needed to get inside the house and fast.

As the thunder rumbled ever closer, the street was rapidly emptying of tourists. Dean glanced around and his gaze quickly settled on an ancient-looking hatchback, not the kind of car likely to have a sophisticated alarm system fitted. As casually as he could manage under the circumstances, Dean sauntered to the car and swiftly broke in—a minute later he was on the move, tires squealing as he sped away.

He parked further down the hill, then made his way up a sandy path toward the large wrap around front porch. As his foot stepped on the porch a shot rang out. Dean whirled around to find Perry standing behind him with a large shotgun trained right at his head.

"Let's not disturb the occupants," she said inclining her head toward the front door of the house. "I would hate to drag more innocent people into this. I mean soon enough, *everyone* is going to be dragged into it. But why single anyone out?"

"This isn't your place?" Dean asked.

"No, silly, why would we have a place out here?" Perry replied.

"Lisa's cell phone?"

"Just dropped it into a garbage truck that happened to be going north. I needed to get you out of Salem. Connie's orders. I was pissed, I admit. I've been taking her shit for hundreds of years. But I'll get to the festivities soon enough. As will you. I'm thinking you will be a special guest of honor. Why don't you walk over here? And no funny stuff, the gun is just for show, but I have no problem roughing you up like I did before. Walk toward me, hands behind your head."

Dean did as he was told. Perry quickly tied his hands together, and then his feet.

"Get into the truck," she said opening the door and pushing Dean headfirst into the large trunk. A cage-like feature had been wound across the back of the car, creating a barrier between the back trunk space and the seats.

"You must have a big dog," Dean said.

"Not yet, but you know opening up Hell might come with some problems."

"Like hellhounds."

"Wow, you know your Hell, Dean," Perry said. "But of course you do."

Dean looked her in the eye.

"I'm going telling you right now—by the end of today—you'll be dead and I'll have killed you," he said.

For a split second a shadow crossed the witch's girlish face.

"I'm the man to do it," Dean continued grimly. "Maybe no one else for a hundred years has known what they were up against with you. But I do. You're going to die today. Trust me."

Perry slammed the back door, hoisted herself into the driver's seat and peeled out of the driveway.

Dean desperately tried to free his hands but he couldn't reach into his front pocket. He was stuck. The only good thing about this situation was that he was getting what he wanted. He was being taken directly to Lisa and Ben.

THIRTY-FIVE

Sam followed the young witch as she drove west out of town. When she pulled off the main road and onto a residential street, Sam slowed, not wanting to follow too closely behind. She knew what he was driving after all. He watched the car take a long curve around a series of tall, brick, residential buildings that made up a planned community, dark woods loomed on the other side of the road.

The girl drove the vehicle around the side of the main building and down into an underground parking garage.

As he approached the main building, Sam noticed that there were a lot of people hanging around: teenagers loitering, old people sitting on benches in the shade of trees or buildings. He couldn't help but think it was a strange place to have a witches' gathering. Sam parked in the shadow of some trees in the far corner of the car park, pushed his sawed-off into the back of his jeans, and walked down the ramp leading into the underground parking garage.

The garage was about half full but the young witch's car was nowhere to be found. Sam walked up and down each and every aisle, methodically checking license plates to make sure he hadn't missed it. Then he caught sight of a wide steel door in the shape of a low arch on the far side of the garage.

Crouching down, Sam noticed a little brake fluid right under the door. This had to be from the jalopy the young witch was driving. Sam pushed against the door, it creaked open just enough for him to see that it was padlocked from the inside.

Sam scanned the cars, and noticed a truck with a "Handyman For Hire" sign on it. He peered into the back of the truck, and was pleased to see it was loaded with tools. Sam pulled out his sawed-off and with the butt of the gun broke the back window, stuck his arm inside and wrenched open the door. He rummaged in the truck bed until he found a pair of bolt cutters.

Armed with the cutters, he pushed on the steel doors again and jammed the bolt cutters in through the opening. The heavy chain broke with a loud CLAP, and fell to the ground with a clatter.

Sam slowly pushed open the steel door to reveal a low cavernous hallway. The space could fit about five cars, but only one was parked inside. The young witch's. Shutting the door behind him he checked the car, quickly establishing that Lisa and Ben were no longer inside it.

Across the hallway was another wide door. But before he could approach it, Sam heard a noise. The roar of car engines coming from the parking garage. Sam crouched behind the young witch's car, listening intently.

Footsteps approached the steel doors.

Sam looked up and spotted an old pipe that stretched across the ceiling. Gritting his teeth, he hoisted himself up and hung on with his hands and legs crossed.

Moments later, the steel doors creaked opened and two cars pulled in, one after the other. From his position on the pipe Sam couldn't see how many people emerged from the cars, but several doors banged shut and the volume of chatter suggested five or six people, and they all sounded female. Knowing what a vulnerable position he was in, Sam willed them not to look up.

The noise level dropped as the women went through the second door and disappeared toward whatever lay beyond. Judging that the coast was clear, Sam untangled his grip on the pipe and dropped to the floor with a THUD.

"Well, what are you waiting for? Let's go," a voice said.

Sam spun around and came face to face with his grandfather.

"What are you doing here?" Sam asked.

"What do you think I'm doing here? I'm making sure these bitches don't actually succeed in raising the four Princes of Hell, particularly the guy who still wants to ride your hide. No need to thank me."

"I don't need your help. I can handle this alone," Sam ground out.

"Yeah, I saw that. Nice bagging of the witch by the way. I mean I had my doubts about you, but I think that cinched the deal. I know things have changed since last time I was around, but I'm pretty sure coitus with a witch is frowned upon. If you needed to get laid that badly, son, I'm sure I could have arranged something"

Sam stood in silence, taking his grandfather's verbal lashing without blinking an eye. *Whatever.* He just wanted to get to the fight. When Samuel paused for breath, Sam took his opportunity.

"Can we talk about this later?" he asked, indicating the door the witches had disappeared through. They were wasting valuable time. Time when he could be killing witches.

"Oh, we're going to talk about it all right. I knew there was something wrong with you the moment I saw you. I don't know what's going on Sam, but once this is done with, we're going to find out."

"I'm fine," Sam said.

"No, son. I may have been dead, but my brain ain't. Believe me, there is something off with you."

The witches had shut the steel doors behind them before heading down the corridor and now a scratching sound came from the other side. Their argument immediately set aside, Samuel and Sam moved silently against opposite walls. Samuel leveled his gun. Sam turned his gun around, stock first. The door inched open. The small barrel of a pistol pushed through the opening. Sam nodded to his grandfather, Samuel swung the door open and Sam brutally bashed the stock of his gun into the perpetrator's face.

THIRTY-SIX

"Where the hell are you taking me?" Dean demanded as he peeked over the back seat. Perry's small frame was almost completely obscured by the large bucket seats.

"You'll see," she said.

After about twenty minutes, she pulled into a mall parking lot, parked and then got into the back seat.

"Hold on, let me get ready," Perry said.

She pulled at her shirt collar tearing it, then to Dean's bemusement she punched herself in the jaw. A large welt immediately formed on the side of her face.

"I bruise easily, sort of the price you pay for being over three hundred years old," she said conversationally, smiling at Dean. He was gradually getting the point.

"Oh, one more thing," Perry said as she opened up a door in the grate separating them. "Now be nice."

"What are you going to do?" Dean asked.

She just smiled wickedly then took out a small vial of

liquid. She grabbed Dean's head with one hand and with the other pried his mouth open. He struggled against her, twisting his head back and forth but Perry had a grip like iron and he was powerless to stop her. She poured the liquid down his throat; he gagged and then swallowed instinctively. She released his head and instantly he fell back, feeling the paralysis spread through his body, until he was completely inert.

After a moment, seemingly satisfied, Perry crawled back into the back seat and shut the cage.

He heard the beeps as she dialed three digits into her cell phone. After a brief pause, she started to speak, her voice small and hesitant with a panicky edge.

"Yes, hello. My boyfriend... my boyfriend beat me up. I don't know. One moment we where kissing and then he just got real rough. Yeah, he just went into the mall. I don't know when he'll be back. Can you come quick? Oh, thank you." She gave the details of their location and then rang off.

"It will wear off by the time the police get here," Perry said to Dean, her voice confident and gleeful again.

Just then the squeal of sirens erupted in the distance. Perry flicked her wrist and the binds on Dean's legs and wrists immediately came off. She hopped out of the vehicle and popped open the back door.

"Whatcha' gonna to do, Dean? Run and hide or face the music? Either way you're not going to see your little GF and son ever again," she gloated.

Dean swung his heavy legs onto the ground, stood up and tried to walk; it was a little more difficult than he remembered it being. He leaned on the side of the car, the sirens were getting closer.

"I'm going to kill you," he croaked.

Perry pursed her lips as if seriously weighing that possibility.

"Eh, probably not. But you can always try. Here they come. Watch and learn, Dean, baby," she purred.

A Salem Police squad car bumped into the parking lot and screeched around in a wide circle clearly trying to locate the emergency caller.

Pushing Perry out of his way, Dean took off in a Frankenstein-like run. He could still feel the paralyzing liquid coursing through his veins, and he had to will his stiff legs to keep moving. He headed for the tree line that ran down one side of the parking lot. He tripped and stumbled down into a ravine and splashed into a polluted little stream at the bottom. He could hear Perry's screams coming from behind him, she was surely pointing his escape route out to the police.

A large drainage pipe led underneath a road, and Dean neaded toward it hoping for a little refuge. Gritting his teeth through the stiffness, he stumbled through the pipe, his boots splashing through the fetid water, and emerged on the other side into a small run-off pond. He struggled to climb up the grassy slopes surrounding it, up and into a fast-food joint's parking lot.

Not far from where Dean paused to catch his breath, a pudgy guy quickly exited his car on a burger run. Dean slid into the driver's seat. He fumbled with a couple of wires underneath the dash, struggling with stiff fingers, but after a few seconds he touched them together. The spark egged the engine into jump-starting. Dean pulled swiftly out of the parking space. Checking his rearview mirror, he saw a couple of cops appear at the top of the grassy bank. He put his foot down and squealed out of the parking lot.

Dean bashed the steering wheel with his fists in frustration. He still didn't know where Lisa and Ben were or what had happened to them—they could be dead by now. The witches' latest sacrifices. He should never have brought them to Salem—what the hell had he been thinking? Family life and hunting just don't mix. It was too dangerous. He had already lost Sam, what if he also lost Lisa and Ben?

He needed to figure out where the witches were. Trying to calm down and focus, Dean decided to head back to the library. He needed a map, an old one.

At the library the same old woman was at the desk. But minus his professorial clothes and clearly looking as rough as he felt, she looked at him much more skeptically.

"May I help you?" she asked.

"I'm looking for any old maps you might have of Salem?" Dean asked politely, trying to keep the edge of panic out of his voice.

"Everything we have can be found on the Internet if you go to—"

"Listen, I don't have time for that," he said urgently. "Where are the maps?"

She pointed to several large cabinets on the other side of the room. Dean nodded his thanks.

Aware of the woman's eyes on him, he tried to be careful as he hurriedly pulled open each cabinet and riffled through the contents, painfully aware that he wasn't sure exactly what he was looking for. Surely he'd know it when he saw it—he usually did. Then he noticed a modern map of the development plans for the Kirkbride Estates, where Perry had her apartment. It showed the series of buildings some of which had been demolished and some of which had been refurbished. His brain made a sudden connection and he went back to another map dating from 1786. It was the oldest the library had. Both the maps were to the same scale. He placed the older one, which clearly outlined old Salem Village, over the new one. Salem Village and the Kirkbride Estates lined up.

The circle in which the insane asylum and then the condos had been built was directly over what used to be Salem Village.

"So Salem Village was torn down?" he called over to the librarian.

"More or less," she replied, "sure there are some buildings in Salem Town that date back to those days, and that were used during the witch trials, but Salem Village where the actual trials took place, those buildings were mostly demolished and left to rot. The insane asylum was built right tip-top on it."

"Well ain't that something." Dean thanked the woman. Then he remembered something else. "Oh I need to see that Campbell journal again, if I could?"

She led him back to the reading room and produced the box in which Dean had left John's journal, then left him alone.

Dean pulled the Campbell journal from his jacket and took one last look at it. His family came from a lineage of hunters who had always sacrificed themselves for the good of others. He only wished he could share his discovery with Sam.

He switched out the journals and left the library. But not without pocketing the last couple of pages of the Campbell journal. They were sort of his by rights, anyway.

Dean got back into his stolen car and headed to the Kirkbride Estates. He was going to have to do some real quick thinking since he was without guns or salt. He'd had to abandon his duffle bag when Perry pulled a gun on him back in Rockport.

As Dean pulled into the estate, he noticed something he hadn't clocked the previous day, when he and Lisa had rescued Ben. A couple of kids were hanging around by the side of one of the buildings. A car approached and slowly came to a stop in front of them. One kid in a baseball cap leaned in through the passenger-side window, and something was passed between the driver and the kid. The kid nodded then went back to his friends. The car pulled away.

These kids were Salem drug dealers. *And where there were drugs, there were sure to be guns,* Dean mused. Thank God, Perry hadn't found the wad of cash in his sock. Dean had never bought drugs; they were not something that was really worked with the hunter lifestyle. Hard liquor definitely, but drugs, not so much.

Dean stopped the car, but kept it idling in case he needed to get out quick. He tried his best swagger approaching the group of kids.

"You got a load in your pants, white boy?" one of the kids said.

Dean pushed down his pride.

"Listen man, I need to buy some shit from you."

The boys laughed.

"You trippin' if you think we're going to sell to a plainclothes. Go back to Captain Crunch and tell him he ain't catching us today," the first kid said.

"I hate that fat freak," Dean said. "I'm not working for anyone but myself, and I need some firepower like two minutes ago."

"Oh yeah?" another one of them spoke up. "What for? Hunting season hasn't started yet."

"Listen, I just need a sawed-off and if you have it, a couple pounds of salt, and anything you have that will blow up."

The kids cracked up in his face.

His patience rapidly running out, Dean approached the closest heckler and elbowed him in the neck. As he fell, Dean pulled him up by the collar then dropped him at his feet. The kid writhed around in pain.

"Hey!" the first kid spoke again. "That some Schwarzenegger shit man. Why you do that to Tiny?"

"Because I'm not kidding and don't have time for this crap," Dean ground out. "What do you have? I have money and I need guns."

"He for real," a tall kid called from beside Dean's idling stolen car. "Car's hot."

Dean looked back to the group of kids. The first kid stepped forward.

"You can go to prison for that shit you know," he said.

"I've been to Hell. Try again," Dean said.

"I believe this guy," the kid said. "Okay, follow me. Just don't wake up my Grams."

Dean followed the kid in through a first-floor apartment door. Inside, an older black woman slept on the couch while the TV blared. The kid gestured for Dean to follow him into another room.

"I'm Tim by the way," the kid said. He laid out two antique guns on his neatly made bed. "I got this and this," he said, gesturing.

"Hey. I'm Dean. And no offence Tim but those are ancient," Dean said disappointed. "I thought we were talking like real guns."

"These are real guns. I only collect classics. This here dates back to the civil war. And this one before that."

Dean didn't know whether to laugh or cry. Instead, he shrugged and picked up the guns. He examined them carefully. They seemed like they would do the job. He placed them back on the bed. Dean eyed Tim, and the pristine condition of his bedroom. He noticed a bookshelf was lined with astronomy textbooks.

"You seem like a smart kid," Dean observed. "Why are you selling guns?"

Tim shrugged. "These are antiques man. I do a lot of research to find good hardware. You won't need anything else but what you have in your hands."

Dean reached crouched down and pulled up his jeans, pulling a wad of cash from his sock, along with a credit card.

He counted out several notes, shoved the rest back into his sock, then handed the kid the cash and the credit card.

"Take this. It's hot, but basically untraceable. I think it's some big agent in Hollywood. Never checks his bills, so feel free to have fun." He inclined his head toward the textbooks. "Get yourself something worthwhile."

"Thanks, man," Tim said, counting the money quickly and easily. He squinted at the credit card. "You can take this too." He pulled out a small pistol. "I don't know how much salt my Grams has in the kitchen, but you can just take what you need."

Dean nodded his thanks, loaded the guns into his pockets and waistband. He then followed the boy into the kitchen where he loaded up on table salt.

Outside Dean offered up his hand to Tim.

"Thanks—you've really helped me out."

"No problem. Hey—what you need the steel for?"

Dean eyed the group of young kids in baggie shorts and big T-shirts. Suddenly they all looked much younger and more vulnerable than they had first appeared. One thing about chasing monsters—makes your average human gang member seem like a pussycat.

"Basically, I think my girlfriend and her kid have been taken by some real bad bitches," he replied. "And I think it's all going to go down somewhere around here."

"No shit. Well you know where to find us," Tim said. "We just chillin', so if you need extra bodies—"

Dean nodded in appreciation, then got back into the car and pulled around the corner to the Kirkbride Estates.

He sat in the car for a short while, checking his weapons and loading them up. Then he got out and walked around the building.

He spied the parking garage and headed down the ramp. Under the strip lighting, Dean spread out the maps he had taken from the library on the hood of a car. He noticed that the development plans outlined the destruction of a large building in the center of the property, in its place a large swimming pool had been dug. But Dean noticed on the older map of Salem Village the very same space once was a fort built for raids against the Indians. The fort's outer walls were much larger than the outline of the asylum building or the pool. Dean wondered if the fort somehow still existed.

A loud thump and muffled voices echoed through the parking structure. Sensing trouble, Dean searched the half-empty garage and noticed the steel doors on the other side of the lot. He grabbed the maps, shoving them back inside nis jacket, took out the pistol and silently slipped past rows of cars to the doors. Inside he could hear muffled voices.

Dean pushed the steel door open an inch. He stuck the pistol barrel through the opening. The next thing he knew the door was swung open and the butt of a gun cracked his nose with a THWACK! Stars exploded in his eyes and Dean fell onto the cement floor.

THIRTY-SEVEN

Sam and Samuel looked at Dean passed out at their feet.

"Now what are we supposed to do?" Samuel asked.

"Lisa and Ben are in there somewhere," Sam said.

"We can't waltz in there and save them—they'll shit their pants," Samuel pointed out.

"I can't. But you can. They don't know who you are."

"Sam, I don't think you understand the gravity of the issue here. There are—I don't know how many witches in there, one man can't do anything. I don't even know what Dean was thinking. He'd get skinned alive. You can't let him go in alone."

Sam looked down at his older brother. Blood trickled from his nose onto the cement.

"We can't leave him here," Samuel went on. "They'll find him. We need to wake him up."

Two minutes later they had opened up a BMW, hot-wired the engine and placed Dean in the front seat. They set all the air conditioning vents toward his face, and blasted the cold air at him. Sam poured a bottle of water over Dean's head.

They then retreated back through the steel doors and opened the second door on the other side of the hallway, stepping into a musty-smelling tunnel with a packed dirt floor, and brick archways that reached across the low ceiling. Stale air washed over them from the dark depths further down the tunnel. Samuel pulled a flashlight from his jacket and Sam led with his gun. As they moved forward, the tunnel seemed to drop downhill, deep into the earth. Sam estimated that they were directly underneath the large brick building. He looked at his cell phone, there was absolutely no reception.

They crept forward in the darkness, until around a corner the tunnel opened up into a large underground cavern. Lamps hung from the ceiling and a crowd of witches was gathered in the middle of the space. They all moved with purpose as though each had been assigned a task. They seemed to be constructing something.

Aware of their exposed position, Sam looked round for a better hiding place. He noticed a narrow passageway built into the thick walls that seemed to cut through toward the main cavern. It looked like the vestiges of another old passageway system. Sam and Samuel squeezed through the narrow gap. They shuffled down the tunnel until they came to a small opening cut into the wall which allowed them to see into the large cavern.

"I don't see Lisa or Ben," Samuel whispered.

Sam didn't respond, because he had spotted Prudence. She stood slightly apart from the rest of the witches, who witches were gathered in a circle. A tall woman stood on a platform. She was chanting from a small book.

"That's it," Samuel said. "That's the *Necronomicon*. We can't let her get through the entire spell."

Sam didn't answer.

"Sam, are you listening?" Samuel hissed.

Sam glared his grandfather.

"Yes, I get it. We can't let them finish."

Sam stared at the book in the tall witch's hands. What he couldn't tell his grandfather was that he didn't care. If Lucifer took back control over his body in some ways he would welcome it. When Lucifer was in him, for the couple days before he fell into the pit, Sam had never felt so powerful. Lucifer was so strong that being filled up by him completely obliterated any need to care about or love anything. The feeling of literally being able to rule the world was exquisite. Addictive. No other human being on earth had ever felt what Sam had.

For that reason, in some ways, he would welcome that feeling again. Being squished into a dirt-packed hole underground with his cranky once-dead grandfather, waiting for his heartbroken and desperate brother to come and stop a bunch of witches from resurrecting Lucifer... wasn't one of Sam's favorite moments.

Dean awoke wet and cold with his head pounding. He opened his eyes and clocked the unfamiliar dash of an unfamiliar car. There was a knock on the window. Dean turned and looked into the face of an extremely angry-looking man clutching a computer case and a suit jacket.

"Hey you, junkie. Get the hell out of my car," the man yelled. He wrenched open the door and pulled Dean out of his seat by his collar.

Dean stumbled and fell into the vehicle in the adjacent space.

"I don't know why management doesn't take care of the trash like you," the guy spat. He got into the driver's seat and slammed his door, then screeched out of the parking lot.

Dean noticed his reflection in the dark window of the mini van he was leaning against. His bruised nose was developing a hideous purplish welt. He had no idea what had happened, but since he was still alive, Dean thought it best to move forward. He checked his guns, they were all still there, still working.

This time, he was slightly more cautious as he pushed open the steel doors. Inside, several cars were parked. Dean instantly recognized Perry's. He made sure that no one else was hiding in the room, then he passed through the opposite door and into a damp underground tunnel.

The tunnel was dangerous, there was nowhere to hide if anyone approached from behind or in front of him. Only the darkness would obscure him. In the distance he could hear the murmuring of voices. Dean crept forward down the sloping dark tunnel.

After what felt like the length of two football fields, the tunnel turned a corner and Dean smelled smoke and found himself looking into a deep cavern and a crowd of witches all chanting in unison.

The figures, all clad in black, encircled a large bonfire. He could see Connie standing on a platform. She was leading the chant from the *Necronomicon*. Perry stood to the side. *She must have fobbed off the cops and then come straight here*, he figured. Lisa and Ben must be somewhere nearby though he couldn't see them.

The bonfire smoke curled up toward the vaulted stone ceiling. Dean estimated the ceiling was about two stories tall but who knew how far underground they were. It would be pretty impossible to mount a large-scale attack from above. Plus, Dean was pretty sure they were almost directly underneath the large community pool.

He looked around the hallway, which was built large enough for a horse cart. Dean had an idea and ran back up the tunnel.

Inside the smoky cavern Lisa and Ben were shackled to the stone wall. Ben whimpered in fear. Lisa tried to soothe her son, but she could only move her hands enough to touch the tips of Ben's sweaty fingers.

"Shush, Ben. It's going to be okay," Lisa whispered.

"I never should have gotten that second helping of fries. Perry is evil."

"This isn't your fault, Ben. None of this is your fault. We're going to find a way out of this. I promise."

"How? Where's Dean?" Ben demanded.

"He's coming, honey. He's coming," Lisa said, hoping that she was right.

* * *

Dean retreated back to the low-ceilinged hallway where Perry's car was parked. He opened up the back of the car and was relieved to find his duffle. He got out his two sawed-offs, made sure they had real bullets in them and then opened up the steel doors leading back into the parking lot. He hopped into the driver's seat of Perry's car, swiftly got the engine going and backed the Escalade into the parking lot. He laid the condo development plans on the seat beside him, tracing the route until he found the building he was looking for.

His headache was receding and he felt a new burst of energy now that he had a plan. Dean accelerated out of the parking lot and headed to the maintenance building. He maneuvered the Escalade up to the garage doors. Inside he found entire barrels of fertilizer, gas and other chemicals— all the gear the maintenance crew needed to keep up the grounds, stacked right up to the ceiling.

Thanking God it wasn't kill-the-weeds day so the place was deserted, Dean hastened to load the large cans of gas and sacks of fertilizer into the back of the car. Then he swung the car back around and retreated with his bounty back to the parking garage.

Dean drove through the first set of steel doors and then opened up the second set of doors leading to the underground tunnel. Hoping his estimations were correct, he flicked on his headlights, gunned the engine and floored it through the doors.

The tires hit the dirt floor of the tunnel and threw the car forward. The tunnel flew by. Dean steeled himself for the turn—the dirt walls didn't afford him any room for mistakes. Mere seconds flew by. Dean held his breath then cut the wheel.

The back wheels fishtailed, and then bumped the truck forward. Dean gripped the steering wheel, punched the accelerator and bombed into the cavern and straight into the crowd of witches.

He stamped on the brakes before he drove into the bonfire. A cacophony of screaming witches shook the cavern. Dean pulled himself out through the sunroof and stood on top of the car. He started shooting.

The women flew at the car, old and young alike they attacked, lips peeled back as they snarled angrily. Dean blew away body after body.

Constance had stopped chanting and stood on her platform scowling. Three of her burly farm hands approached the car, Dean got one shot off before they grabbed him by the foot and pulled him off the roof. The six-foot drop landed him on his back.

Constance stepped off her platform and walked over to Dean. She towered over him.

"I'm not into this whole two girls one cup angle, could you maybe move?" Dean said.

Constance kicked him in the ribs. Dean rolled over and blood dribbled out of his mouth.

"I don't find you funny," she said. "But I'm delighted you're here. It is very appropriate that a descendant of those who ruined my quest the first time, will be sacrificed when I succeed this time."

Dean struggled onto all fours, spitting blood, and looked up at Constance.

"I don't know what kind of junk you've been smoking," he croaked, "but raising Lucifer is just about the worst idea I've ever heard. Trust me."

"I didn't ask for your opinion. All I need is your blood. Tie him up with the others," Constance instructed.

The burly guys dragged Dean by the feet into a corner where he saw to his relief that Lisa and Ben were shackled. They might be prisoners but they were still alive and apparently unhurt.

Lisa glared at Dean.

"This was your idea of a rescue?" Lisa said. "To drive into a cave full of witches without any backup?"

"I didn't have much of choice, Lisa. Sort of light on brothers to back me up. It's not like I can go out and hire anyone to help," Dean replied.

The burly guys finished shackling Dean to the wall, then walked away.

"It's fine anyway, I have an idea," Dean said, trying to sound confident.

"I'm not feeling so fine," Lisa said.

THIRTY-EIGHT

Constance stepped to the edge of the platform and hushed the gathering. She raised her hands up in supplication and began to speak. Her ice-cold voice echoed loud and clear around the walls.

"To all my sisters, we have waited years. The time is nigh. Our great Princes will rise up and under our power create the world in their image. Darkness will reign. No longer will we have to live in the shadows. Sisters, since we came to this land we have suffered and cowered in the corners. Never gaining the respect or the resplendence we are due. After three hundred years the alignment is clear. Sixty-six seals were broken and though the Prince of the South was returned to the underworld—his resurrection is imminent. We will finally have the dark power to create a New World in which we can live freely without the reigns of the light and the Godly. As we go forth, spread the darkness before you like seeds, dear sisters. We are the chosen queens of darkness. The power is ours for the taking. We are the spouses of the Four Princes, and they will do our bidding and build the world of dark, crushing the light. Bring forth the first sacrifice."

A scream echoed through the cavern. A young girl, presumably the one from the Amber alert Dean had heard on the trucker's radio, was dragged up to the platform. Constance began her chant one again. With one hand she brought out a long knife, with the other she held the neck of the girl over a large brass bowl.

"Close your eyes, Ben," Dean said. "Now."

Ben squeezed his eyes shut. The girl continued to scream.

The rest of the witches joined in the chanting, louder this time, their voices echoed off the walls so the noise was unbearable.

Dean tried to move closer to Ben as the boy started to visibly shake with fear. Dean looked at Lisa and saw her eyes were full of tears. The guilt squeezed his chest—how could he have let this happen?

Constance shouted over the chanting and the girl's hysterical screams.

"We call forth the Four Princes of the Darkness. The rulers of Hell, the sons of darkness. Rise up from your unearthly shackles. We call forth and command you to rise. We call all the forces of darkness to rise. To the prince of the North, Belial, I command you to rise. I invoke thee. I summon thee. I conjure thee. With this life blood, manifest thyself. With this sacrifice, manifest thyself. Come forth, Belial. Come forth, Belial."

The girl fought like a young goat, but Constance held her firmly by the nape of the neck and in one deft cut she slit the girl's throat from side to side. Lisa whimpered and buried her head in her chest.

Constance held the dead girl's hair, the body plunged forward and blood poured from the gaping neck wound into the bowl. A dark-red drop splashed up across the lip.

Constance started to shout.

"Belial, I call you forth. I have raised you, I am your Queen, I am your bind to this earth."

There was a rumble from all sides of the cavern. Small pebbles shook loose from the ceiling.

"What's happening, Dean? What did she mean by the princes of darkness? Is that Lucifer?" Lisa whispered.

Dean looked at her.

"Is that why we're here? Were you going to try and do this? Raise Lucifer to get Sam back?" Lisa's eyes were wide with fear and disbelief.

"It crossed my mind," Dean admitted.

"Are you crazy? I know you miss Sam, but were you really prepared to do *this*?"

"I had no idea it meant sacrificing people—I would never do that. You know that, don't you?"

Lisa turned her head away from him.

"I don't know anything anymore, Dean. I'm so scared I can't think."

Another great groan emanated from the ground. Belial was slowly rising up. They needed to get out of there.

"Trust me, please, baby. It's going to be fine. I'll get us out of here—I promise," Dean said.

Just then two of the burly guys walked over. One grabbed Lisa by the waist and pulled her up, as the second struggled to unlock the ancient iron shackles that held her feet and ankles. Lisa started screaming, she kicked her legs and struggled to escape.

"Mum!" Ben called as he tried to pull free of his bonds.

"Leave her alone," Dean growled at the men. "Take me instead." But the guys ignored him.

Lisa spat and fought, she pulled her leg back and managed to kick one of the guys in the nuts. The guy doubled over. Neither of the attackers noticed as a small key dropped to the dusty cavern floor. The guys pulled Lisa away.

Dean looked at the key and looked at Ben. The boy's eyes were full of terror but he wasn't hysterical. He understood Dean's meaning straight away and placed his sneaker over the key.

"Can you get it over to me?" Dean whispered.

Ben steadily wrapped his sneakers around the small object and pushed it toward Dean's hands. Dean felt the tip of Ben's sneakers, then the cool metal of the key. He pulled one hand through the shackles as much as he could, then twisted his hand with the key into the keyhole of the opposite shackle. The iron clap unlatched with a soft click. Dean threw a glance in the direction the men had taken Lisa, he saw she was still fighting. Dean undid the other shackle, then his feet. No one was looking at them—all eyes were on Constance.

Dean shuffled over until he was beside Ben. He quickly undid the boy's shackles. Dean looked around—how was he going to get them out of here unharmed? In the corner Dean spotted a nasty, ripped old dress. Dean crawled over to it and brought it back to Ben.

"Put this on. Quickly," Dean directed.

"I don't want to put on a dress," Ben said.

"Just put it on," Dean insisted, eyes flicking back and forth to make sure no one was looking at them. Ben pulled the dress on over his T-shirt. "Put this on, too." Dean handed him a bonnet he had also retrieved. Ben begrudgingly put on the bonnet.

They stood up slowly and carefully, Dean's gaze taking in the whole room. But the commotion in the center of the cavern was drawing everyone's attention and they began to move slowly and silently toward the corridor.

"Hold my hands like they're still shackled," Dean murmured. "When we get near the opening, let me go and then I need you to do something for me."

"What about Mom?" Ben asked.

"Don't worry—I'll take care of her," Dean replied.

The chanting continued. In the center of the bonfire the earth below had started to give way again.

Dean saw that Lisa was being forced onto Constance's podium. He didn't have much time. He eyed the *Necronomicon* at the tall witch's side. She was still giving directions to her underlings.

Dean whispered instructions to Ben, still dressed in the filthy dress and bonnet. If you weren't looking carefully, he could have been one of the witches. Dean waited a moment.

"Okay, now," he said.

Ben let go of Dean, and walked toward the podium. His hand shook as he reached out and grabbed the *Necronomicon* that lay near the dead young girl's head. He flinched at her dead eyes, that were looking upwards right at him.

"You girl, bring me that book," Constance said spinning around to face Ben. "Don't dawdle, give me that book."

Ben grabbed the book and approached her.

"Give it here," Constance directed. Ben stepped toward her, but misjudged the uneven dirt floor, he tripped landing on all fours. "Oh you stupid child, can't seem to resurrect a competent witch these days," Constance said.

Ben struggled to get up. He rearranged his "skirts" then drew himself up before Constance. He held out the book for her. She grabbed it and stuck it under her arm. Then she directed the two burly men to bring Lisa to her. Ben swung around on his heel and walked in the direction of the door. The Escalade still stood inside the entrance. As Ben walked past Dean he handed the *Necronomicon* to him.

"Good job, now get out of here," Dean whispered.

Ben nodded and walked into tunnel. The darkness swallowed him.

He made it five feet into the tunnel when two young girls appeared out of the darkness.

"Where are you going, girl?" one of them asked.

Ben hid his head and shrugged.

"These old witches are weird. Do they even speak English?" the other one said.

"I don't know," the first one replied. "But she shouldn't

be leaving. Keep her here. I'll go ask." The first girl walked into the cavern, the other watched her.

Ben was about to flee, when someone grabbed him by the arm.

Ben struggled against his abductor until the guy turned him around and gestured for him to be quiet. He had pulled him into the side tunnel off the main corridor. Ben couldn't see much but he could tell this guy was old, bald, and definitely not a witch.

"I'm going to get you out of here," the man hissed. "Follow me."

Not having an alternative, Ben did as he was told and followed the old guy. They ran up a long, dark tunnel, through two sets of doors and out into a parking structure.

There they paused to catch their breath. Then the old guy bent down and spoke to Ben.

"I want you to go back above ground. And no matter what you do, do not come down here again. You understand me?"

Ben nodded. "Who are you?"

"Friend of Dean's. Now go," the man said sternly. Ben wasn't going to be told twice. He ran up the ramp and out of the parking garage to the lawn outside. There he plopped down on the grass, still trying to catch his breath. He looked down at his improvised disguise and then quickly tore off his dress and bonnet.

"What the hell are you?" a voice said.

Ben swiveled round. A gang of boys stepped forward and encircled Ben. They were much bigger than Ben, and though he'd been bullied a couple times on the playground, Ben knew he was being confronted by a group with a lot more street cred.

"We haven't seen you around here before. You know you gotta ask permission before coming outside, right." one of them said.

In the last six hours Ben's skin had grown a tad thicker than it had been before.

"Dude, leave me alone. There's some shit going down and I really don't need your crap too."

"Hey, you know some white guy, Dean, came here looking for trouble round here?" an older kid said, stepping forward.

"Yeah, Dean's my mom's boyfriend. He's down there," Ben said pointing to the parking garage.

"Where? Down in that locked cavern shit?" another kid said.

Ben nodded. "These real bad witches have my mom. I don't know how Dean's gonna stop them. Some old bald guy just took me up here and told me to stay. I think he went back in there."

The older kid held up his hand. He was clearly the leader.

"What do you mean witches, little man? Like Halloween witches? You trippin'?"

Ben shook his head emphatically.

"No, I mean *real witches*. Like want to bring the dark days upon this whole town, upon this whole world kind of witches. Believe me, there isn't going to be any candy given out."

"Well, I'm up for a little beat down. If that white dude is

down there, we're going to go help him. Tiny get some steel up in here," the kid said.

"Sure thing, Tim." Tiny, who was anything but, popped open the back trunk of a Caddy. Inside was an impressive weapons cache. Ben got up and stepped toward the trunk.

"Back away, little man. This is our fight now. No freaks are going to take over our homes," the older kid said.

They all grabbed street weaponry and disappeared down the ramp and into the parking garage.

Ben sat on the bumper of the car and said a little prayer that Dean and his mother would reappear soon. This vacation really sucked.

Samuel and Sam crouched at the cavern entrance; they were taking potshots at any witches trying to leave the cave.

They heard a noise behind them, and turned to see a group of boys were approaching through the tunnel. Samuel stood up to meet them.

"Be careful in there boys," Samuel said.

"Why aren't you in there, old man?" the oldest-looking kid asked.

"Believe me, I'm doing my part," Samuel said as he pointed his gun at a runaway resurrected hag and pulled the trigger. Her dusty head slit in two and she dropped at the boys' feet.

"Good enough," the kid said.

Crouched in the shadows, Dean thumbed quickly through the *Necronomicon*. He found the spell Thomas had described in the journal that Nathaniel had used to send Belial back to

Hell. Dean realized he had one small problem; he didn't have anyone to sacrifice—except himself.

He was going to have to rethink this—but fast. Very fast. Constance was hushing the chanting crowd of witches. She had pulled Lisa up on the platform. In the center of the cavern, the earth started to move around in a circle. The fire squelched as a blast of heat poured from the hole opening up in the center of the room. Belial was rising.

Constance started to chant again. Dean saw a shadowy figure lunge forward in the darkness.

Then he saw them. The kid who had sold him the guns and his gang ran into the cavern, guns blazing. They started shooting.

Enraged, Constance released Lisa and leapt off the podium. Dean was relieved to see Lisa still had the presence of mind to seize an opportunity, as she too jumped off the podium and retreated into the corridor, back toward safety.

Dean ran toward the group.

"Dude, arm me!" he yelled at Tim.

Tim swiveled around and threw Dean a sawed-off.

"Now this is more like it," Dean muttered. He turned around and started blasting at encroaching witches. He climbed back up onto the Escalade and started shooting at the center of the writhing fiery pit.

"This is some shit," Tim called.

"All in a day's work," Dean yelled back.

The gang members had some great hunting skills. One old witch flew at Tiny, who tried to swat her away but was caught offguard by her strength.

"Die, witch bitch," Tiny said, pointing his gun at the resurrected creature's head and blowing her dusty brains out.

Another kid with a red do-rag ran into the center of the cavern.

"Don't!" Dean yelled. But it was too late, the kid jumped over the ring of fire and landed in the center of the resurrection. The ground gave way and a blast of fire spit up as the kid slid into the pit.

Tiny steeled himself as another witch jumped on his back.

"Duck!" Dean yelled.

Tiny ducked down, leaving an open shot for Dean. He blasted the witch.

"They're weakened by all their energy going toward the resurrection," Dean explained. "Just keep blowing them away."

Constance flew at Dean and toppled him off the car, knocking the breath out him. The tall witch knelt on top of him and held the knife to his neck.

"When are you Campbells going to stop causing problems for me?" she hissed. "I'm getting pretty sick of it."

"Get sick of this bitch," Tim said, shoving his gun into her head. But Constance was too quick; she spun off of Dean and swiped at Tim with the knife. A crimson ribbon of blood appeared across his chest. The boy looked down in surprise, and ineffectually put his hand to his chest. A little bubble of blood spit out his lips.

"No!" Dean rushed to Tim's side. "We'll get you out of here."

He shook his head.

"Too late, man, too late. I ain't going to make it. Just use me, okay?"

Dean looked into the kid's eyes and nodded. He knew what he was saying.

"Take care of my Gram." The life was quickly draining out of him.

At that moment the rumbling became more intense. From the center of the cavern a geyser of fire shot up from the floor, the figure of Belial—half-goat, half-man—appeared from the earth. Though surrounded by fire, the figure was darker than dark. It turned toward Constance in a shower of brimstone.

"I have raised you, I am your Queen, I am your bind to this earth," she cried.

"Belial is yours to obey. You have unchained the first Prince of Hell." Belial's voice shuddered over the cavern.

"Do it. Do it now," Tim whispered to Dean.

Dean pulled out the *Necronomicon*, and started reading out loud.

"Oh god of dark and god of light. You are summoned no more. Hide your evilness in the cage from which you came, you are not wanted on this mortal plain. I forbade *vos of atrum pergo huic regnum. Vos es inconcessus ut ingredior inter lux lucis. Vos es inconcessus ut futurus in is terra. Vado tergum qua vos venit. Vado tergum ut vestri cage. Vos es non volo. Per vox of lux lucis quod filiolus of Olympus quod bonus verto tergum ut atrum.*"

Belial swung his mighty head and the enormous blackness headed toward Dean, but Dean continued, struggling to keep his voice steady.

"You are not needed in this world. Go back from which you came. Take this sacrifice and be gone."

With that Dean sliced Tim's throat and the blood spurt from his neck over Dean's hands. It dripped onto the dirt floor, seeping into the dust. Belial gave a great roar. He moved toward Dean, and as he passed through the ring of fire, he transformed. Suddenly standing in front of Dean was the figure of John Winchester.

But the figure's voice wasn't his father's; it belonged to something dark and unearthly.

"Dean, why have you forsaken your father? Why not create Hell on Earth, and then your family can be together again?" it said.

Dean turned his head away and repeated the last sentence of the incantation.

"*Non opus in hoc mundo. Revertere unde veneris. Accipe sacrificium et recedemus.*"

Belial bent down and shot his hand out, grabbing Dean's chin. He pulled him toward the fire.

"I haven't forgotten you, Dean. We're still waiting for you to come back."

With that he let go of Dean and stepped back into the fire and disappeared. The brimstone died down into embers, the earth closed back up and the ground re-coagulated into solid earth.

Constance screamed in anger. She wielded her knife and sliced off the closest young witch's head in one motion.

"You won't get away with this!" Constance yelled to Dean. She flipped open the book in her hands. "What is this? This isn't my book. What is this Winchester journal?" She threw the book onto the ground. Dean smiled. He hadn't taught Ben much, but he had picked up some neat slight of hand.

Dean felt someone grab his hair and jerk his head back.

"You made her mad," Prudence said. "And you've really disappointed me, Dean. Why are you always screwing things up for me?" With a powerful swing she threw Dean across the cavern. He hit the rock walls and slid onto the ground.

I'm getting really tired of being thrown around like this, Dean thought.

Prudence stepped over the dying fire and marched toward him. Dean shook the cobwebs from his head. He was still holding the *Necronomicon.* He flipped to another page and started reading.

"God of darkness, God of light bring forth the witness this one night. Those that have died at the hands of the undone. Bring them forth for them to shun those that have trespassed against the good and innocent. Bring them forth for the world to once again gain equilibrium."

Prudence stopped in her tracks.

"You wouldn't."

"I just did," Dean said. "I think some people have a score to settle."

Dean pulled a canister of salt out of his jacket and poured a ring around him. Prudence raced forward, but he closed the circle before she could reach him. Dean smiled and pointed behind her. Prudence swung around.

The witches stood still as the spirits of the long-dead residents of Salem Village appeared. Bridget Bishop, the first to be hanged, approached Prudence.

"I remember you. You sent me to hang. I was innocent, yet you used your cunning and wit and let me hang."

"You slit my throat," a young voice said. Prudence spun again and came face to face with Abigail Faulkner. "I trusted you. I did everything you said, and how was I repaid? I became your first sacrifice."

Prudence shrugged. "Come now, Abby. I was only doing what I was told. It was Constance who picked you to sacrifice."

Abigail shook her head.

"No, it was you." Abigail shot her hand through Prudence's chest. Prudence tried to struggle, but her strength had already been drained by the resurrections. "I could have lived a long and happy life. I should have. Well, now we'll make sure you're shown the same justice as you showed the innocent people of Salem."

Abigail thrust her hand deeper and Prudence's skin began to lose its healthy pallor. Her eyes grayed over, her skin cracked and flaked. Abigail continued to hold Prudence until her body fell into a thousand dusty pieces at her feet.

Abigail looked at the walnut-sized shriveled heart in her hand, and she let it drop to the ground. She then looked at Dean and the ring of salt around his feet.

"I don't remember you," she said.

"I'm just here to observe. It's your fight now," Dean replied.

Abigail nodded, turned and sped toward Constance. The

tall, fearsome witch was hissing and spitting as she fought off a dozen angry Salem ghosts all at once.

"Get off me you fleabags. You were worthless bags of skin in life and now you're worthless specks of dust. Get off me!" she screamed.

Bridget Bishop jumped onto Constance's back. She reached over and thrust her hand into her chest. Constance thrashed and fought, but the angry spirit held on. Other ghosts piled on top of her, until Dean couldn't even see the witch beneath layers of ghostly flesh.

Finally, one last scream of agony and anger echoed through the cavern as Constance suddenly aged to her three-hundred-and-fifty years, and crumpled into dirt.

The cavern was suddenly eerily quiet. With their leader gone, the few witches that remained evaporated.

The gang members surveyed the scene and then gathered their weapons and limped back toward the tunnel. Dean looked around the echoing space that was littered with bodies. Some of the resurrected witches had merely turned to piles of dusty clothes. Dean shook his head.

Abigail approached him once again.

"Are you a Campbell?" she asked.

Dean nodded. "Yes, I am."

Abigail smiled. "Thank you. Thank Thomas and Caleb for me too."

Dean nodded, he didn't want to correct the poor ghost and tell her they were long gone.

Their work done, Abigail and the other ghosts of Salem disappeared into thin air.

Dean stepped out of the salt circle. He searched the ground for John's journal and finding it, tucked it safely back into his jacket. Tim's body lay prostrate at Dean's feet. Dean took his Zippo and tore a little piece of cloth from his shirt. He opened the back door of the Escalade, set the burning piece of fabric in the trunk next to the explosives and shut the door.

He then crouched down and swung Tim's body onto his shoulder and started jogging up the tunnel. He knew he didn't have long to get out.

Thirty seconds later, the percussive explosions started. Dean ran full force with the kid's six-foot frame bumping against his. He headed through both sets of doors, swinging them closed behind him and then ran out of the parking structure.

Dean hauled ass up the parking ramp just as the BMW douche from before was pulling in. Dean stood in front of the car.

"Don't go in there man," he yelled.

"What are you saying to me?" BMW said. "Is that a dead body?" The guy indicated the figure thrown over Dean's shoulder.

"I warned you," Dean said, moving away and walking onto the grass.

With that a massive explosion ripped through the parking structure. The BMW blew backwards and Dean was thrown to the ground, Tim's body crumpled beneath him. He stood up as the rest of the gang appeared and surrounded the body. They ceremonially placed a sheet over it.

"He was a good kid. A hero," Dean managed to say.

The kids nodded.

"Dean!" Ben shouted, running toward him. Lisa followed and they both hugged Dean. "You made it," Ben said. "I knew you would. The old guy did too."

"What old guy?" Dean asked.

"Your friend. The bald old guy," Ben said hugging him.

Dean looked at Lisa who shrugged.

"That was some nice hand work, Ben," Dean said, referring to the switch Ben pulled on the *Necronomicon* and the journal.

"Thanks," Ben said. "But next vacation I think I'm going to stay home."

"Me too," Lisa said with a sad smile.

"I think I owe you both a real one," Dean said.

"Yeah, we're going to have to talk about that," Lisa said.

They started to walk away, then Dean halted.

"I gotta make one stop first." He left Ben and Lisa and jogged over across the lawn to the Tim's grandmother's house. He rang the doorbell.

A moment later Tim's Gram answered the door. She took one look at Dean and seemed to know immediately what had happened.

"I'm so sorry," Dean said. "He was a good kid. There's some money on his bed."

The old lady shook her head.

"I don't need no money. I need my grandson alive."

"He sacrificed himself for me and my family. He was a real brave kid," Dean said.

She nodded, then shut the door on Dean. He walked soberly back to Lisa and Ben and they started to walk down the road. Dean wished once again that he had bought the Impala.

Dean picked up his phone, he ached for someone, anyone, to call. But who would that be? Bobby would be glad to hear from him, but it wouldn't be the same. Dean needed his brother back. He sighed. And yet he had made a promise to him. Dean decided to keep it. He pushed himself off the couch, went outside and into the garage. A few seconds later he had the mower out, and was pushing it across the lawn.

If this was the life Sam wanted him to lead, then he was going to do it. For Sam.

"Well I can't say it was a job well done, but you did manage to keep Lucy in his cage, so I guess kudos to you." Crowley stepped out of the shadows of Samuel's office.

Samuel stared up at him, a glass of whiskey in his hand.

"Dean almost got killed," Samuel said. "The kid, too."

"Ah but he didn't, old boy. You did your job and now we have to get back to work don't we? Must keep our eyes on the prize. Your darling Mary."

Samuel jumped out of his seat with such force that the chair knocked over and his whiskey glass spun like a top on the table. He was chin to chin with Crowley.

"Don't ever say her name again," Samuel warned.

"Well since I don't take to reading the Bible each night, I won't have much trouble with that. Sit down and get your smelly meat mouth out of my face before I get upset," Crowley said with an edge.

Samuel backed off.

"Now I think you have some monsters to catch." Crowley flashed a crooked smile.

"I'm telling you this now," Samuel said, "as soon as Mary is returned to me, you better watch your Limey ass. Because I'm going to hunt it down and send it back to Hell."

"I'll look forward to that," Crowley spat. "Very much."

And with that the demon disappeared. Samuel picked up his chair and sat back down. There was a knock on the door. Samuel grumbled some sort of acquiesce and Sam entered. He closed the door behind him.

"Thought you might like to know, there's a nest of vamps in Oklahoma City. You want to come?" Sam asked.

Samuel shook his head.

"You can take care of it without me. You know the drill."

Sam nodded. He paused a moment.

"You okay?" he asked.

"I'm fine," Samuel replied, not looking up.

Sam nodded. "Be back by noon tomorrow."

Outside, Sam gave a quick nod to Gwen and Mark, and they headed toward the truck. Sam breathed in the crisp morning air, it felt what he imagined was "good." He got in the van.

As they pulled away from the compound, Sam's mind stayed on the sad look on Samuel's face. A flicker of sympathy passed over his face, like a quick zap of static from a socket on a dry day. Then as quickly as it came, it was gone.

EPILOGUE

Fall 1705

Caleb and I rode into Philadelphia under the cover of darkness. Though only late September, the weather was unusually cold. Fog pushed in from the river and rolled down Market Street making the cobblestones wet and slick. We had been called to town by one Mrs. Webster Moreland. Her letter, hand-delivered to our inn by a servant boy, had asked that we come immediately.

She had recently arrived in the town of Philadelphia and had left a sizeable estate up the river in the care of her son, Arthur. It seems that she had become rather frightened of her only son; that he was not himself. Once a gregarious, kind-hearted young man, he now seemed sullen and mean, and was seized by frequent violent outbursts. Not knowing if a disease had taken over her son, Mrs Moreland had fled to her city house.

Caleb believes she is mad, and has made a bet with me to prove it.

"This will be a waste of our time," Caleb said, "you'll see. She will turn out to be a fussy old hen who is making up stories."

I told him we would see for ourselves.

As it turned out Mrs. Moreland was neither fussy nor an old hen. She was a stocky and sane woman who seemed to have her household in order. Her son was her main concern.

We arrived at seven, just in time for dinner, and she invited us to join her. Caleb and I looked out of place in our leather coats and canvas trousers at her polished dinner table, piled high with roasts and pies. After a meal that rivaled our Christmas feasts, we sat down to speak about her son. After some discussion, it was decided that Caleb and I would ride up to her estate and survey her son's behavior.

It seemed however that Arthur had other plans.

Arthur arrived at his mother's brick townhouse, unannounced, just after ten. He seemed surprised that she had visitors, namely two gritty gentlemen like Caleb and myself, but he put on his best face to hide his disgust.

It was decided that we would spend the night. Caleb and I shared a room which contained two of the largest beds we had ever seen. Arthur slept across the hall. Or so we thought. At around two in the morning we heard him sneak out of his room, creep down the stairs, and then we heard the click of the front door latch. Caleb and I jumped into our boots and followed him.

The fog hadn't dissipated any as we followed Arthur down the damp streets. At some point he turned a corner into a darkened alleyway. Not having been in the town of Philadelphia before, Caleb and I were unfamiliar with its streets. Perhaps there was another way around, but we didn't know for sure, and since we risked losing Arthur's trail, we followed.

We made our way after Arthur as quietly as we could. The narrow passage stunk of wharf rats from the nearby piers. Behind a brick house we saw Arthur steal into a recessed basement of some sort. When we were sure he was shut inside, we peered into the street-level windows: inside was full of merry men and women, dancing and drinking. Not so unusual, we thought, he's just a regular young man out for a night of fun.

But then from behind us came a sound. We hid behind a couple crates of trash and watched a young man in upper-class finery walk to the same door. He looked in our direction and though I'm sure he couldn't see us we were caught with a most surprising site. His eyes were black—jet black as the night.

Dearest sister, father once told us of demons, but we have never encountered them ourselves. We are in need of any and all of the Latin exorcism texts, as well as your expertise.

We are afraid there is a scourge of demons in Philadelphia. Please come quick.

Your dearest brother,
Thomas

SUPERNATURAL™

THE OFFICIAL SUPERNATURAL MAGAZINE

features exclusive interviews with Jared and Jensen, guest stars, and the behind-the-scenes crew of the show, the latest news, and classic episode spotlights! Plus, pull-out posters in every issue!

TO SUBSCRIBE NOW CALL

U.S. 1 877 363 1310
U.K. 0844 844 0387

For more information visit:
www.titanmagazines.com/supernatural